FOOL'S GOLD

By

Dennis Collins

Also by Dennis Collins

Turn Left at September
The Unreal McCoy
The First Domino
Nightmare

ISBN 978-0-692-42137-6

Cover photo by Dennis Collins
Interior design by Susan Leonard

Printed in the United States of America

ACKNOWLEDGEMENTS

This was a fun novel to write but not without its challenges. I was able to frame the story thanks to Rick Mixter who provided film excerpts from the Unsolved Mysteries television series. I did my best to create an interesting plot while staying true (mostly) to the legend. I'd like to thank Monica Blackwell for an offhand remark that led me to change the whole direction of the story. And hats off to Jennifer Hartley, who so willingly helped me find my way around Escanaba as well as all of Delta County, Michigan. Big thanks to Andy Guaresimo. (President of Blue Water Rescue and Salvage) who walked me through search and salvage techniques. And then there's Susan Leonard of Rose Island Bookworks who put up with my punctuation and actually built my story into a book. Finally I salute Capt. Mike Quinn of the North Star Great Lakes Ferry Boat who's knowledge of nautical navigation and Great Lakes tendencies kept me from sinking my ship.

FOREWORD

The lore of the Great Lakes region is full of legends, many of them involving ships and shipwrecks. Perhaps the most enduring story revolves around the Poverty Island treasure. One version of the tale says that in 1863 the Confederacy, strapped for cash negotiated a loan or possibly a gift from the government of France and that a ship carrying five chests of gold and silver bullion was being sent to help the south with their war effort. At that time the value of the cargo was said to be over five million dollars.

The treasure laden ship secretly entered the Great Lakes through the Saint Lawrence River and made its way across Lake Erie and northward through Lake Huron. After crossing into Lake Michigan through the Straits of Mackinac, the ship sailed northwest into Little Bay de Noc and into the harbor at Escanaba Michigan. The cargo was then transferred to a sixty foot schooner for the remainder of the journey to Chicago, through the Illinois Waterway and down the Mississippi River.

As soon as the schooner sailed out into Lake Michigan, she was intercepted by a vessel carrying French mercenaries or pirates who planned to steal the treasure. The crew of the schooner, fearing for their lives dumped the gold filled chests over the side. That action so angered the pirates that they slaughtered the entire crew and scuttled the ship. And that is the legend.

Perhaps it's true or perhaps it's just such a good story that it has simply refused to die. There are further adventures that add fuel to the tale. In the early nineteen hundreds there are a couple of more rumors that the gold was found only to be lost once again to the icy waters of northern Lake Michigan. One such story involved a salvage tug from Toledo Ohio that supposedly floated the chests to the surface and tried to tow them to a shallower location for recovery. However, word of their plan had leaked and the United States Coast Guard observing the operation from the cover of Poverty Island moved in swiftly. The tugboat had not even got under way when they saw the Coast Guard cutter bearing down on them. They immediately severed the air lines and tow cables allowing the treasure to sink once again.

Over the years, a lot treasure hunters both amateur and professional have tried unsuccessfully to find the gold. Several different operations have spent twenty or more years searching to no avail. Many say that it's all a fairy tale while others have taken it seriously enough to file litigation challenging the State of Michigan over the ownership of the yet to be discovered treasure.

There are just enough clues, facts, and newspaper reports dating back to the day that the original ship was lost to keep the legend alive. Perhaps somebody will put an end to the speculation and find the riches. Perhaps sooner than we think...

FOOL'S GOLD

CHAPTER 1

There were four dead ones laying on the afterdeck of the big cruiser. Crack! Five.

A voice came from the dock above. "One of the greatest inventions in the universe, the flyswatter is."

Michael shaded his eyes against the sun. "Ranks right up there with the back-scratcher, I'd say." He got up from his canvas deck chair and smiled at the silver haired old man who seemed to be studying the lines of the boat. "Roamer. Chris-Craft, steel hull forty-two feet."

The big man nodded. "I know. Had one at one time. Nice boat. Any rust problems down below?"

Michael shook his head. "Naw. That's one of the big reasons I bought this one, everything's real solid. I'd say she's never seen saltwater."

"That's the way a lot of these Great Lakes boats are. They live their whole lives just sailing around the mitten."

After a short silence, Michael asked, "Wanna come aboard and look around? She's probably gonna be for sale this fall or next spring."

The old man smiled, stepped off the dock onto the gunwale, and hopped down to the afterdeck. "Not a fisherman, eh?" His hand swept around the aft of the boat questioning the absence of downriggers and rod holders.

Michael chuckled. "Never wet a line over the side of this boat. I actually just bought it about six months ago. It'd been sitting in dry storage for at least eight years. Had both

9

engines overhauled and just got 'em re-installed in the boat a week or so back. They start and run just fine but I haven't had the maiden voyage yet. I've been sorting out the electronics and adding a few things here and there to bring it up to date. Pretty sure I've replaced every inch of wiring. It'll be ready soon."

The man's gaze scanned the entire vessel, even managing a quick peek into the salon and cabin below. "I'm George Snyder from Grosse Pointe." He stuck out a meaty hand to meet Michael's. His grip was firm but not overpowering.

"Michael O'Conner. Detroit."

"Hey, we're neighbors. How come you've got your boat way up here in God's Country?"

Michael laughed. "Hell, Escanaba ain't so far up north. I've got a place about another hundred miles northwest of here. Really though, the boat's here because I bought it right here at this marina and I've been working on it trying to get it ready to sell. Both engines were seized up because they hadn't been started in a number of years so I had them totally rebuilt and the transmissions have been rebuilt as well. Had both propellers reworked and then had them and the prop shafts magnafluxed. No cracks or weak spots. The entire drive train is like new. I got a real deal on this baby, under ten grand. It's been strictly a project."

"Thinking of selling it, are you? I just might be interested. When do you think she'll be ready for a little sea duty? A week? Two weeks?"

Michael put his hands on his hips and looked around. "Could be two weeks, probably more though. Depends on how much time I have to work on it. I could have a few things down in Detroit that need taking care of too so I'm not sure."

Resting against the helmsman's seat, George asked. "If I decide that I don't want to buy it, would you consider taking on a charter?"

Michael shook his head. "Naw, I don't have a charter license and I have absolutely none of that type of fishing gear. I'm a fly fisherman, I don't do fishing boats. It's waders and a creel for me. But there are plenty of charter boats in the harbor and I'm sure that they're not all booked."

"I wasn't thinking about a fishing trip. I want to do a little exploring. A museum has asked me to investigate some things in this area and beyond. I've got all the stuff I'll need cameras, a team of divers, sonar equipment, everything but a big enough boat. It's a low key thing. Call it a historical expedition if you like. A little bit secret too because a magazine reporter got wind of it and has been asking a lot of questions. Museums don't like sharing until they have their prize in hand. Too many public failures would severely dampen benefactor enthusiasm."

"Sorta like a treasure hunt, eh?"

The old man smiled. "I suppose if you consider a bunch of broken and waterlogged planks and rusty spikes treasure, it could be a treasure hunt. It's mostly an historical quest though. We're looking for a significant key to the past. I have a reasonably open checkbook for this venture. What do you say?"

Michael shifted his weight to his left foot. "I dunno. The idea's intriguing. I love a good mystery. Could be fun. I've got to do a pretty good shake-down first, make sure everything on the boat works okay. You sure you don't mind waiting a couple of weeks?"

George held up his hands like a preacher blessing his congregation. "I've got a ton of preliminary work to do.

Some of it I can do from my thirty five foot fishing boat but it doesn't have enough open space for everything I'm going to need. I won't really need a big boat until we start working with the heavy equipment. Then I'll need room for a couple hundred feet of communication cable for the underwater video camera and a place for all of our spare air tanks and a couple of gasoline powered compressors. But until then, I'll be doing a bunch of quick little day trips to get things set up. I'm guessing that I'll be ready for you in two to three weeks. It could even be four."

"No promises but I'll see what I can do." Michael scribbled his cell phone number on the back of a receipt from the gas dock. "Here's my number. I might be back and forth between here and Detroit so this will be the best way to track me down. Gimme a call in about a week and I should have a better idea if I can be ready."

The big man named George Snyder handed Michael his business card, nodded climbed over the side and hopped back onto the dock. "My boat is in this marina too so I think, it would make sense for me to get a room at the motel right here. I'll be staying in touch."

Michael watched him walk to the end of the dock where a silver Mercedes with darkened windows sat idling. He couldn't help but notice that George's curly hair perfectly matched the color of the car. As he opened the passenger side door and the car Michael caught a glimpse of a reddish beard on the man behind the wheel. His eyes were covered in wrap-around mirrored sunglasses and a dirty looking baseball cap was pulled low over his brow. Snyder said something to the driver and climbed in. The Mercedes silently drove off.

CHAPTER 2

George Snyder might be described as the quintessential self-made man. He began his career as a teenager fresh out of high school working for a trucking company, starting out as a helper on the tire truck. His job was to assist the tire man who responded to highway tire repair situations. When a truck had a flat tire on the road the company would dispatch the repair crew to change the tire. George had been with the company for almost ten years and just worked his way up to the top seniority tire man when the trucking company decided to downsize their repair department and farm the work out to contractors. George had the foresight to buy the tire repair truck along with the wrecker that the company no longer needed, all financed with favorable rates through the trucking company. With his strong connections in the trucking industry he didn't miss a beat, picking up towing and tire service contracts with several outfits. George built his business on reasonable rates, prompt responses, and hired only the most reliable, competent, and conscientious workers. His company prided itself in professionalism and efficiency which translated into dollars saved for his clients. As time went on George bought out several of his competitors and expanded his service to include a wide variety of roadside repairs. His fleet eventually grew to four tire trucks, four tri-axle wreckers, and three fully equipped repair trucks, all of which operated twenty-four hours a day and covered three states. He named his company, "The Road Wrench."

And then about two years ago George bought out a small towing company in Toledo, Ohio called Admiral Salvage. It had been a family owned company for more than a century and had actually begun its life as a marine salvage company. Their old tugboat still sat on a timber crib in the storage yard. The owners hadn't engaged in maritime recovery since sometime before the Second World War, focusing their efforts on the trucking industry to help the war effort. George bought all of the assets including four large tow trucks and the original and only office building that the company ever had, a dingy but sturdy and roomy old building sitting on three acres on the banks of the Maumee River.

George Snyder planned to take anything useful and then investigate the possibility of auctioning off the building or maybe hanging on to it, after all there was one former Admiral employee still there acting as a caretaker so he wouldn't have to hire anybody new. The large storage yard as well as the three oversize repair bays just might come in handy one of these days. The office could be upgraded although the furniture wasn't worth saving. But it was a long forgotten old safe, tucked away in a storage room that would change George Snyder's life forever.

CHAPTER 3

It was after midnight when Gypsy walked out of the Stick & Stein bar in Homestead, Florida. His Harley Davidson Heritage Softail patiently waited for him at the curb. He opened the big leather saddlebag and began digging out his leather jacket and then looked up at the lighted sign on the bank across the street. The temperature said eighty-four degrees. He certainly wouldn't need the heavy jacket. The peaceful night was suddenly interrupted by the sound of Gypsy's cell phone ringing. He looked at the number and recognized it as that George guy from up in Michigan. George had offered Gypsy a lot of money to do some salvage diving somewhere in Lake Michigan. Gypsy had been making a living doing freelance salvage diving for several companies and finally opened his own business over in Key Largo almost twenty years ago. He had built a decent reputation as a somewhat surly but efficient and reliable diver. He tried to keep a low profile over the years, mainly because much of his diving involved illegal salvage. Along with a couple of cohorts Gypsy supplemented his income by pilfering from several of the undocumented shipwrecks that were scattered around the Florida Keys. Nobody suspected him of anything and he wanted to keep it that way. Some of his dealings were serious enough to merit some major time if he got caught and nobody knew his whole story. He wasn't worried about his two hired divers exposing him because, during one of their exploits the pair had murdered a local sheriff's deputy and Gypsy had helped them dispose of the body. It was a blood bond.

Gypsy was a little nervous about the call from George because it was never made clear to him how he could have come to the attention of a contractor way up north but even though he didn't know what George had in mind, there was one Great Lakes treasure that intrigued him enough to make him curious.

He answered his phone. "This is Gypsy."

"Hello, George Snyder here. I know it's late but I wanted you to know that I'm ready for you whenever you can get here. Just let me know how soon you can get away and I'll have a ticket waiting for you at the Miami Airport.

"Just a minute now. I haven't decided whether to accept your offer. I don't even know what the job is. We need to talk about this."

George was silent for a moment. "If it's a matter of money..."

"It's not that. I want to know how you heard about me and why you can't just hire a local guy."

"I see," answered George. "I'm in the transportation service and salvage business myself and I honestly can't remember who gave me your number but I'm sure that it must have been somebody in the salvage industry down there. I know a lot of people in Key Largo and put the word out last spring that I'd be needing a man with certain skills. Somebody sent me your name. The job that I'm engaged in requires a high degree of technical knowledge, you know, side-scan sonar and that sort of thing and that's why you were recommended. As a matter of fact, I believe that you were recommended by at least two salvage outfits. I've got all the equipment and all the diving gear.

I don't want to use anyone from around here because the project is somewhat sensitive. If you'll just fly up here, we can have a face-to-face meeting and I'll fill you in. If you decide not to accept my offer, I'll fly you back home and pay you for all of your time and expenses. No hard feelings. What do you say?"

"Give me an address and keep your airfare. I'll ride up. It'll take me a couple of days, maybe three."

An uneasiness swept over George as he ended the call. He had never met Gypsy and his manner on the telephone was anything bur reassuring. There was something about Gypsy's tone that suggested a dark nature. It went deeper than just a gruff demeanor.

George had relied on his honesty and integrity to build his sizable fortune and had never resorted to unethical or illegal practices. But this new adventure was far less clear. When the situation had first presented itself, George contacted his attorney to research the legality of the whole thing and the results of the lawyer's investigation while somewhat encouraging, were still not final. Now he wondered if he'd moved too quickly. Could he trust this Gypsy character? Was it too late to turn back? George shook his head. He'd play it by ear, but carefully.

CHAPTER 4

The first meeting between Gypsy and his new boss got off to a rocky start. It was obvious that George had not expected his elite salvage diver to look like an outlaw biker. Gypsy didn't seem to ask many questions other than wanting a full list of equipment that would be available to him and things like the depth of the dive. It was as if he didn't seem to care what needed to be salvaged from the bottom of the lake, or maybe he already knew. He also wanted to know how many divers would be on the job.

George told him that there would be one other diver and that he was a good one. The other mans name was Charlie Kelly and he had spent over thirty years as a diver for the Harbormaster Division of the Detroit Police Department. Gypsy stiffened when he heard the name. "You really should get acquainted," said George. He gave Gypsy a slip of paper with Charlie's address and directions to his secluded cabin. "You can stop in about any time. Charlie lives alone and he's almost always home. He reads a lot."

"Should I call first?"

George laughed. "After years of being on a leash, old Charlie decided to cut things loose. He doesn't have a phone, not even a cell phone and his place is really in the boonies. He's only got electricity because the power line runs through his property. He's so remote that they don't even read his electric meter. He drops off the readings himself once a month when he's in town."

Although it hadn't been discussed, Gypsy was sure that the prize George Snyder was seeking was the Poverty Island treasure rumored to be worth around five hundred million dollars. The list of equipment that George read to him suggested a heavy load to be lifted from the bottom. It had gold written all over it. He wasn't about to let that opportunity escape and he was prepared to kill to protect his chances.

Charlie Kelly's cabin was really off the beaten path. Gypsy had to ride almost three quarters of a mile down a twisting sand two-track before the log cabin popped up in a small clearing. Remote couldn't begin to describe it.

When he knocked on Charlie's door, it was obvious that Charlie felt that he knew Gypsy from somewhere but couldn't quite put his finger on it. Charlie had been the guy who broke him in many years ago. Gypsy went by a different name back when he was a diver for the Detroit Police Department. They called him Ping, short for Pingree. He was supposed to be some distant relative of Hazen Pingree, one time governor of Michigan. Gypsy knew that it would be only a matter of time before Charlie made the connection so he quickly devised a plan. Charlie would have to be dispatched right away. He told Charlie that he had a meeting in town but would be back later to discuss the project.

Gypsy had the forethought to come to Michigan prepared for any encounter and had packed his trusty old hogleg, a sawed of twenty gage shotgun loaded with buckshot.

He walked out to his motorcycle and slid the shotgun out of the saddlebag keeping it covered with a jacket that he threw over his arm. Acting as if he needed help, Gypsy wandered back up to the cabin door and asked Charlie for a hand getting his bike started. Charlie claimed to know nothing about motorcycles but Gypsy responded by saying it's simple and offered to show him. When they got to the sandy driveway, Gypsy turned around, shoved the shotgun right into Charlie's face and pulled both triggers.

After hiding his motorcycle in the weeds on the other side of Charlie's cabin, Gypsy loaded the body into the back of Charlie's pickup, covered it with a tarp and proceeded to sweep the area with a leaf rake to cover any evidence of the killing.

Driving Charlie's pickup, he got to the harbor just as the sun was disappearing into the bay and parked in the shadows on the east side of the marina. It was well after midnight when things got quiet enough for him to slide the body out of the truck bed and drag it down to the seawall. By two A.M. he had deposited the truck back in Charlie's driveway and hauled his Harley out of the weeds. He was sound asleep in his room at four o'clock.

CHAPTER 5

"I'm not getting involved. I'm not getting involved." Michael O'Conner repeated the phrase softly. "I'm not getting involved." He watched the scene from the afterdeck of his cruiser. Two police divers were loading the body into the Stokes litter. Even from the thirty foot distance O'Conner could see that the man had met a violent death. In the brief moments before the body was covered with a blanket, it looked like he had taken a shotgun blast square in the face at close range. The dead man was wearing blue jeans and denim shirt. He wasn't dressed like a boater even though he had been found floating between the docks at the marina. Boaters don't usually wear cowboy boots.

Michael silently promised himself that he wouldn't ask questions and wouldn't engage in the marina gossip. He was here to get his boat restored to pristine condition so that he could get a good price for it. He had work to do. There was no time for dead bodies and no time for solving murders. That was the cop's job. He wasn't going to get involved. Michael turned his back to the grisly scene and tried to concentrate on getting the binnacle compass mounted. Even at this early hour the docks were filling with people, primarily men and a few young women. Most of the kids had all been whisked away by mothers concerned about nightmares.

He felt the boat rock slightly and turned to see a man in a uniform with a gleaming deputy sheriff badge climbing aboard. The man wasn't smiling and held a notebook in one hand and a pencil in the other. His voice was raspy and tired sounding. "I need to ask a few questions." Michael was now involved.

The man introduced himself as Deputy Haynes. "This your boat?"

Michael nodded.

"How long have you been on here? I mean on this boat."

Michael answered. "I've been staying here since we put it in the water about ten days ago. Been right here every day. I don't sleep on board though. I've got a room in the marina motel." Michael pointed back at the motel at the end of the dock.

"Close enough. Were you there last night?"

"Yep. All night"

"Okay. Did you hear or see anything unusual during the night?"

"You mean like a shotgun blast?" asked Michael.

"Who said anything about gunshots?" fired back Deputy Haynes.

"Look deputy, I'm a licensed private investigator and a City of Detroit reserve police officer. I'm not trying to give you a hard time, just hoping to keep my distance from this whole situation. But to answer your question, it was a peaceful night and I sat right out on my balcony that faces the bay sipping Margaritas and chatting with an old friend until almost three o'clock this morning and then went to bed. I never heard anything."

"Who was the old friend?" asked the deputy.

"John Strong," replied Michael. "He owns this place."

The Deputy scribbled a few notes and then asked "Can I see your Detroit ID?"

Michael fumbled through his wallet and finally produced his Detroit Police Department identification tag. "Here you go,"

"Okay Mister O'Conner. I guess it's okay to share a little with you. Preliminary information is that the body that we just hauled out of the harbor was quite possibly a retired Detroit cop, Harbormaster division.

CHAPTER 6

Little Bay Marina on Little Bay de Noc in Escanaba, Michigan is less than twelve years old but it has already more than tripled in size. Built on the twelve acre site of an old deserted coal terminal the new marina brought a sophisticated aura to the once barren waterfront. Featuring two hundred deep water slips and eighteen transient berths it is easily the largest and most modern marina in the area. It is capped off with a tasteful ninety room motel and crowned by "The Ship's Anchor," a beautiful nightclub at the far end of the longest pier in the facility. A smaller, year round restaurant sits next to the motel office. Tying the entire complex together was a large combination party store and marina supply store that anchored the gas dock. A person could buy anything from a six pack of beer and a deli sandwich to water skis and beach towels.

Originally built as a fisherman's marina by the owner of a local lumberyard, it was sold to an industrious couple from a farming community in Michigan's Lower Peninsula and it was then that the business blossomed. Fred and Sarah Strong retired from a large and successful dairy farm and needed to invest some of the profit from the sale of the farm. It was a big jump from milking five hundred cows every day to becoming a landlord for floating tenants but the Strong's recognized the potential and didn't hesitate. Their only son, John, a business school graduate agreed to help them launch the enterprise. John saw the dangers of running a seasonal business and depending on the weather for success so he made sure that the facility would offer attractive recreational activities year round. He joined with nearby ski lodges to offer skiing and snowmobiling packages, bought dozens of ice fishing shanties to place throughout the harbor, and even organized a winter festival. It was John's forward thinking and aggressive style that catapulted the little marina into an empire. Rather than rely on local trade to sustain the business, John embellished the facility with amenities that would attract business from Milwaukee and Chicago as well as all of Michigan and the rest of the Great Lakes. Along with the sizable investment his parents provided, he was able to draw investors from all over the Midwest. Providing a free shuttle service between the Marina and the upscale local casino furnished the catalyst that sealed the deal. The business still had plenty of room for growth but the docks boasted close to seventy-five percent occupancy which comfortably paid the bills and provided a nice living for the proprietors. The future was bright.

Three years into their ownership, Fred Strong, not yet sixty years old suffered a fatal heart attack. The tragedy changed a lot of things. John sold his home back in Elkton, Michigan and with his wife Sandy, he moved to Escanaba to help his mother manage the marina complex. A popular place known for its luxury, Little Bay Marina due to John's efforts was even featured in a major boating magazine. John and his mother had carved a diamond out of the northern Michigan granite.

Back when John was in college he played the keyboard and sang the lead vocals for a little campus band. They were pretty good and very popular with the college crowd. John harbored a not so secret desire to someday become a recording star. As time went on his dreams of show business fame and glory faded but now that he owned his own nightclub he installed himself as the Friday night piano bar artist from Elkton, Michigan. He billed himself as "Elkton John."

John was sitting at the piano in the nightclub on a Tuesday around noon going over a couple of old songs that he wanted to include in his repertoire. As with most weekdays the place only had a few customers, a half dozen or so at the bar, a few scattered couples who had stopped by for lunch, and a two men who sat at a table in a corner who seemed to be in deep conversation.

When Michael O'Conner walked into the club, John immediately broke into a rendition of Johnny Mercer's classic, Tangerine. The familiar melody brought a smile to Michael's face, it had been Michael's college theme song and John had always played it when Michael entered the bar. He crossed the room and joined his old college room mate at the baby grand.

"How's the yacht coming?" asked John

Michael leaned on the piano, "All of the cleaning and painting is done and the engines are installed and ready for testing. It looks great but I'm just getting into the finer details now so progress is slowing down. Some days it looks like nothing gets accomplished but it's all stuff that needs doing. I'm getting very close."

"Have you decided what you're going to do with it? If you want to get rid of it, I'm sure I could line you up with some great buyer prospects."

"Y'know, the more I work on it, the more attached I become. I know that I bought it purely as an investment but now I'm not so sure I want to sell it. A guy stopped by the other day who might be interested in it. His name is George Snyder. He gave me his card. But if you see me painting a name on the transom, you'll know I've decided to keep her."

John moved into a slow quiet rendition of Hoagy Carmichael's "Skylark." "I think it'd be great if you hung onto it. There's plenty of business in this area if you wanted to start pulling charters."

"Nah, you gotta be a lifetime Great Lakes fisherman to have any success in that kind of business. If I hang on to her, she's gonna be strictly a pleasure boat. I hear they can be a real chick magnet," grinned Michael.

John stopped playing for a moment and looked at his friend, "I guess that Sheriff's deputy talked to you about the guy they found out there in the marina harbor. Said that you used me as your alibi. He questioned me for about a half hour this morning. I couldn't help him at all. I haven't seen or heard anything out of the ordinary. How about you?"

"Not a thing. I'm sure I would have heard a shotgun being fired."

"Shotgun? What's up with that?"

Michael realized that John hadn't seen the body. "I'm sure it was a homicide," said Michael. "Looked like the guy took a full load of buckshot to the head, not much left. They think that they might know who the victim was though."

"Oh brother. Was it somebody from around here?"

Michael thought for a moment. "I don't think so. The deputy said that it might be a guy who retired from the Detroit police force. I don't think they're sure yet."

John began playing the piano again, quieter this time. "The only thing I know is that it wasn't someone who was staying here and I haven't heard any talk so I don't think it was anyone connected with any of the boats. As far as I'm concerned, the less said, the better. I'm sure that the newspapers and television reporters are gonna want a statement from me. Haven't a clue what I'm going to say though. And it couldn't have come at a worse time No disrespect for the deceased but I'm kinda hung out to dry on this big 'Shoreline Festival.' Back last November when the chamber of commerce came up with this idea of some kind of summer festival to promote boating and fishing and stuff, I volunteered to be the chairman. Figured that our business had the most to gain. We got a lot going on. There's a carnival that's going to set up at the back corner of our parking lot and the rooms in our motel will surely sell out by the end of next week. I just don't need any bad publicity right now."

CHAPTER 7

"Hello Otis? This is Michael. I tried to reach McCoy but my calls keep going straight to his voicemail."

"McCoy is headed your way. He has just been told that his promotion was approved and he'll be moving up the ranks in about a month. He decided he'd better burn up his vacation while he had the chance. I think he's got over two weeks coming. Said he was gonna head up there and give you a hand with your boat project."

"That's great. I guess I'll be staying up here until I get it finished then. But the reason I called was to find out if you ever knew any cops in the harbormaster division? Any that retired recently?"

"Yeah, I know Charlie Kelly," answered Homicide Lieutenant Otis Springfield "he retired about three or four years ago. If I recall correctly he was originally a Yooper. Last I heard he was traveling the world looking for the greatest scuba adventures on the face of the earth. Said he'd paid his dues in the muddy waters of the Detroit River. Wanted some of that crystal clear Caribbean or northern lakes stuff. Why? Did you run across him?"

"Well, I'm not sure but if I did it's not good news," answered Michael. "They've just found a body in the harbor here in Escanaba and it looks like it might possibly be him. It was a homicide."

"Aw geeze. We keep losing all the good guys. Any arrests? Suspects?

Michael wasn't sure how to answer "As far as I can see, there aren't even any leads at this point. So far there hasn't been a positive ID. I'm not a hundred percent sure that it's your friend. I'll keep you posted."

"We're still planning to come up there in a few days for a couple week's vacation. Marla and the kids are really counting on it. Everybody is looking forward to the big festival. Will this change anything?

"Not at all" said Michael. "I've got the two adjoining rooms right next to mine reserved for you, Marla and the twins. The extended weather forecast is full of above average temperatures and lots of sunshine. I'm sure you'll all like it here. Aside from the fact that there's a first rate night club just up the dock, there's a great bathing beach for the kids, lots of nearby shopping for Marla and you and me can see if this tub will make it in and out of the harbor."

Otis sighed, "If it's going to be your first venture into the bay, I'm not so worried about making it out of the harbor, it's bringing it back in that concerns me."

After Michael hung up, his thoughts wandered back to the body that he had seen being recovered in the harbor. There was no face for him to recognize yet there was something disturbingly familiar about the victim. Perhaps it was the way he was dressed. Or maybe it was the cowboy boots. Michael couldn't connect with any of it. Charles Kelly certainly didn't ring any bells. The guy with George Snyder, the driver of the Mercedes had been dressed a lot like the guy floating in the harbor. Michael realized that had forgotten to mention his contact with George Snyder when the deputy questioned him earlier today. He dialed the Sheriff's office.

"I'd like to speak with Deputy Haynes please." Michael tapped his foot while he waited for the deputy to come to the phone.

"Haynes."

"Hello deputy. This is Michael O'Conner, the guy you interviewed on board the boat at the marina this morning. I may have a little more information for you. There was a man inquiring about chartering my boat for a diving expedition and I think that his partner was wearing the same kind of clothes as the guy you found in the water. I'm not positive but I've got a feeling that it could have been him."

"Well, we haven't got the final results on the fingerprint identification yet but we'll take any information we can get. Can you locate the other man that was with him?"

"I think so, He left me his business card. How about if I just give you the information and let you make the contact?" Michael was still determined not to become involved.

"Okay, let me have it."

Michael read off the contact information from "The Road Wrench" business card, ended the call on his cell phone and said a silent prayer that he'd heard the last of it.

CHAPTER 8

The knock on Gypsy's door at five o'clock in the morning was barely audible. A skinny, grizzled old man stood outside reeking of whiskey and filth. "We need to talk mister."

Gypsy stared at him for a minute and then looked up and down the sidewalk in front of his room. Satisfied that nobody else was around he stepped back and said, "Come on in."

The old man settled into a chair and began, "I was just finishing off my evening refreshments when I saw a man get out of a pickup truck, haul something out of the bed and roll it into the water. Stayed hid until the pickup left and then I went over to the seawall to check if I could see anything. Sure as hell looked like a body floatin' out there. A while later a motorcycle pulled in and the guy who got off of it walked just like the guy in the pickup truck. I followed him right to this room. Sat out there most of the night tryin' to figure out what I should do."

"So you came here to talk about it?" asked Gypsy.

The old man laughed a drunken giggle and said. "I see a chance to make a little something here. If your buddy overdosed on something and you wanted to get rid of the body, I don't blame you. But if you want me to keep quiet about it, we need to talk money."

Gypsy decided to play along. "I don't have a lot of money here so I can't help you. All my cash is in a lock box in my cabin over in Bark River."

The old man's eyes lit up. "Then let's go get it."

Gypsy stroked his beard. "You got any transportation?"

"My car's right outside."

The two men walked out into the parking lot, climbed into the old Chevy Nova and drove off into the night.

CHAPTER 9

"Well, did you have a good conversation with Charlie? Was he any help to you?" George Snyder was digging away at a large slice of cantaloupe.

"Never hooked up with him," answered Gypsy. "I got turned around a little bit trying to follow your directions and pretty soon I found myself in front of a place called The Island Casino and Resort. Decided to stop in and try my hand at the slots. I started getting hot and stayed there til damned near midnight. It was too late by then so I guess I'll have to compare notes with this Charlie guy some other time." Gypsy sat across the table sipping his coffee.

George paused for a moment, pondering his response. "Oh well, I was really hoping you'd be able to stop by his place last night. I figured you'd be anxious to meet him."

Gypsy waved his hand. "Doesn't matter, I'll catch up to him eventually. Anyway, I need to know just what it is that you need me for"

George polished off his breakfast before he spoke. He decided to lay out his story and study Gypsy's reaction. "There's a shipwreck out there in Lake Michigan that I'm very interested in. Lots of people have tried unsuccessfully to find it over the years but I have reason to believe that they've all been looking in the wrong place. I'm pretty sure that I know where it lies."

"Poverty Island wreck?"

George smiled and nodded "You've heard of it, I gather."

"I think everybody anywhere near the Great Lakes and certainly anyone involved in marine salvage has heard of it. Why do you think you know more than the other salvage guys? Some people have done tons of research and invested thousands of dollars but everybody comes up empty." Gypsy was now slumping in his chair.

"If it had as much treasure on board as the legend says, it's surely enough to make this search well worth the investment. And to answer the other part of your question, I think I've come across some information about the actual location that the other folks just don't have."

Gypsy shifted his weight and his eyes brightened. "Sunken treasure, eh? You've got my attention. It's supposed to be a really big prize. How many people are in on this deal?"

"Right now it's just you, Jake my advisor, me, and Charlie. Wasn't planning on getting anyone else involved. Well, I've talked to a guy about chartering a boat but he doesn't have any idea what it's all about."

Gypsy sat up straight. "What's in it for me? What are you willing to pay?"

George leaned toward Gypsy. "If we find what I'm looking for, I'll pay you two hundred thousand dollars."

There was a long pause before Gypsy answered. "And if we come up empty handed?"

"Four hundred a day plus expenses," answered George.

Gypsy nodded. "When do we get started?"

George was glad that he was able to get some facts out in front of Gypsy and judge his reaction. The diver seemed to be happy with the cash offer although he'd probably insist on a bigger share when they found it. But for now, no alarms went off in George's head and so he relaxed a little.

"I'm headed out to Charlie's cabin right now. You want to come along?"

"Naw. I think I'd better go back to my room and get cleaned up. I checked in right here last night. You can fill me in later. Maybe the three of us can have supper tonight or something."

When George arrived at Charlie's secluded cabin he found a Sheriff's Department cruiser parked in the driveway. Charlie's old Ford pickup was parked in its normal place next to the cabin. A man in a uniform standing at the front door turned and looked when he heard George drive up. George got out of the car and hesitantly walked up to the deputy. "Is there some kind of problem, officer?"

The deputy looked George up and down. "This your place?"

George shook his head. "No, a friend of mine lives here."

"I'm trying to establish an identity. What's the name of this friend of yours?" The deputy gestured toward the cabin.

"His name is Charlie Kelly. Can you tell me what's going on?"

The deputy glanced at his notes, "Would you be George Snyder?"

George was clearly shocked that the deputy knew his name. "That's right. Is something wrong here?"

"We need to talk. I may have some very bad news for you.

The clouds of doubt were in George's mind once again.

CHAPTER 10

The old Admiral Salvage Company of Toledo only had one full time employee left on the payroll when its investors decided to unload the business. Jacob Marley has been teased about his name for most of his lifetime. His namesake, the partner of Ebenezer Scrooge appears as a ghost in the Dickens classic, A Christmas Carol. But he's also a soothsayer and that description fits Jake Marley. Jacob, in his late thirties with a workingman's muscular build on his six foot two inch frame. His narrow waistline suggested the daily workouts of a boxer but his demeanor tells a gentler, almost timid story.

When Admiral Salvage was sold to that Snyder guy from up in the Detroit area, Jake had managed to stay on as the Toledo site manager and assist with the transition. Jake's great grandfather had been one of the original employees of the company back in the early nineteen hundreds. He served as the first mate and navigator on the company's salvage tug. Old Harry Marley was probably the best navigator on the Great Lakes. It was said that he could pinpoint the location of a wreck within ten feet in the middle of Lake Superior. The accuracy of his secret system of celestial navigation was legendary.

The rusted old tugboat had at one time been the pride of Admiral's fleet of tugboats but after a costly encounter with the United States Coast Guard almost a century ago, she was hauled out of the river and cradled on the shore. She was lucky to have not been impounded and hadn't moved since. Without the use of their prized tugboat, Admiral Salvage was forced to shift its focus to rolling stock, concentrating on the trucking industry and operating a small salvage yard.

One of Jake's first assignments from the new owner was to get the ancient tugboat ready for sale as scrap. All he had to do was measure all of the bulkheads and compartments and calculate the volume of scrap metal. Outside of the propeller and the old model 129-6 Winton Diesel Marine engine which was undoubtedly seized up from non-use, there certainly couldn't be much of value still on board but he was told to see if there was anything worth saving. Jake really hated the thought of the old tug being cut up to make razor blades. As a kid he used to play on her decks when his dad worked for Admiral Salvage. He figured he'd remove the ship's wheel and see if the new owner would let him keep it as a childhood memory. Some of the primitive instruments might possibly have some value. There are plenty of collectors who'd be interested in that stuff.

It was while he was disassembling the pilot's console that he discovered the notebook tucked deep inside. The only reason he could think of for it being hidden was that it must contain some very secret information. Jake is not the type to take on any responsibility unless he's directed to. Notebook in hand he hurried back to the office and called his new boss.

"Snyder here," blared in Jake's ear.

"Oh, hello mister Snyder. This is Jake Marley from Admiral Salvage and I've found something that you might need to know about"

"Okay, tell me about it."

"Well, I was taking apart the pilot's station on that old tugboat and I found an old notebook hidden inside."

"Cool. What's in the notebook?"

"Well sir. There's just a few words. It says, 'In the silver,' And then just some numbers and letters. I think it could be the combination to that old safe in the back room."

Snyder laughed. "What's in that old safe anyway? I've wondered about that thing ever since I first laid eyes on it."

"I've worked here for twenty some years, Mr. Snyder and I've never seen that safe opened. From what I heard, nobody could remember ever seeing it opened. No one here knew the combination."

"Hmm," mused Snyder. "I'll be down that way in a couple of days and you and me can check it out."

It was two days later when Jake and Snyder crouched in front of the safe and Jake read the numbers from the book. "Thirty-two R. twenty-two L. and twelve R."

"Sounds simple enough," commented Snyder. He smiled when the door swung open effortlessly. "You must have oiled the hinges before I got here," he grinned.

The safe was mostly empty with just a tin can containing eight stacks of silver coins from the early nineteen hundreds up through the twenties and what appeared to be a ship's log, its leather cover carved with the words Log Book.

"Why don't you put on a pot of coffee and then you and me can see what's so mysterious in here," said Snyder holding up the logbook. He walked into the front office and plopped down in the big swivel chair behind the desk.

Snyder was soon buried in the tugboat log. For the most part, it contained details of hard hat dives on sunken freighters and lists of clients and salvaged items. But when he flipped through to the last few entries there were references to large crates full of gold bullion and more containing gold and silver coins. The estimates were in the tens of millions of dollars. There was a mention of Poverty Island. He checked the date of the entry and it was August nineteen twenty-nine. The report went on to say that a crew of hard hat divers had lashed the crates together with cables and had installed a large float collar around the entire package. The on deck compressors worked all day and the next night to raise the treasure from the bottom. It was a little more than two and a half hours before dawn when the top of the first crate reached the surface. The air pumps were adjusted to maintain neutral buoyancy and the tug began to tow its treasure on a westerly course. They had made their way close to thirty five miles when the sunrise revealed a column of black smoke on the grey horizon off of their stern. The Captain ordered one of the divers to keep the other boat in the telescope and told his navigator to keep a running fix on their position. Within forty five minutes the watchman had identified the unknown vessel as a Coast Guard cutter and it was definitely in pursuit. The captain told Harry Marley, his navigator to determine a firm and exact fix on their position and then he ordered the crew to sever all of the air lines and tow cables and allow the crates to sink. He then set a northward course while the Coast Guard cutter was still well over a half hour away. There was a vague reference to Beaver Island off the starboard bow in the log book but nothing concrete. There were no more entries in the log.

When Snyder looked up from the log book he was greeted with the sight of Jacob Marley sitting directly across the desk, staring at him. Snyder cleared his throat, "There's a Harry Marley mentioned here. Any relation?"

"Yep, my great grand daddy. Probably the greatest navigator the Great Lakes ever saw. A real innovator who was way ahead of his time, he even had a custom made sextant, made to his own specifications. His was the only sextant ever built that would work on the Great Lakes. They're all made to operate at sea level and the lakes are about six hundred feet above sea level so all of the relative star positions needed to be recalculated. It was a tremendous mathematical challenge and he had his figures verified by no less than four different engineering colleges. His name is mentioned in several books about navigation. I can just barely remember him. He died when I was like six or seven."

"Interesting," commented Snyder. "The big question will be, 'What are the coordinates?' The log book says that the skipper had your great grandfather get a fix on their position but it's not entered in the log. Strange."

"From what I've seen of old Harry's personality, he could be pretty cryptic. I'd bet everything's in there. You'll just have to find it."

"Ever had any luck figuring out his secret codes?"

Jake displayed a sly grin. "I've had some success but I'm the only one, nobody else has ever figured out any of his old notes and stuff. I've been studying his work all my life. I guess I think a lot like he did. Must be in the genes"

Snyder tossed the log into Jake's lap and said. "I'm trusting you with something highly important. I'm not sure if I believe one word of what I just read. If it turns out to be true, I'll make you my full partner in this. Like you said, you're probably the only one who can figure this out. Just be completely honest with me, okay?"

Jake nodded. "You can trust me. I've never done a dishonest thing in my life and I never will."

CHAPTER 11

The log book from the tugboat intrigued George enough that he made copies of all of the final entries and took them home with him. When he began to investigate the Poverty Island connection he stumbled across the highly debated story of the treasure. According to one of the reports, in about eighteen sixty-three the Confederate Government had put together four or five crates full of gold and smuggled them aboard a ship in the Chicago Harbor that was scheduled to set sail for a port somewhere in Canada. At that point the Confederates planned to use the gold to purchase muskets, canons, gun powder, and other munitions. But word of the gold had leaked and the ship was intercepted by pirates just off of Poverty Island in northern Lake Michigan. When the captain saw the pirate ship approaching he ordered the gold dumped over the side in an effort to save the lives of him and his men, The tactic backfired and angered the pirates who slaughtered the entire crew and then sunk the ship. The story was covered by a few local newspapers but due to the sensitivity of secret wartime strategies major news outlets avoided it. Another account had the gold coming from the other direction, a loan from France that was being smuggled down through Canada. But all reports had their endings in the Lake Michigan waters near Poverty Island and all of them had five crates of gold. Either way, if true, the incident could have very likely changed the outcome of the Civil War. It was an historically important legend.

Over the years, hundreds of treasure hunters have searched in vain for the lost gold. From time to time there are reports that evidence of the treasure's existence has been found but never anything substantial.

One story particularly intrigued Snyder. Back in about nineteen twenty-nine there was a report that a tugboat possibly named The Maumee Princess and owned by a salvage company in Toledo, Ohio may have located the wreckage and deployed divers in the area. According to the report the divers had floated 'something' to the surface and had attempted to tow it away. A coast Guard vessel had observed the activity moved in to investigate. Before they were able to intercept, the tug became separated from its tow and whatever it was that was being salvaged was claimed once again by the cold waters of northern Lake Michigan. The notes were not an official Coast Guard report but simply excerpts from a Yeoman's log. There was no firm location given for the incident but it was implied to be in the vicinity of Poverty Island.

It was almost Christmas before Jacob Marley contacted George Snyder with the solution to his great grandfather's navigational riddle.

"Okay Mister Snyder, I'm pretty sure I've got the answer you were looking for."

Snyder's smile could almost be heard over the phone. "Lemme have it. I'm all ears and I've got a pencil in my hand."

"Here we go then. Latitude, forty five degrees, thirty eight minutes, and forty nine point two nine two eight seconds North. Longitude is eighty five degrees, thirty three minutes, and nine point five, three, seven, eight seconds West."

"How in the hell did you come up with that?" laughed Snyder.

"Well sir, the note book that I found hidden in the old Princess said 'In the silver.'" Since those were the only words in the book and somebody went to great lengths to hide the damned thing, I figured it might mean something. Then I remembered those old silver coins that were in the safe. When I took the can out I saw that there were little cardboard dividers between the stacks so's that they wouldn't get mixed up. It took me a long time to put it all together though. Probably couldn't have figured it out except I've done a fair bit of navigating myself."

"You got all this information from a can full of old coins?"

"It sure wasn't easy mister Snyder. I musta tried over a hundred ways of arranging those coins. Sometimes I did it by date and sometimes by the face value. I finally wound up using a combination. Some were stacked heads up and others were tails up. That was part of his code. Had to be awful careful to always put 'em back in the same order they were in when I found 'em. Even the way that the tin can was positioned in the safe meant something. The coins in the north end of the can were used to figure the latitude and the other row of coins were on the east side of the can. They were the longitude. Everything that old Harry Marley did had a definite reason, y'know. When I got done, I checked everything against a NOOA nautical chart and it makes perfect sense. The location is just west of the southern end of Beaver Island. Looks to be between fifty and sixty-five feet of water in that area"

"You referred to that old tugboat as the 'Princess,' is that her official name?"

"No sir," answered Jake. "Her name is the Maumee Princess."

George was stunned. That was the name mentioned in the old Coast Guard report.

"Well Jake, I have to tell you that I'm truly amazed. You know, of course that you can never share this information with anyone else. Anyone at all, even your wife and children,"

Jake chuckled. "Don't you be worried about that mister Snyder, I've never been married and have no family at all. And one of the reasons that I've been able to keep this job all my life is that I know how to keep my mouth shut."

"If this turns out to be what I hope it is, you will be richly rewarded for all you've done. I won't leave you in the dust my friend."

George Snyder used the remainder of the winter to accumulate underwater search gear. He spent countless hours in dive shops picking the brains of staff members. It seems that the story of the Poverty Island treasure was widely known, especially after the network television show "Unsolved Mysteries" did a segment on it. Every dive shop he visited had outfitted at least one expedition of treasure hunters. The treasure hunt had become an industry unto itself. And they were all looking in the wrong place.

In quiet times George reflected on his discovery. If it was true it could make him wealthy beyond his wildest imagination. But along with obscene wealth came obscene problems. He would need to hire professional help to retrieve the treasure. During the recovery he wouldn't be able to fully trust anyone. He would need to be vigilant at all times. George didn't have any family to turn to and his dedication to his career had not afforded him the time to develop any trusted friendships. He was virtually alone and at the mercy of his own character judgment when bringing partners on board. A heavy burden indeed. His thoughts drifted to Michael O'Conner, the boat owner. George's gut feeling told him that Michael was upstanding and trust-worthy. But he didn't know for sure.

CHAPTER 12

Michael O'Conner was having lunch in the marina sandwich shop when George Snyder walked in the door followed by a husky guy dressed in well worn jeans, sleeveless t-shirt, leather vest, and a ball cap with a skull on the front. His muscular arms must have carried a dozen tattoos displaying dragons and snakes. He wore dark sunglasses and a beard so thick that the only exposed skin on his face was a prizefighter's crooked nose.

George spotted Michael, waved and headed straight over to his table. The new guy stood just inside the doorway. George spoke quietly, "It looks like I've got a problem or two. One of my divers has died suddenly and I'll need to find someone to take his place. It's not really of any concern to you but I thought I'd let you know in case it causes a hold up."

"Would that be the body the Sheriff's department recovered from the harbor?" asked Michael.

"That's right. Nobody knows what happened but it's certainly a tragedy. I'd gotten to know Charlie and felt that he was a guy I could trust. I really liked him. I guess the only family he has is an older sister in a nursing home in Arizona. They're not sure if she's strong enough to be told about it."

Michael pointed with his chin, "Is that fellow one of your divers?"

George turned to the man standing by the door and hollered, "Hey Gypsy, c'mon over. I want you to meet someone."

Gypsy walked slowly and deliberately over to the table. He nodded at Michael.

Michael smiled.

"This is Gypsy," said George. "And this is Michael. Mike has a good size motor yacht in the marina here and we're hoping to use it as our search vessel."

"It's not quite ready," said Michael but a friend is coming up to help me. It should move along quicker once he gets here. He's a Detroit cop on vacation. I guess this is his way to unwind."

Gypsy nodded again. "When you gonna be ready?"

"Maybe pretty soon. When McCoy gets here we'll do a test run on the engines, one at a time. You know, make sure they're running smooth and cooling okay and the oil pressure stays constant. Then we'll finish wiring in the electronic stuff. There's two of everything because of the dual command stations so we have to make sure that everything's in sync. Then we check out the transmissions and we'll be ready for our maiden voyage. Probably have to do a few shake-downs before we declare it ready."

George sat down in the chair opposite Michael. "I'll need to come aboard tomorrow if I can. I want to take a few measurements in your afterdeck area. It looks plenty big enough but I've ordered a portable gasoline powered air compressor that we'll be needing for the operation and I want to make sure we have a good spot to lash it down."

Gypsy cleared his throat. "This friend of yours, I think you said it was McCoy. Where will he be staying?"

Michael turned. "Right in our motel. He's got the room next to mine."

Gypsy nodded.

George stood up to leave and added, "As soon as I can hire another diver, we'll be getting together for some planning sessions. Gypsy, here knows a couple of guys down in Florida who might be willing to sign on, We'll see. Take care." He turned and walked out the door. Gypsy followed him.

Gypsy tried to remember if he'd ever run across a cop named McCoy. It didn't sound familiar at all but he sure wasn't happy about all the Detroit cops he was encountering. When he left the Detroit Police force in disgrace thirty years ago he had been at least twenty five pounds lighter with a slim athletic build. No tattoos back then, he also had worn his hair in a military cut and he was clean shaven. He looked a lot different today than he did back when he was a diver with the Detroit Harbor Master Division. His voice had become much deeper as well, the result of breathing mixed gases during deep dives.

CHAPTER 13

The breeze played with McCoy's sandy blond hair as he tightened the final mounting screw securing the satellite telephone booster antenna. "So tell me about all these dead bodies you been tripping over."

Michael smiled as he peeked around the corner of the command station. "It's not quite that bad. There's only one body and I never got near it."

"I hear it might have been a Detroit cop," said McCoy.

"Nothing official yet but it's looking like that. A guy named Kelly from the Harbormaster division," answered Michael.

McCoy paused, staring into space for a moment. "Never hung around with those guys much. Can't say that the name rings a bell."

"Ahoy there."

Michael looked up to see Deputy Haynes standing on the dock next to the boat. "C'mon aboard, Deputy. What brings you down here this morning?"

Deputy Haynes hopped down to the afterdeck. "More bad news, I'm afraid. You know a guy named Freddie Henson?"

"There's a Freddie that kinda hangs around the marina picking up odd jobs from the boat owners. He's done a couple of lifting chores for me. Hard worker and all he ever wants is a few bucks for a bottle of whiskey. I think he lives in his car most of the summer. Never knew his last name."

"Well, he was found in his car on a deserted road a few miles out of town this morning," said the deputy. "Strangled. He had your name on a slip of paper in his wallet. When was the last time he worked for you?"

"Geeze, I guess it's been a week or so. He helped me install the bilge pumps and sniffers down below. It was kind of a two man job," answered Michael. "I've seen him around the boat yard lately but haven't talked to him."

"That's kinda what I expected. I've known the guy for close to ten years. Had to throw him in the drunk tank once or twice but he was never a problem type. Always trying to pick up a few bucks doing odd jobs. Claimed the marina was a great place to find work because boaters were always fixing things, paid in cash, and they liked having him around, probably because he didn't steal things. I understand that he had a deal with the owner of the marina that he would mop the floor every morning in the men's dockside bath house in exchange for a key to the place so that he could use the bathroom and shower. He used the marina laundromat too. That would kinda go along with what you said about living in his car. Had a good heart but a weakness for the grape. My understanding is that he came from a privileged family up in Marquette but was cursed with a very low IQ and was sorta shunned by his folks and siblings. Too bad because he was really a decent guy. When was the last time you saw him?"

"A couple of days ago. He was sitting out on the break wall drinking out of a paper bag. Didn't talk to him though."

The deputy nodded and shrugged.

Michael moved toward the engine hatch. "Sorry I couldn't be more help but I just didn't know him that well."

It's okay, I'll interview the marina owner and see if I can make the picture a little clearer," replied the deputy. He gestured toward McCoy. "You haven't introduced me to your friend."

"Oh, yeah. This is Detective Sergeant McCoy of the Homicide division, Detroit Police Department."

The deputy extended his hand and the two men exchanged hellos.

After the deputy climbed back up to the dock, McCoy grinned at Michael and grinned. "See what I mean? This place is just like Cabott Cove, you can't turn around without seeing a body. You guys get all the interesting cases. Back in Detroit most of our murders can be pigeon holed into just two categories, boy/girl murders where husbands kill wives and vice versa or street gang murders. Solving the domestic ones is almost always a slam dunk because passion inevitably leaves a trail but tons of the gang killings never get solved and nobody seems to care. The street is not known for producing witnesses. Homicide investigation can be very frustrating."

Michael hurriedly changed the subject. "George Snyder is supposed to stop by sometime this morning to do some measuring on the boat so that he can plan on how to arrange his equipment."

McCoy wiped the sweat from his forehead. "That's the guy you told me about? The one who wants to charter this thing?"

"Yep, that's him. He wants to make sure that he can get all of his gear on board. I guess that finding a shipwreck takes a lot of equipment."

What do you know about this guy?" asked McCoy. Did you check him out?

Michael pondered the question. Didn't really think about it. I guess I should have. I'll get on it tomorrow. I won't be doing anything with him for at least a week. I've got time. All I know right now is that he lives in Grosse Pointe and that he owns a fleet of service trucks and takes care of the big rigs when they break down on the road."

McCoy nodded. "Sounds like a legitimate business. Should be easy enough to get a handle on it. Want me to do it for you?"

"Be my Guest."

A silver Mercedes glided to a quiet stop next to Michael's slip. Both doors opened and two men climbed out. The older one waved and walked toward the boat while the other guy just leaned on the fender and looked around the marina. McCoy watched them both with interest.

"Greetings," said the older man. He held up what looked like a one hundred foot tape measure and asked, "Can I come aboard?"

Michael waved him welcome.

The man produced a notebook from his shirt pocket and started looking around the afterdeck. "Sure looks plenty roomy enough. The biggest things I have are the compressor, a rack for a dozen or so spare tanks, and the tub for the coils of cable. If we get to a point where we need to bring anything to the surface, I'll need room for my lifting collars but that will be later on." He handed one end of the tape to Michael and asked him to hold it on one corner of the transom. He then stretched measurements in two directions, smiling as he wrote in his notebook. "Plenty of space. I might even have room for a cooler full of egg salad sandwiches and some iced tea."

McCoy walked over and introduced himself. It was only then that George Snyder seemed to remember his partner. He turned and yelled up to the parking area. "Hey Gypsy, wanna meet the guys we'll be working with?"

Gypsy had been studying McCoy since he got out of the car and seemed comfortable climbing down on the boat and shaking hands with McCoy and Michael. "Pleased." Was his one word greeting.

McCoy nodded and smiled.

Snyder spoke up. "Any idea when you'll be ready? A couple of Gypsy's dive buddies from down in Florida will be here in a day or so and we'll be making a preliminary exploration with my runabout. If all goes well, we'll be ready soon after that."

"Well, said Michael, "I was planning to take tomorrow off because another one of my friends is coming up with his wife and kids and I want to spend the day with them. I plan to try our maiden voyage the following day and then I'll know if we're ready."

Snyder smiled, "Sounds like a plan. We're definitely on the same page. I'll check back in about three days." The two men returned to the Mercedes and drove away.

McCoy spoke up. "Your main guy seems to be okay but I'm not too crazy about his right hand man. Wonder where he dug him up?"

"I talked to George about that guy and he tells me that one of his contacts down in Florida recommended him. Says he's a top notch diver even if he is a little on the weird side. George says he'll make sure that he tows the line"

"I sure hope you're right," answered McCoy.

CHAPTER 14

Gypsy was at the airport waiting to pick up the two new divers that he and George had hired. George only wanted to bring one more person into the project but Gypsy convinced him that it was better all around to have three qualified people on the job. He was still deciding how much information to share with his partners.

Eddie and Sam had done a lot of diving with Gypsy, they had been his employees for a number of years down in Key Largo. The two men looked enough alike to be brothers but they weren't related. About five feet ten inches medium build with brown hair. No tattoos or piercings. Two very nondescript looking guys. In the early days it had been all about legitimate salvage but then Sam started getting greedy.

On a routine dive to recover a pleasure boat belonging to the son of a wealthy real estate developer, Sam discovered two large tightly wrapped bundles of what looked like marijuana. He slipped them into his net dive bag and then snuck them back aboard the salvage vessel. The only person to notice was his pal Eddie, who remained silent until the two men were alone together later that day. When Eddie confronted Sam saying he'd seen him hiding something, Sam offered to cut Eddie in if he could keep quiet and Eddie reluctantly agreed saying that he didn't want to be caught doing anything illegal.

"Let me get this straight," said Sam. "You don't want to do anything illegal or you just don't want to get caught doing it?"

Both men laughed and the pact was sealed. From that day on pilfering became routine. Things went along smoothly until a day when Gypsy was working as their dive master, he approached them and told them that he was fully aware of what was going on and if they wanted to continue working anywhere in the Keys they would need to pay him a tribute. The men reluctantly agreed.

And then one day their world changed. Eddie and Sam had come across a large jewelry collection while working on the wreck of a commercial vessel. The treasure was far too large to sneak out of the depths so they consolidated it in one spot and left an underwater marker on it. The water was only about thirty feet deep so it would be easy to retrieve using a minimum of equipment. After the end of their shift, the rented a small boat from a local fishing livery and went back out to claim their prize.

A local sheriff's deputy who happened to be cruising the shoreline saw the two men leaving the dock and something about their demeanor and the fact that they didn't have any fishing rods aroused his interest. He decided to park his cruiser out of sight and wait for their return. He left his gun rig along with his uniform shirt in the trunk of the car, slipped his Walther .380 backup into his pants pocket and sat on the dock, his bare feet dangling in the water.

It was late afternoon when the boat returned to the now deserted dock, both men were looking at him a sure sign that they were up to no good. Instead of veering away from him the boat glided up right along side and Sam immediately grabbed the deputy's legs while Eddie gunned the engine and pulled away from the dock. The deputy was dragged off the dock and found himself upside down with his upper torso completely submerged and totally helpless. He drowned in almost no time at all.

The two men looked around making sure that no one had witnessed what just happened and then tied the body off underneath the dock and out of sight. The next thing they did was call Gypsy.

Gypsy arrived at the dock just before dusk noticing the parked Sheriff's cruiser a couple of blocks away. "This place is going to get red hot as soon as they find that empty cop car," he said. "We'd better work fast. First, one of you guys grab a rag and completely wipe down that boat and the other, back your car right up to the dock like we're loading fishing tackle into the trunk." Eddie and Sam did as directed and within minutes they had the boat cleaned of prints and the body wrapped in a plastic tarp and hidden safely in the trunk."

Sam piped up, "One good thing is that when I rented the boat I told the old guy behind the counter that I'd left my wallet in the car and couldn't give them any ID. The man told me not to worry about it. They don't even have my name."

The men drove off and cruised the back roads until they found a secluded and unattended landfill and then buried the body under a good size pile of putrid garbage.

"You guys owe me big time now," said Gypsy

Both men responded, "We know."

And now as they got off the airplane, the three of them are together again, this time in northern Michigan. Gypsy only promised them a big payday and didn't give any details on the job. He was unsure about how much he wanted them to know. For now, the less they knew the better. All he would tell them was that the job was top secret that they were lucky to be included. There would be plenty of time to discuss treasure once the diving began.

CHAPTER 15

Otis Springfield, his wife Marla and their ten year old twins arrived at the Little Bay Marina just before noon. Their oldest boy, a freshman at Michigan State wasn't with them. He had taken a summer job with a lawn care company and was trying to earn some extra cash before reporting to the dorm. After settling into their adjoining rooms, they met Michael and McCoy for lunch at The Ship's Anchor, the club on the end of the pier.

Anytime the couple entered a room, heads turned. They were certainly impressive looking. Otis resembled the ex Oakland Raider turned actor Carl Weathers in his prime when he was costarring as Apollo Creed in the 'Rocky" movies and Marla was a dead ringer for Halle Berry, smile and all.

"This reminds me of a place called Portofino downriver from Detroit," said Otis.

"It should," responded Michael. "It's a carbon copy. It's as if the same guy designed it. Caters to a pretty sophisticated crowd but it's not too upscale for the locals. Probably the most popular restaurant in town. Everything from lobster to burgers and pizza on the menu. On nice evenings the big windows in the front open up so that it's an indoor/outdoor thing. They have dancing under the stars on the big circular deck to a sixteen piece band playing here most of the summer."

Marla smiled. "Great for dancing. Sounds like my kind of place."

McCoy turned to Otis. "Mike and me have got just about all the important work done on the boat. By this time tomorrow we're hoping to cast off the lines and see how far it will float."

Otis turned in his chair to look out over the marina. "Can you see it from here?"

Michael jumped to his feet. "For sure. It's just the second dock over all the way out at the end." He pointed to the blue and white Roamer.

Otis whistled. "Man, that's a pretty big boat. Looks like you need a full crew just to run it."

"Nah, with twin screws and those hydraulic transmissions, she handles like a runabout. Want the grand tour?"

The twins were jumping up and down in anticipation of getting aboard a real live yacht and Marla smiled and sighed her approval.

In spite of the fact that, aside from the carpeting the interior was pretty bare bones. Everybody seemed impressed with Michael's latest toy. "We'll be putting in the microwave and other stuff in the next couple of days and then, assuming there are no glitches, she's ready for the high seas."

McCoy added, "Mike's even got his first charter lined up. It's an archaeologist's treasure hunt."

"Really?" asked Otis.

"It's not exactly a charter. The guy says he might be interested in making an offer on the boat so it'll be somewhat of a demo run. I'm not completely sure what it's all about but a guy is doing some historical research for a museum and he needs a big boat. Don't know any more than that right now."

Otis laughed. "Now you're telling me that this is a treasure ship?"

While Michael opened the hatch covers to show Otis the sparkling clean V-8 engines, Marla explored the cabin, inspecting the salon, galley, and the head. "Not much of a shower down here," she hollered.

"It's a whole lot more than you'd get with a boat that was ten feet shorter," answered Michael.

When they were all back topside Michael pointed to a boat leaving the harbor and headed toward Lake Michigan. It appeared to be good size offshore runabout, maybe thirty five feet or so. "There goes the guy who wants to hire this boat," said Michael. The three men with George Snyder were all wearing wetsuits. Michael recognized one of them as Gypsy. The other two were new faces, probably in their late thirties or early forties. They both had their backs to Michael's boat.

McCoy stood next to Michael. "Those must be the other two divers that came up from Key Largo."

"And Snyder called that a fishing boat," said Michael. "It's a Donzi. Looks like a ZF model. Those babies can run close to sixty miles an hour and they'll get up to top speed in a heartbeat. Fishing boat, yeah, right."

"Why would they be bringing help up from Florida? There are plenty of qualified divers around Michigan," said Otis.

"A little mystery thing going on," answered Michael. "According to Mister Snyder some historical publications got word of this search and they're kind of prying. I guess the museum wants to keep it under wraps until they have something in hand. The magazine reporters don't know about Snyder or this boat. Hush-hush."

"By the way," said McCoy. "I checked Snyder out and he seems solid. Didn't come up with any connection to museums or historical societies. But then he's in the salvage business and could have picked up a lead anywhere and took it to a museum."

Michael responded, "The way I read him, he's one of those businessmen without a label. He's interested in turning a profit and he'll swing with any breeze that smells like money. I guess we'll know in a couple of days. Are you coming with me?" he said to McCoy.

"I suppose I'd better just in case there's a mutiny. You'd be pretty helpless with four against one."

"I hadn't thought of that," said Michael "but it's certainly something to keep in mind. But that's a story for another day. What are we doing tonight?"

"Well, how about cocktails on my balcony this evening?" said Otis. "My treat. We'll drink to the success of this here voyage."

CHAPTER 16

Keeping an eye on his GPS and the nautical chart at the same time, George cut the power on the runabout a little sooner than he had originally planned. He was beginning to have an uneasy feeling about this whole adventure. For one thing, he never felt really good vibes about Gypsy. There was something about the man's manner that suggested a mysterious history. The two men that he brought up from Florida seemed polite and respectful enough but they didn't act like they were very smart, always turning to Gypsy for answers to even the most simple questions. Gypsy assured George that the two men had no idea what the object of the search was and their casual, almost uninterested behavior reinforced that notion.

And then there was the maze of legal details to work through. Treasure hunters from all over had been battling the State of Michigan for the rights to the yet to be discovered treasure. Lawyers had been haggling the ownership issue and were constantly stonewalled by attorneys for the establishment.

George's lawyer was planning to use a totally different approach arguing that Maritime law always took precedence. Nobody had ever presented the case from this angle. The attorney pointed out that the original ship had a French registry therefore had to be considered a foreign vessel establishing foreign entities as the original owners. Secondly, the crew had intentionally dumped the treasure overboard in hopes of avoiding being massacred. Therefore the gold became classified as jetsam and governed by entirely different rules than flotsam. Since the ship had voluntarily jettisoned the cargo, ownership automatically transferred to whoever recovered it. The designation as jetsam made the treasure subject to maritime law, thereby voiding the state's claim of ownership. The same claim could be made for the salvage tug The Maumee Princess back in the twenties. They cut the crates loose on purpose and the logbook supported that position. The requirements for jetsam were satisfied in both instances. The legal staff had not yet filed a brief as they were still searching court records for precedents. But George's lawyer assured him that they had some good information already and seemed confident that the worst they could do would be some sort of compromise where the state would have legal claim to a token amount, just enough to save face. George hoped he was right but would definitely feel more comfortable if he could see a few successful cases that had been argued that way.

George pondered his dilemmas as the boat rocked gently to a stop. Jarred back to the present, he fished the transducer out of the tackle box, attached the cable and lowered it over the side. He booted up the screen on the onboard unit and began to scan the bottom some forty-five feet below. Allowing the boat to drift he watched the GPS until he was within twenty or thirty feet of the desired location.

One of the new divers, a small GPS nestled in his hand moved in to look over George's shoulder. "What are we looking for?" he queried.

"Trying to find some historical artifacts, nothing special," claimed George. I'm looking for irregularities on the bottom."

The diver stared into the screen. "Good luck, it looks like a pretty rocky bottom down there. Everything is going to be irregular."

"You might be right," muttered George as he re-checked his GPS. He reeled in the transducer. "Let's move a couple hundred feet northeast." They repeated the process several times of moving a short distance and then reading the bottom. The process consumed over three hours and produced nothing.

Finally Gypsy stepped forward and in an irritated tone said. "All you're doing is reading the contour of the bottom. You'll never find anything that way. I had Eddie and Sam bring up some of our gear from Florida. We have metal detecting capabilities and visual if needed. This water ain't that deep and it's pretty clear. There's no reason we couldn't just dive and have a look around. And now we've wasted a whole day."

George appeared cool to an actual dive but just nodded his head and retrieved his cable from the water. "Okay, we'll pack up and go home for the night. Tomorrow's another day and winds are predicted to be calm. We'll hit it bright and early with more equipment and see if we can't do a little better."

He started the motors and swung the bow around to the west. The powerful engines immediately brought the boat on plane. Gypsy moved back to join George at the control console. "You're acting like you don't want us to dive. Why is that?"

George made sure that the other two men were too far to hear over the hum of the engines. "I'm just worried about how those two might react if they see crates full of gold bullion. That's the kind of thing that can make a man crazy and cause him to do crazy things."

Gypsy nodded. "I wouldn't worry about those two. I can handle them. Besides, I'm assuming that a treasure like that was crated in some pretty substantial containers. I wouldn't be surprised if they were made of iron and completely sealed. Nobody will know what's inside. But I need to see them and get some measurements so that I can calculate the weight and determine what sort of lift collars we'll need to bring them to the surface. By the way, have you got a plan for them once we get them off the bottom?"

"I'm working on that right now," said George. I've got a friend over in Charlevoix who has a private dock and I'm negotiating with him to buy it. It's a secluded area and the only building on the property is an old warehouse that went out of business a decade ago. Most of the time there's nobody there and it sits way off the beaten path. There's nothing around it. Right now I have a pre-purchase lease arrangement. I specified privacy in my interim agreement. The guy trusts me so there should be no problem there. I had my drivers bring some of my company trucks up there and park them where we could transfer the crates. I'm just hoping that my lawyers can get a decision or at least a qualified opinion on the legality before that happens."

Gypsy sat upright. "Lawyers? What lawyers? I thought you said that nobody else knew anything about this."

"Calm down and think," said George. "If this thing is what we believe it is, it's going to be way too big to hide. Besides, where you gonna fence five hundred million dollars worth of gold? It has to be done this way, above board and legal. It's the cheapest way to go because, if everything goes like I expect we won't have to share it with anybody. And besides, only one attorney and a couple of very trusted staff members in the law firm know what we're doing and they won't reveal any information to anybody."

Gypsy frowned. "This is going to change some things."

"Like what?" asked George.

"Like my cut of the action. Now that you've got lawyers involved this money is likely to be tied up in court for years and we may never get it. I'm taking on this job because it pays well. I gotta tell you that the price just went up... way up."

George could feel the trap closing. Gypsy already knew way too much to think of cutting him out of the action. A guy like Gypsy surely could cause big trouble and definitely wouldn't go quietly. He was in over his head. Hiring Gypsy may have been a mistake and George's instincts had told him that from the beginning. George had always been an honest man and planned to remain that way. He had the feeling that once the treasure was recovered, his life could very well be in danger. He had to devise a plan to protect himself.

George almost wished he had never gotten into this thing to begin with. If he had been smart he could have teamed up with one of the established treasure hunters and used his information to leverage a partnership with someone who was legitimately searching. But that option was hindsight. He'd have to deal with the monster that he had created.

Perhaps Michael, the young man with the boat might come in handy. He seemed very honest and above board. Besides, his buddy was a cop and Gypsy knew it. If he came along it might provide some insurance.

He thought about his options all the way back to the harbor. If he was going to depend on Michael for help, he'd have to let him in on the entire plan. He'd have to be completely honest and share every detail. But then Michael might very likely back out of the whole deal. Who could blame him? What had started out as a dream of riches was rapidly turning into a nightmare. If only he would have thought things through more carefully. Oh well, he'd address it tonight before going to bed and see if it would look more friendly in the morning.

CHAPTER 17

Michael, McCoy, Otis, and Marla sat around the big table on the second floor balcony that overlooked the harbor but also had a nice view of the nightclub and the horizon beyond. Marla had concocted Margaritas, Strawberry Daiquiris, and Shirley Temples for the children. A large bowl of fruit graced the center of the table.

"If it wasn't for the winters," commented Otis, "this place would be an absolute paradise."

"The lakes are a couple of degrees cooler when you get this far north" replied Michael, "but the Bay is fairly shallow here and the sun, reflecting off the sand bottom warms it up quite comfortably on cloudless days. But, you're right, the winters can be brutal. Of course there are still plenty of outdoor things to do when the snow falls. Things like skiing, ice fishing, snowmobiling, and all the winter festivals with their beer tents. Polar Bear dips, and Polka bands out on the ice."

Otis smiled, "Thanks but I think I'll stick to bowling, darts, and pool in the winter."

"So tell us about this great adventure of yours," said Marla

Michael sat back and folded his arms. "It all started a little over a week ago when this guy named George Snyder stopped by my boat to see about chartering it. I told him that I didn't have a charter license but he said he wasn't looking for that kind of charter. Seems that he has a deal with a museum somewhere to find some sort of historical artifacts that are supposed to be on the bottom of the lake somewhere near here. It's supposed to be kept under wraps because they're worried that a failure could lead to reduced funding in the future. George seems to be an all right sort of a guy but his diver is kinda creepy."

"What do you mean, 'creepy,'?" asked Otis.

"Well, he hardly ever talks and when he does it's only a word or two. He dresses like a one percent biker and he's got these weird tattoos all up and down his arms. And he doesn't seem to even have a real name. Calls himself, 'Gypsy'".

"He's staying at this motel," added McCoy. "His room is on the lower level at the other end of this wing."

"I'll have to remember to lock our doors," chimed in Marla.

Michael continued. "It may not be nearly as bad as it seems. This George guy appears to be an okay guy and he's the one calling the shots."

A sound came from Michael's room. Someone was knocking on the door. Michael jumped to his feet. "Wonder who that could be?" he rushed inside.

It was George Snyder who stood in the hallway with a worried look on his face.

"C'mon in," said Michael and he led George out onto the balcony. George acted surprised to see other people enjoying cocktails and snacking on grapes.

"Oh' I didn't know you had company," said George. "Perhaps some other time."

"Nonsense," responded Michael. "These people are all my friends from Detroit. Pull up a chair, grab a drink, relax, and tell us all about your adventures on the high seas this afternoon."

"I suppose I do need to unwind. Maybe a drink would help."

Let me introduce everybody," said Michael. "You met McCoy and, if you don't mind, he'll be coming with us when we go treasure hunting."

George nodded and gave a thumb's up.

"And this is Otis and Marla Springfield and a couple of their children. They're some very dear friends of mine. Otis is a Lieutenant in the Detroit Police Homicide division."

"I see," said George. "Perhaps I could burden you all with my concerns after all since you all seem quite trust-worthy" George's growing confidence in the group was obvious.

"Go ahead and unload," invited Michael.

George sighed a very deep sigh. "This isn't going to be easy. First of all there is no museum, there's well, only me. I'm the treasure hunter and it's a really big one, maybe the biggest ever inside the United States."

"You must be talking about the Poverty Island Treasure," said Michael I think we've all heard about that one." Everybody nodded.

"But I have inside information," said George. "Everybody is searching around Poverty Island and that's not where the gold is. It's all the way on the other side of Lake Michigan near Beaver Island."

"What makes you think that?" asked Otis.

George took a deep swallow of his Margarita. "Almost two years ago I bought out a towing and salvage company whose focus at one time had been marine salvage. They were kind of forced out of that side of the business back in about 1930 after having a run in with the U. S. Coast Guard. Seems that it may have involved that Poverty Island treasure. The Coast Guard reports say that their tugboat, The Maumee Princess was intercepted trying to tow the treasure away but that they dropped it back to the bottom when the cutter appeared. The Coast Guard documents are very unclear and incomplete. You might even call them sketchy. From the way the event is described, one would assume that it all happened in the Poverty Island area. The implication is clear although no exact location is noted. The salvage company that I bought still had the logbook from that tugboat in their company safe and it told a very different story."

Aside from George's voice, the balcony was absolutely silent.

George continued. "The legend is that the navigator for the salvage company was unusually gifted and his calculations were always quite precise. He used celestial navigation but he had a custom made sextant that had been built specifically for the elevation of the Great Lakes and it utilized more stars than anyone else for more triangulation options. He marked the location and I have his coordinates. It's miles from the area everyone else is searching."

Michael interrupted. "How many people know what you know?"

George thought for a moment. "Well, there's the guy who figured it all out. He's rock solid, the great-grandson of the navigator who marked the spot. And then there's my attorney because I want to keep this thing all legal. And there's Gypsy and he's the problem. I don't feel comfortable trusting him."

"Can you just fire him?" asked Michael.

"It's not that simple," said George. "I actually sought him out down in Florida and asked him to come up here.

I've probably confided in him more than I should have and now he knows the exact vicinity of my search grid. We were out there today and I saw him both him and one of his partners checking their hand held GPSs. Like a dummy, I got us within about thirty or forty feet of the exact position. Him and his buddies have some pretty sophisticated search equipment and I'm afraid they may sneak in and steal the whole thing. Gypsy has as much as told me that he's not interested in doing it the legal way."

McCoy spoke up. "I can understand that. The State of Michigan will undoubtedly lay claim to it and they likely have the law on their side."

"My attorney thinks he's stumbled on a little known precedent that would throw things in favor of whoever recovers it," said George. He's putting his case together right now."

"How much do you know about this 'Gypsy' guy?" asked Otis. "What's his real name?"

"I wish I knew," said George. "I just make the checks out to Premier Salvage Divers of Key Largo. When he first got here I asked him what his name was and he said, 'just Gypsy.'"

"That's bullshit," chimed in McCoy. "Even Elvis had a last name. He's hiding something."

There was a brief silence and the George said, "I guess my big question is, are you still willing to help me out even if I can't get rid of him?"

Michael looked at McCoy. "My biggest concern is that two guys who hung around this marina have been murdered less than a week apart. From what you know about Gypsy, do you think he's capable of having anything to do with that?"

George seemed to struggle with his answer. "I've always fancied myself a pretty good judge of character but Gypsy is really hard to read. According to the people who recommended him, he's highly qualified, very reliable, a hard worker, doesn't do drugs, not a drinker or troublemaker but sometimes he can be quite hard-headed. My personal observations lead me to the same conclusions. He's certainly intelligent but as far as being violent, he hasn't shown anything that would raise a flag. I'd say he's probably not involved."

McCoy said to Michael, "You decide. I'll have your back any way you want to do it. It will sure keep my vacation from getting boring."

Michael glanced at McCoy and then Otis. He turned back to George. "I'm in."

CHAPTER 18

Michael, McCoy, and Otis were on board the boat at eight o'clock in the morning. Michael had picked up three Italian submarine sandwiches and two six packs of Dr. Pepper. McCoy examined one of the sandwiches and read the label aloud, "Submarine. I certainly hope it's not an omen." The weather was supposed to be hot and still today, no wind and temperatures in the mid to upper eighties.

Marla would spend the day on the sugar sand beach with the kids as they all paraded their new bathing suits. It promised to be a beautiful day.

Michael had the bilge blowers running immediately and his air quality gauges showed a safe environment in the engine compartment. He brought the big V-8 engines to life one at a time and then kept a close eye on the gauge panel as the oil pressure stabilized and they slowly rose to operating temperature. When everything settled in at optimum he told McCoy to cast off the lines and they were under way. He cautiously maneuvered through the marina and harbor at no wake speed before gently bringing the hull on plane. It was his first time at the helm of his newly acquired yacht. In his younger days he had piloted similar but somewhat smaller boats and so he felt comfortable even though this boat was bigger by six feet than anything he had run before. The big vessel's deep vee hull easily sliced through the calm waters leaving a miniature rainbow in its wake. Michael wanted to test everything on board and had a large notebook sitting on the control console. He made entries from time to time noting the speed of the boat against the RPMs in calm waters. Once out in the open bay, he made a few turns. Gentle at first and then gradually more aggressive until he was in full evasive maneuver mode forcing Otis and McCoy to hang on. Settling back down to a steady and true course, he tested the depth sounders for synchronization with McCoy hollering readings down from the fly-bridge while Michael monitored the instruments at the main command station. It was a good shakedown with all systems responding in textbook form. Michael had replaced or upgraded all of the original electronic and operating systems and had expected no less.

The radios both checked out just fine and the GPS agreed with all of the compass headings.

Michael pointed the bow for Lake Michigan so that they could get out of reach of the cell phone towers and he could check the range of his radios and see if his satellite phone was still showing a signal.

Once they had the boat on a steady heading the three men gathered around the command station to talk.

Otis was the first to speak. "After our little get together broke up last night I called down to the precinct and had them run a check on this Premier Salvage outfit in Key Largo. Their record is clean and the reputation is fine but the ownership is pretty cloudy and I find that bothersome. It's owned by a group of other corporations as part of a large conglomerate. The names on the title are bankers, investors, commodities brokers and that sort. No clear ownership at all. There doesn't seem to be a name exclusive to Premier Salvage Divers. But on the other hand, I couldn't find any skeletons in their closets. No lawsuits, no Better Business Bureau complaints, nothing. I get the distinct feeling that your Gypsy guy is the main man and all the rest are just shadow investors."

"Kinda bears out what George says about the place," said Michael. "Nothing that points to trouble at all. But that Gypsy character still gives me the creeps. I'll be keeping an eye on him the whole time."

McCoy joined in. As long as we're prepared, there will be no reason to be caught off guard. I'd like to have another meeting or two with all of them before we're alone together on a boat, miles from land."

"I'll talk to Mr. Snyder," Said Michael.

"Even though I won't be joining you on your adventure, I'd like to be at your meeting too," added Otis.

CHAPTER 19

George Snyder awoke at six in the morning to the sound of his cell phone ring tone. Checking the caller number, he saw that it was an Ohio area code. "Snyder here," he answered.

"Hello Mr. Snyder? This is Jacob Marley from Toledo. Um, I was wondering maybe if I couldn't lock this place up and go along with you when you go out looking for that stuff. I mean I'm a pretty good sailor and a better than average navigator. Spent lots of time all over Lake Erie, ya know. And I'm a certified scuba diver too."

"Geeze, I never even thought about asking you along but it certainly doesn't sound like a bad idea. Besides, I owe you. There are a few vacancies at this motel. I'd be thrilled to have you along. I'll book you a room and you can head up this way."

Jacob's reply even sounded happy. "It'll take me all day to get there. I checked the place out on the internet and printed out driving instructions. I can be there sometime tonight if I leave right now."

"Okay," responded George, "I'll have a room waiting for you. Just check in at the desk and give me a call when you get here."

George hung up the phone with a smile. Having another guy along that he could trust made him much more comfortable. Even if Gypsy's diver pals sided with him, they'd now be outnumbered. He hurriedly reserved a room with his credit card and headed for the shower to begin his day.

He decided to throw Gypsy a bit of a curve ball today. Gypsy wanted to make a dive on the treasure site and have a look around. The northern Great Lakes are quite clear and visibility is excellent especially since the winds had been calm for more than a week.

George decided that he would take them at least a half mile north of where they were yesterday. Gypsy would notice but George had a story prepared.

The three divers were already wolfing down big helpings of pancakes and sausage from the breakfast buffet when George got to the restaurant.

"Carbing up," Gypsy explained. "We'll be exerting lots of energy underwater and we need carbohydrates."

George scooped up some scrambled eggs and a big bowl of fruit and joined them at the table. "Looks like another bright and sunny day with no wind. We've been pretty lucky so far. I figure we'll get a full day's work in today."

"And hopefully a productive one," added Gypsy. "The water's pretty shallow in the area where we're looking. We'll be able to stay down longer and use less air. We're bringing two extra tanks each. We'll be good for probably two full hours or more of bottom time."

"I've got a little new news for you too," said George. "Gypsy, do you remember me saying that I have a partner down in Toledo?"

Gypsy nodded.

"Well he'll be joining us here tonight and will be helping out with the search."

Gypsy frowned. "That boat is gonna get pretty crowded out there. Why is he coming along?"

"He's the guy who made all of this possible," said George. "He found the logbook that tells the whole story and he's the one who figured out the exact location. He's pretty vested in the whole project. We can't exclude him."

Gypsy shrugged. "I guess it's your banana, you can peel it any way you like."

George swung his big runabout around to the gas dock. After topping off the tanks he climbed up on the dock to go inside the large convenience store and pick up a few sandwiches and some soft drinks. After seeing those divers devour a huge breakfast this morning, he walked back to his boat dragging his large cooler completely stuffed with food and carrying a plastic bag full of sweet snacks. He motored back to the main dock where Gypsy and his pals stood waiting. After everyone was aboard, George navigated his way out of the harbor and toward the open waters of Lake Michigan. Both Gypsy and Sam had hand held GPS units in front of their faces for the entire journey.

Once they got near the search area George altered his course slightly northward and shut the engine down about five miles from yesterday's position. Gypsy was at his side almost instantly. "Why are you stopping here? This ain't anywhere near where we were yesterday."

"I know," answered George. "We have an alternate location. The figures we're working from aren't exact. But there's only these two hot spots so it's not too bad." Gypsy stared at George for a long time before moving back to where his scuba gear sat. H e slowly slid into the buoyancy compensator and tank harness. "Suit up guys, it's time to get wet."

The three divers slipped into the water and disappeared below the surface leaving only a trail of bubbles and leaving George topside to ponder his dilemma. It was clear that Gypsy wasn't buying his story. He'd have to think fast before things got out of hand. He wished that Jacob was here with him. Maybe things will get better when he gets here. All he hoped for at the moment was to make it through today.

CHAPTER 20

On that same morning Michael exited the "Ship's Store" in the marina with a giant plastic bag slung over his shoulder. "Picked up a couple of junior size lifejackets so the kids can come along on today's cruise."

Yesterday's shakedown had been nothing short of perfect with everything performing flawlessly on Michael's prized boat. "I guess attention to detail and replacing everything that's suspect pays off in the long run," he said. Today's trip would be a little farther ranging with the only test being a call from Michael's satellite phone to the land-line manned by his friend John, owner of the marina. The water was as flat as a sheet of glass and there wasn't a cloud in the sky.

Marla and the twins were about to embark on their first trip ever aboard a motor yacht. At forty two feet, the boat exuded confidence and safety. Marla's early fears quickly evaporated once she realized the stability that the big hull offered. The twins were just excited and grinning. They couldn't wait for the adventure to begin. Otis, saying nothing, proudly watched his family overcome their needless fears.

It was a gorgeous day out on Lake Michigan. Michael followed the coastline northward at an easy cruising speed and then east to pass underneath the Mackinac Bridge and into the waters of northern Lake Huron. Turning back southwest at Nine Mile Point, he hugged the lower peninsula coast taking in an up close view of Fort Michilimackinac, the home of the infamous lacrosse game played by the Ojibwas as part of the Pontiac uprising thirteen years before the Revolutionary War. With the straits behind them Michael sailed past Sturgeon Bay and down to Harbor Springs where he turned back to the west for the trip across Lake Michigan and home. Once again, everything performed without incident and when they tied up back at the dock, Michael declared his craft fit for sea duty.

Once the boat was properly moored and all systems secured, Michael, McCoy, and Otis joined Marla up on the motel balcony for pizza and refreshments. The twins, exhausted from their active day went to bed early without protest.

Marla once again demonstrated her skill in concocting exotic drinks for the group as she gushed over the unexpect-ed pleasure of her all day cruise on Michael's yacht. "I could become a sea wench," she commented. Michael had finished installing all of the salon furniture complete with bar and a sound system full of Caribbean music. It truly felt like a yacht now, at least to Marla. When everyone was served she curled up next to Otis on the wicker loveseat and toasted the day's success.

Michael's cell phone chimed. It was George. "Yeah," said Michael. C'mon up. We've got plenty of pizza and a few cocktails to boot."

Within minutes George Snyder appeared at Michael's door and he had a stranger with him. "Hi everybody. This here is Jacob Marley, call him Jake. He's my partner. It was his great grand daddy who marked the location of the things I'm hunting for."

Jake spoke up. "I'll probably get all of your names con-fused but please bear with me. I'm not used to crowds."

McCoy chuckled. "That why all us cops carry note-books. We'd never remember all the names."

"I have a few concerns," said George. "Gypsy, my diver, I think I can trust him okay but I don't know anything about the two guys he's brought on board. Today I took them to a spot a few miles away from my target location and they went over the side to see if they could find anything on the bottom.

"Why'd you do that? Take them to a place where you don't expect them to find anything?" asked McCoy.

"Let's just call it a precautionary move," said George. "But anyway they came across the skeleton of an old schoo-ner that's just about the right size and age. You know, civil war era. Anyhow they went over the wreck pretty good and all they could come up with was some rusty old spikes and some hardware. When they got back aboard my run-about I could tell that they were mad. They must have been expecting to find the treasure right away. All the way home I assured them that there was something down there, we just hadn't located it yet, Treasure hunting takes time."

"Did they buy it?" asked Michael.

"Not sure. Gypsy seemed satisfied but the other two just sulked for the rest of the trip. I told them that we were dealing with eighty year old information and that it just might take some work. That seemed to sink in a little bit.

Otis spoke up. "Do you think they'd all be receptive to a pre-dive meeting with Mike, McCoy, me and everybody concerned?"

"Hell, it's my dime," replied George. "I'll schedule it and tell them to be there."

CHAPTER 21

The UPS truck arrived about noon and Gypsy took charge of overseeing the unloading. There was a crate with a space-age looking JW Fishers Dual Frequency Side Scan Sonar, another crate with three hundred feet of cable, and yet another containing MFP-1 pingers. There was also an underwater surface penetrating radar with a Hummingbird side imaging sonar system which would provide a 3-D picture. Gypsy smiled. With this kind of equipment nothing on the bottom, or below it would escape his eyes. He had his two underlings unload everything and take it to his room. George Snyder had paid for all of this stuff but had no idea how it worked or what to do with it. It belonged in Gypsy's room where he could read the manuals and make sure that everything was in good working order. And as a bonus, ownership of the equipment would automatically transfer to Premier Salvage divers of Key Largo at the conclusion of this project.

Within the hour a freight truck arrived carrying a Max-Air 90 compressor for filling scuba tanks along with a larger two-stage high volume compressor for inflating floatation collars. George was there to meet the truck and had the cargo transferred to the marina pickup truck. He contacted Michael to arrange getting it installed on the afterdeck of the cabin cruiser.

The next few days brought freshening winds and turbulent seas. There would be no diving excursions until the breeze subsided. George decided to make judicious use of the time by scheduling a team meeting. He wanted everybody in his motel room at eight o'clock this evening to discuss strategies and schedules.

Michael, McCoy, Otis, and Jacob brought the deck chairs in from George's patio while George and Gypsy sat at the kitchenette table. Sam and Eddie flopped onto the leather couch. Jake looked over at George and said, "By the way, Mister Snyder, I've got most of the dimensions on that old tug written down. I've just got to measure the hull and interior bulkhead thicknesses and I'll be able to calculate total weight."

George thanked him and said that it could wait until things here were all wrapped up.

George opened the meeting by saying that the winds were supposed to subside within the next two or three days so that would give them a little time to install all of the equipment and to fully provision the boat. Michael told them that he had topped off the fuel tanks as soon as they had returned to port so everything aboard his boat was ready to roll. Sam piped up, "What's the big deal all about? What exactly are we looking for and why is this being planned like some kind of a military mission?"

George looked over at Gypsy and then slowly began. "We're looking for five crates full of museum artifacts. They're extremely fragile and very valuable."

"How valuable?" asked Sam.

Gypsy took over. "Could be as much as a half a million. But the stuff is only valuable to a museum and they know we're looking for it."

Sam wasn't satisfied. "If it's fragile, it's probably all busted up by now. I've recovered a lot of stuff and breakable things always get broken. It never fails."

"That's my problem," retorted George. "Your job is just to get it off the bottom."

Sam folded his arms and sat back, obviously not happy with the answers.

Gypsy held up the instruction manual for the surface penetrating radar and side imaging scanner reading the cover and saying. "I'll have all of this figured out before we leave the dock." It was the first time he'd taken his dark sunglasses since he'd been there. Otis studied his eyes. There was something vaguely familiar but Otis couldn't place it. Acting as if he wasn't even aware of Gypsy's presence, he catalogued it in his mind for future scrutiny.

Gypsy scanned the room and seemed to fix on Otis. The expression on his face saying that there was some recognition. He quickly put his dark glasses back on but kept his gaze focused on Otis.

The group agreed that Michael, McCoy, and Jacob Marley would take care of getting the air compressors secured in place and that Gypsy would bring Sam and Eddie up to speed on the use of the new searching gear. They were experienced divers and had used similar equipment but the new stuff was high technology and they hadn't worked with this latest version.

Michael stood up. "It looks like we've got at least two days before we can get back on the water so let's all try to use the time wisely. George has rented a car for you divers so that you can get around. I think we've got everything covered. I'll stay in touch with George and that should be good enough. Agreed?"

They all nodded and the meeting broke up. Gypsy was the first out the door.

Michael, McCoy, Otis, and Marla retreated to Otis's balcony for a nightcap.

What'd you think?" asked Michael.

"I think it's a good thing that Jake decided to join you guys," responded Otis. "He looks like he can handle himself and you'll want him on your side."

McCoy asked. "Did you see something we didn't? Expecting trouble?"

"Not necessarily but I wasn't crazy about that Sam guy. He acted like he was looking for something to complain about."

Michael said. "Look, these guys are all used to being someone else's employees. They're always paranoid about 'the man' and maybe that's why they're a little antagonistic."

"One other thing," said Otis. There's something familiar about this Gypsy guy and I'm getting bad vibes from it. Keep a close watch on him. I peg him as your main problem."

"Well," said McCoy. "We've got two days to observe and take notes. We're all detectives so shame on us if something slips past us."

Everybody laughed.

"Well said," replied Michael."

A knock at the door signaled the arrival of George and Jacob.

"Come on in and have a cocktail," said Otis. "It's not a school night so we can party until dawn if we like."

"Spoken like a man on vacation," said Marla.

George sat down. "Well, it wasn't as bad as I expected but I didn't like that Sam guy questioning everything we're doing. I'm just glad that Gypsy had enough sense to keep those two out of the loop for now."

"Don't worry about it," said Michael. "McCoy and I know what to do and we'll make sure everybody stays in line. Do you have a plan for the moment you find the treasure?"

"I just talked with Gypsy about that and he says that the other guys likely won't know what they've found until we have it on dry land. By then, I'm hoping that I'll have a court order that will let us lock it up in some major bank vault until we sort out the ownership details. By the way, on the way up to your room, I got a text message from my attorney saying that he thinks he's found a case that sets a rock solid precedent in our favor, He's checking for challenges right now but the future looks awfully bright at the moment."

"Sweet" said Michael.

CHAPTER 22

Sam and Eddie climbed into the rental car and headed for the Island Casino. "What did you think of that meeting?" asked Eddie.

"They're hiding something," replied Sam "And I think that Gypsy's in with them. You and me gotta watch one another's back."

"Right," said Eddie. "Why would they fly two guys all the way up from Florida if they didn't have some kind of secret? Maybe we can ask around a little bit and see if there isn't some sort of local mystery going on."

"Be cool," said Sam. "This just could be a pretty good gig so let's not screw it up. Me, I'm kinda torn between just keeping my mouth shut and collecting my paycheck or having a good hard look at things and seeing if there isn't something more to this deal. For now, it's probably best that we don't do anything that might get Gypsy breathing down our necks. Think, we gotta think."

Eddie didn't respond right away. After a few moments he said. "What about that Snyder guy? He sure doesn't seem to mind throwing his money around. Big spenders like him don't get to be rich by making bad bets. I'm guessing he's got this treasure hunt figured as a sure thing. What do you think these 'historical artifacts' are anyway?"

Sam shrugged. "I've been wondering about that myself. Couldn't be paintings or anything. You know, it ain't stuff that can be damaged by being under water. It's gotta be jewelry or something like that. Maybe old guns and swords or something. Who knows? This used to be Indian Territory so it could have something to do with that. I guess we'll find out when we drag it out of the lake."

They pulled into the casino parking lot and circled it three times trying to find a vacant spot close to the building. Sam finally gave up and parked in one of the few empty spaces at the far end of the lot. The pair sauntered across the brightly lit parking lot and into the casino.

"What's it gonna be? Slots? Blackjack? Roulette?" asked Sam.

"I always have my best luck with the poker machines," answered Eddie. "I'll just stick with those. Besides, I can control the pace when I'm playing a machine. The live dealers are always moving the games along too fast."

"Not if you're winning," countered Sam as we worked his way through the crowd. "I'll meet you over at the bar in about an hour, okay?"

Eddie was already sliding into a chair in front of a twenty-five cent poker machine. "Sounds good."

In spite of Sam's warning to play it cool, Eddie continuously queried the stream of patrons who stopped by to drop a few quarters in the machines. "Hey, have you heard anything about a shipwreck over on Lake Michigan?" Nobody had an answer for him but it didn't stop Eddie from pestering everyone he saw. He only quit bothering people after a member of the security staff informed him that anybody harassing other customers may be asked to leave. After the warning he gambled in silence. His luck at the poker machine was pretty much up and down and at the end of an hour he found himself ahead by about thirty-five dollars. He cashed out and headed for the bar.

Sam, a beer sitting on the bar in front of him was smiling as Eddie approached. "Do any good?" he asked.

"Maybe up a few bucks," answered Eddie as he climbed onto a barstool. "How about you?"

"A little over two hundred on the blackjack table," said Sam, waving a fistful of bills in Eddie's face.

Eddie smiled and ordered a Bud from the patiently waiting bartender. "Well, tomorrow we get our refresher course from Gypsy on the new equipment. I think we've both used those things before but the stuff we have now is the new, improved version and we'll have to learn all the new wrinkles."

"Yeah," said Sam. "Gypsy wants us to get together in his room right after breakfast, around ten o'clock. I figure it should only take an hour, two at the most and we'll be outta there by noon. Then we have about a day and a half all to ourselves before the wind dies down and we have to go back to work. What do you want to do with all that time?"

"We could do a little snooping around, I'd sure like to have some idea of what it is that we're looking for. I'll bet it's some kind drugs sealed in watertight packaging."

"Y'know, you might just be on to something there. Gypsy says that one of the guys on the boat will be a cop so that makes sense. It would also explain why they're not using any locals. Yeah, drugs."

The two men went back to their car and headed back to the motel, stopping on the way to pick up a twelve pack of beer. After returning to their rooms and putting the beer on ice, the decided to check out The Ship's Anchor, that neat looking nightclub out on the end of the pier.

The place was about three quarters full with waiters and waitresses scurrying back and forth delivering drinks and meals prior to the last show of the evening. The entertainment during the week consists of a five man combo and a talented cabaret singer. The weekend fare included a full dance band and a stage show that was overseen by a standup comic who doubled as the emcee.

Sam and Eddie chose to sit at the bar. As soon as they sat down Eddie poked Sam and pointed to a ringside location. Seated at the table were George Snyder and his sidekick from Toledo along with the owner of that big cruiser and his two cop buddies. There was a woman with them too. "Hmm," mused Sam. "Gypsy's not with them. Wonder what he's doing tonight?"

CHAPTER 23

Gypsy spent a little over an hour going over the nuances of the equipment that had arrived yesterday. It wasn't too much different than the stuff that they were used to working with, just a few refinements here and there. Sam and Eddie had brought underwater video cameras with them when they flew up from Florida. Now the expedition was equipped with ground penetrating radar, sonar, 3D imaging and video gear. If there was anything to be found within seventy-five feet of their search grid, above or below the sandy bottom they'd see it. The meeting wrapped up right about noon.

"What are you guys planning to do for the next day or so?" asked Gypsy.

Sam replied. "Well, we've still got a little money left over after last night and we were thinking about a return trip to the casino. Want to come along?"

Gypsy didn't smile. "One thing that you guys have absolutely got to understand is that you have to stay out of trouble. As a matter of fact, I don't want you even noticed around here. Am I clear?"

"Yeah but why all the secrecy?" asked Sam. "It's just a routine salvage job. At least that's what you've told us."

Gypsy sighed. "Here's the deal. A museum wants this stuff and is paying the bill for us to salvage it. They don't want anybody to know about the search just in case we don't find it. Museums get their money through donations and benefactors want to see results. Too many failures and their money dries up. You guys should understand. The whole world runs on money. This could be a big new market opening up for us and success will certainly look good on our resumes. Now go have fun but stay below the radar."

Sam and Eddie left the hotel and decided to cruise around town before heading back out to the casino. They stopped at a big rustic looking place called the Buck Inn.

"Looks like a hamburger and beer kind of place, don't ya think? said Sam as he climbed out of the car.

"Sounds like just what I need," said Eddie.

The two men entered the log building and sat at the bar asking for menus.

"See?" said Sam. "Look at all the different hamburgers on the menu, doe burgers, buck burgers, moose burgers. What'd I tell you?"

A guy who the bartender called Vinny, sitting a few stools away was carrying on a fairly loud conversation with a friend. "Yeah, it looks like some new treasure hunters must have landed in town. My brother-in-law is a UPS driver and he said that he just delivered a load of high end underwater search equipment to some guys over at Little Bay Marina. Says that it's real expensive stuff, the kind that only the real pros use. And he'd know cause he's a diver himself."

"More Poverty Island freaks?" asked the other man.

"Sure looks that way. Another bunch with more money than brains wasting their time and cash hunting for non-existent gold. I wish I owned the dive shop that equips all these guys. They're the only ones getting rich."

"Excuse me," interrupted Sam. "Did you say treasure hunters?"

"Right," answered Vinny. "The Poverty Island thing."

Sam remembered seeing Poverty Island on one of the

nautical charts that Gypsy was studying but that's not the area that Snyder had taken them to for his search. "We're not from around here. Can you bring us up to speed on this here treasure?"

"Geeze," said Vinny. "I thought everybody in the world knew that story. Confederate gold from back during the civil war. Supposed to be worth around a half a billion in today's money. I don't think it really exists though. If it did, somebody wouldda found it by now."

"Not necessarily," said his buddy. "The bottom changes in sixteen year cycles out there in the lake. It could be lying out in plain sight one year and buried under ten feet of sand a couple years later and then pop back up again in a decade or so. The lake is shifty that way."

"So a lot of people have tried to find it?" asked Sam

"For generations" said Vinny. "One guy, comes in here, guy outta Detroit has a big old fishing trawler chocked full of gadgets for hunting treasure. Been coming here for five weeks every summer for over twenty years. Always shows up with some new contraption that can't miss. Has a big smile on his face when he gets here and is still smiling later in the summer when he leaves empty handed saying he'll be back next year. It's like a disease."

"And you say that this treasure is near Poverty Island?" asked Sam

"I say there is no treasure," answered Vinny. "But the scavengers all say it's within a mile of Poverty Island."

"Interesting. Thanks." Said Sam

Sam and Eddie ordered loaded cheeseburgers and Budweiser and had their lunch in quiet conversation. They tipped the bartender and complimented the cook before heading back out to their car.

"When they pulled out of the Buck Inn parking lot and set their course for the casino, Eddie asked. "Should we tell Gypsy about what we just heard?"

Sam thought it over and replied, "Let's just keep quiet and not even mention it. My guess is that Gypsy already knows the whole story and is keeping it between him and Snyder. I'm not really buying his museum song and dance anyway. It just ain't important enough for all of these elaborate precautions. As far as I can tell that legend we just heard is a big part of the local history and in a small community like this, everybody knows the story. As a matter of fact I would be damned surprised if that's not what we're looking for. And Gypsy wouldn't be involved if he didn't think he had an edge. This Snyder guy might have found something that sheds new light on this whole thing. After all, we're searching on the other side of Lake Michigan. That's nowhere near Poverty Island but it's in a pretty straight line across the lake. We're going to have to play it careful from here on."

The new information caused enough of a distraction for the casino to lose some of its luster. When they started gambling Sam stayed away from yesterday's productive blackjack tables and just pumped twenty dollar bills into the slot machines. Eddie stuck with the poker machines betting seventy-five cents a hand. By the end of the night both men were ahead by at least three hundred dollars. It felt like they had already found the gold.

When they got up to leave, two men who looked to be in their early twenties followed them out into the parking lot. They closed in quickly as Sam and Eddie walked to their car. It wasn't much of a fight. The two younger men seemed to know exactly what they were doing and the brass knuckles made short work of their victims. In less than two minutes both Sam and Eddie lay unconscious on the asphalt, their pockets turned inside out and all of their money gone.

The ambulance arrived almost fifteen minutes later. By then Sam was sitting up but Eddie was still writhing on the ground, his eyes not open. Casino security had administered first aid but insisted that the men remain where they were until paramedics arrived. At St. Francis hospital a Sheriff's Deputy interviewed the men and took statements but neither man could offer any help identifying their assailants. It had all happened so fast that they couldn't even give a description. Fortunately, the only thing stolen was cash. Credit cards, cell phones, and identification were not bothered. Eddie was having problems focusing his eyes and was undergoing further testing and Sam had fared only slightly better and was showing signs of traumatic head injuries.

There was a newspaper reporter at the hospital smelling a juicy story while the public relations manager from the casino did her best to hush him up.

Neither of the men knew Gypsy's real name so when asked whom the hospital should notify, they gave George Snyder's name at Little Bay Marina and Motel.

CHAPTER 24

The motel restaurant was finally quieting down after a brisk lunch crowd left in twos and fours. Michael had his nose buried in the Daily Press barely listening to McCoy, Otis, and Marla as they gossiped over coffee. "Two murders in one week is totally unheard of in this part of the country," he said as he folded the paper and laid it on the empty chair next to him. "It's all they can talk about. It will be on the front page for weeks. At least they're not tying anything to the marina yet. The story just says that one of the bodies was found in the bay and the other on a lonely stretch of dirt road."

"I'm sure you'll find another cadaver soon just to spice things up," said McCoy.

"Seems like you have quite a knack for that," chimed in Otis.

Michael smiled. "I'm just glad that sheriff's deputy hasn't felt the need to ask me any more questions. Gives you an uncomfortable feeling. Know what I mean?"

"I wouldn't start feeling too cocky," said McCoy. "It looks like you spoke a little too soon." He pointed at the entrance.

Deputy Haynes spotted Michael as soon as he entered the restaurant and was making a beeline for his table. At least he was smiling, thought Michael.

"Good afternoon folks. I'd just like a minute or two of your time, okay?"

"Whatever you need," answered Michael.

The deputy picked up the newspaper that Michael had discarded and sat down. "We've had crime scene guys out looking over the two sites. They're not a hundred percent positive that Charlie Kelly's cabin is an actual crime scene but they took some samples of some suspicious looking sand from the driveway and it's at the lab right now. It looks like somebody went to a lot of trouble to clean up the area. Makes you want to take a closer look. All the tire tracks have been raked over and the road leading in and out has had so much police traffic that it's a waste of time even looking for evidence there."

McCoy and Otis nodded in agreement.

"Not much help on the other scene either. Freddie Henson's car was wiped clean and the hair samples we found inside turned out to be dog hairs. Dead ends everywhere we turn."

"I know the feeling," said McCoy.

Deputy Haynes, smiling shook his head. "I'm wondering if you guys can help me out a little bit. I understand that this George Snyder fellow has brought some hired help in from out of state to assist him with a salvage operation. I'd like to get a handle on them. Do you know their names?"

"I can get them for you," said Michael. "Well, most of them anyway."

"Most of them?" asked Haynes.

"There's one mystery man in the group who just goes by the name of Gypsy," said Michael. "We've checked him out as best we can and he comes up clean so far."

"Is he the motorcycle guy?" asked Haynes.

"Yup" answered Michael.

"I've got the license number off the bike. I'll see who it's registered to," responded Haynes. I'd appreciate if you can get the other three guys names though."

"Two," said Michael. "The guy from Toledo is named Jacob Marley and I'll be surprised if he doesn't come up squeaky clean."

After Deputy Haynes left, Michael called George Snyder and told him what he needed. He wasn't surprised that Snyder didn't know their last names but he was assured that he would have them within twenty-four hours.

Snyder was just about to call Gypsy when the phone in his room rang. It was the Sheriff's department. He listened intently, scribbled down some notes and then told the Sheriff's department that he would be sending a car to the hospital to pick up the two men and that he would be available to answer any questions once he had more information.

Before calling Gypsy, he pondered the situation. Current events seemed to throw the control back into George's lap. He'd need to use his leverage judiciously.

Gypsy answered on the first ring. "Hello, Gypsy. This is Snyder. Your two divers have gotten themselves mugged in the casino parking lot. They're being treated at St. Francis hospital and we have to pick them up. I'm going to drive you to the casino where their security people have the keys to the rental car and then you can go pick them up. I don't even want to see them. Meet me at my car right now." He hung up before Gypsy could respond.

When Gypsy arrived at Snyder's Mercedes it was clear that he didn't like being put in a defensive position. He climbed in and slammed the door staring straight ahead. "You got directions to this hospital?" he asked.

Snyder handed him a piece of paper with the hospital address on it and said. "There's a local street map in the glove-box of the rental car and you've got a GPS. They're expecting you at the casino. I'm sure they can give you directions too."

Not another word was spoken by either man until Gypsy got out of the car at the casino entrance. "I'll fill you in when I know something," he said.

"You do that," said Snyder.

The security officer didn't want to accept Gypsy's signature on the receipt for the car keys. "I need a complete name," she argued.

Gypsy grabbed the paperwork out of her hand and wrote 'John Smith' on the bottom line and handed it back to her. She surrendered the keys without looking at the signature.

There was very little conversation at the hospital. Both Sam and Eddie were quite subdued as they signed their discharge instructions. Gypsy paid to have their prescriptions filled at the hospital pharmacy and the pair was given emergency contact information if certain symptoms should appear. They both sat in the back seat of the rental car as if neither wanted to be within reach of Gypsy's fist.

"Okay, let's hear it," barked Gypsy.

"There's nothing to tell," answered Sam. "We won a few hundred bucks, not that much, and a couple of guys must have been watching and followed us out to the parking lot and waylaid us. We never seen it coming."

"That the way you saw it?" Gypsy asked Eddie.

"He's telling you like it is," said Eddie. "We were caught totally by surprise. Never had a chance."

"What about inside the casino?" pressed Gypsy. "You must have flashed the money around or something to attract attention. I told you guys to keep a low profile. Now the cops will want to know what two guys from Key Largo are doing in northern Michigan."

"Nothing," said Sam. "Nothing at all. We just cashed our play slips at the ATM machine, stuffed the cash in our pockets and walked out the door. We didn't even talk to nobody while we were in there."

"It's worse than you think," said Gypsy. "You must have told somebody that you were salvage divers and now the doctor is saying that you shouldn't be diving for maybe as much as two weeks and Snyder knows that too. He's not gonna even let you guys put on wet suits. The doc wants another look at you in a few days."

"But we couldn't help it," said Eddie. "I'm telling you the there wasn't a thing we could do about it. We were ambushed."

"We'll talk later," said Gypsy. "Looks like we're going to have plenty of time."

CHAPTER 25

The wind stayed at a steady twenty miles an hour for the next three days, throwing the lake into a frothy turmoil that defied man made challenges. The marina fleet remained tethered to their docks.

The break gave Michael a little time to get to know Jacob Marley and they seemed to develop an almost instant bond. They found themselves to be very much alike in many ways. Both were college graduates with business degrees, Jacob preparing himself for a management career at Admiral Salvage and Michael working toward becoming an insurance underwriter. Both of their career paths were derailed by circumstances beyond their control and both found themselves headed in new directions these days. They were content to forge ahead and see where the world took them. Michael introduced Jake to John, the marina owner and the three of them entertained McCoy, Otis, and Marla with their zany humor. It was almost enough to make them forget the gravity of the times. But not completely. Deputy Haynes saw to that.

"Things are getting more confusing by the minute," said the deputy. "Two murders, two muggings and I still haven't got a firm identity on this Gypsy character" Haynes sat in the motel restaurant nursing a large coke while Michael, McCoy, and George Snyder had lunch.

"I thought you said you'd get it from his motorcycle registration," said McCoy.

"Aw, the damned thing is registered to some salvage diving outfit down in Key Largo. But at least I've got full names for his two buddies."

Snyder asked. "Are there any problems with any of these guys? Criminal type problems, I mean."

The deputy pulled a notebook from his shirt pocket. "Nothing too worrisome. Seems that one of the divers, Eddie Karas was involved in a minor theft deal when he was a teenager. Smashing a pay phone for the dimes in the coin box. Drunk at the time. That's it."

George waved his hand in dismissal.

"They seemed okay to me," said Michael. "I just wish I knew more about Gypsy."

"I'm working on that," said Deputy Haynes. "I've contacted the Monroe County Sheriff's department down in Key Largo to see if they had a book on the alias and asked them to dig into Premier Salvage Divers while they're at it. I expect to hear something in a day or so. Oh, and I checked that Jacob Marley guy out. You were right. Clean as the driven snow. He was even an Eagle Scout."

Michael laughed. "I could have guessed that."

Gypsy walked into the restaurant followed by Sam and Eddie. When he spotted Michael's table, he veered his course to the other side of the dining room, his two disciples obediently bringing up the rear.

Later, as the sun was setting, Otis, Marla, McCoy, and Michael gathered in the familiar setting of the balcony outside Otis and Marla's room. It made sense because the twins room was right next door where mom and dad could keep an eye on them.

"What are you hearing about the weather?" McCoy

asked nobody in particular. "Is the wind ever going to die down?"

"The radar on the six o'clock news made it look like the breeze is almost out of here," said Marla. They're predicting more sun and warm temperatures by the end of the week. That's only a couple of days away."

"It's not going to help us if we don't have divers that can dive," said McCoy. "Any word on how our two crash dummies are doing?"

"Ya know," said Michael. "We actually have another certified scuba diver among us. Jake Marley has taken advanced open water classes and has even done some ice dives. He's just waiting for an invitation. We might want to give George Snyder a call and see if he wants his right hand man to be underwater with Gypsy."

"Do it." Said McCoy

Michael placed the call and within fifteen minutes Snyder and Jake joined them on the balcony. "My turn to order pizza," Snyder announced on his arrival.

"I'll mix the Mai-Tai's," announced Marla.

"Jake, have you talked with mister Snyder about helping out with the diving?" asked Michael.

"Not yet," answered Jake. "I was kinda waiting for him to bring it up."

"I've given it some thought," said Snyder. There are some technical things involved though and I wasn't sure if Jake was up to speed."

"I guess I should have said something," said Jake. "I'm familiar with just about all of that stuff that you just bought. Before Admiral Salvage decided to close its doors, there was some discussion of resurrecting the old marine salvage part of the business. They were getting bids on a new salvage tug and they sent me to school to learn all that stuff before they scrapped the idea. I actually have done quite a bit of diving for the company. When we'd get a call about some ice fisherman's car going through the ice, I was the guy who went under to hook up the tow rig. Of course it was usually less than twenty feet of water though."

Snyder sat pondering his hands in his lap. "My biggest problem is sending you down there with Gypsy. I'm not completely sure I can trust him. Although he's been a lot less antagonistic lately, ever since his friends got bushwhacked. How about I talk to Gypsy and see if I can get a feel for his receptiveness? You got any reservations, Jake?"

"Gypsy doesn't bother me," said Jake. "I personally feel he just likes to intimidate people. If I think he's dangerous or more than I can handle, I'll know it after the first dive and that will be the end of it."

"Okay, I'll give Gypsy a call when I get back to my room and lay it out for him. Looks like we might be able to start diving the day after tomorrow or so and I know that those other two won't be cleared to dive by then. Now let's get that pizza."

CHAPTER 26

Gypsy sat on the couch in George's room while George and Jacob occupied the kitchenette chairs.

"So," began George. "We've got two guys out of action and you can't do this thing alone. Jake here, is a certified diver and has done some pretty challenging stuff like cutting holes in the ice so he can get down under a car whose driver thought the ice was three feet thick."

Gypsy chuckled. "How do you get them things back up on top of the ice anyway? I've never done any ice diving."

"We begin by finding some thick enough ice to support our wrecker and then drive stakes into the ice to lash the wrecker down. Then we roll out a long runner made out of five foot wide rubber and fabric conveyor belt material. We try to get it over the edge of the hole that the car went through and as far under the car as we can. That's when I get underneath the car and rig the tow cable. The hookup's gotta be pretty hefty because everything weighs about five times its normal weight when it's full of water. Then we start up the winch and start dragging it up the conveyor belt real slow. Lots of times it will pull hard enough to lift the front wheels of the wrecker up in the air. Once the car breaks the surface, we slow it down even more so that the water can drain out of it. It's a hard pull because the cold water shrinks the air in the tires and they usually go flat. It's a long, slow process and we normally wind up working way into the night when the temperature really drops down. Not my favorite job for sure."

"Sounds like an expensive operation," said George.

"I wasn't involved in the billing part but my understanding is that it started at about twenty-five hundred and then there was an hourly charge after that and it generally takes a long time," answered Jake.

Gypsy whistled. "An operation like that could easily reach ten grand for one day's work. Seems like it would be cheaper to just leave the damn thing down there."

"Not an option. You just can't do that any more," said Jake. "The local counties won't allow it. They would have it hauled out. Likely hire us to do it and we'd charge them a higher rate. Then they'd add their charges to the bill and make the owner pay it. It's better to leave your car on dry land and haul your stuff out there on a sled."

"Okay, so what's the deal?" asked Gypsy. "Is Jake here going to be my dive buddy?

"Just how many choices do we have?" answered George. "Your guys won't be off restrictions for close to a week at the earliest and I want to get this thing done."

"Guess you're right," sighed Gypsy. "You had any time working with search gear?" The question was aimed at Jake.

"As far as actual searches go, I've never done one. But I've had all the training on everything you've got, provided by the manufacturer and have done a bunch of simulated searches. That's the best I can offer," said Jake.

Gypsy sat quietly for a few seconds and then said. "Then it looks like that's the best I can do. But before we go all the way across the lake, I'd like to have a few practice sessions together. Any problem with that?"

"None at all. As far as I'm concerned it's the best way," said Jake.

"We can use my fishing boat and do whatever we need to do right out here in the bay," added George.

Jake went out to his car and hauled in all of the diving paraphernalia that he brought from Toledo. Gypsy was pleased to see that it was all professional quality gear Dacor and ScubaPro, top of the line stuff that said Jake was no amateur.

They went back to Gypsy's room so that Jake could have a look at the new search equipment. The evening ended with everybody seemingly satisfied.

CHAPTER 27

Sam and Eddie weren't happy with their situation. Snyder had given each man a four hundred dollar advance to make up for the stolen money but Gypsy had told them to stay away from the casino and had pretty much limited their travels to within the city limits. The two Florida natives found that they had a lot to learn about Michigan's Upper Peninsula. The regional pride took some getting used to. There were pastys and the Packers and Minnesota beers. The 'Yoopers' as they called themselves did not assimilate with the 'Trolls' as they referred to lower peninsula residents. The culture was both amusing and challenging. They took to hanging out at the Delta County Historical Museum and Archives looking for anything they could find on the Poverty Island Treasure. There efforts yielded frustratingly wispy results. If there truly was a treasure, why wasn't there more information? An attendant at the archives said that it was a wartime top secret mission and there just wasn't any detailed information to be had. She offered that there were several volumes of historical notes and letters donated to the archives many years ago that had never been reviewed and so it was entirely possible that there was more information on the subject but nobody had ever read it. When Sam and Eddie saw the shelves of unexplored information, they decided that it was just too much to deal with.

Disappointed in the fruits of their research, the pair headed back to the Buck Inn where they first heard the story. Hopefully, local gossip would produce more answers than some stuffy museum.

The guy named Vinny was sitting at the bar on the same stool that he was sitting on the last time Sam and Eddie were here, obviously a regular. He nodded to them as they walked in. Sam took the empty barstool next to Vinny and Eddie squeezed in beside him.

"How you doing?" asked Vinny.

"Just great," answered Sam. We were kinda hoping to find out more about that sunken treasure. Feel like chatting?"

"There ain't much more I can tell you except there are people looking for it all the time. It's been going on for at least a hundred years and nobody's come up with anything yet."

"But there must be something to it or they wouldn't keep coming back," said Sam.

Vinny looked at the ceiling and then said. "The way I see it, it's like the old Dutchman's mine out Arizona way in Superstition Mountain. It's a great story and everybody wants it to be true, especially since it involves gold that's just there for the taking. But they're all just kidding themselves. There ain't no gold."

"So nobody's even gotten a nibble?" asked Sam.

"Well," said Vinny. "There are stories that back about seventy-five, eighty years ago that some salvage tug hooked onto something out there and tried to float it to the surface. They weren't real good about details back then so it's a little foggy about what really happened. Anyways, the way I heard it is that the Coast Guard got involved before the tugboat could get away and somehow the treasure got dropped right back to where it came from. They claim that there was gold in them crates. Don't know how they could be sure though."

Sam took a swallow of his Budweiser. "Is that the only treasure out there? I don't mean just around Poverty Island, I'm talking about the whole area, all the way across the lake."

Vinny shook his head. "If there is, I've never heard about it. There are sure plenty of wrecks scattered over the bottom but they're mostly old grain haulers and lumber barges. There's only the one by Poverty Island that attracts any interest."

"Nothing on the other side of the lake, eh" asked Eddie.

Vinny spent several seconds contemplating his response. "Why, what have you heard?" he asked.

"We haven't heard a damned thing," said Sam. "We're just curious, that's all."

Sam thanked him for the information and motioned for Eddie to follow him to a table off in a corner and away from the other patrons. When they were out of earshot Vinny snatched his cell phone from its holster and punched in a number.

"Kind of a waste of time, eh?" commented Eddie

"Not necessarily," said Sam. "I picked up on one thing he said that could mean something. When he was talking about that salvage tug that almost found the treasure he said it was seventy-five or eighty years ago."

"Yeah?" said Eddie.

"Don't you remember? When we went out to dive the other day and didn't find anything but crumbs from a really old wreck, we was frustrated because we wasted a whole day for nothing. On the trip back home, that Snyder guy tried to make me feel better by telling me that the search information he had was eighty years old. Ties right in with what Vinny over there was saying."

Eddie frowned. "Kind of a stretch, dontcha think?"

"Not at all," answered Sam. "I told you in the beginning the Gypsy wouldn't be here if he wasn't damned sure about this thing. My guess is that Snyder has stumbled onto something good. And that buddy of his that he brought up from Toledo, he worked for a salvage company. I heard him and Snyder talking about an old tugboat before our meeting the other day. I wonder if there's some kind of connection there."

"I guess all we can do is keep our eyes and ears open," said Eddie.

"You got it."

Two women who looked to be in their late thirties or early forties wandered into the bar and hoisted themselves up onto a couple of barstools. One of them was very blonde and the other a bright redhead, both obviously dyed. They were pretty but not beautiful and each could stand to lose somewhere near five pounds. Both of them sported gorgeous sun tans accentuated by their sexy white shorts. Sam couldn't take his eyes off of their legs. The blonde noticed Sam and Eddie staring at them and she smiled and winked.

Eddie was on his feet immediately and headed for the bar. Sam was not far behind. "You girls from around here?" asked Sam.

"Nope," replied the redhead. "Alvin, Wisconsin. We heard that there was some kind of festival going on over here with a bunch of concerts and stuff so we're here for the music."

"And whatever else we can find," Giggled the blonde.

"Two beautiful young ladies looking for a party," said Sam. "What a coincidence, so are we."

"You local?" asked the redhead.

"Naw, we're from Key Largo. Just up here for a job," said Eddie.

"Cool, I love Florida," said the redhead. "Where are you staying?"

"We're at the Little Bay Marina and Motel."

The redhead answered. "We couldn't get in there, tried but they're full up. We're still looking. That's why we stopped in here, to see if anybody knew of a good place."

"We passed a Best Western just down the road," Sam pointed to the west.

The redhead signaled the bartender and asked for a phone book. He retrieved one from under the bar and she quickly found the number and called the Best Western Motel. When she got off the phone she was smiling. "We got the last room." She high fived her girlfriend and then Sam and Eddie.

"This calls for a celebration," said Sam. "Can we buy you girls a drink?"

"Hell yes," said the blonde. "If you're buying we'll drink all night Two Captain and cokes," she yelled to the bartender."

"What do you do when you're not partying?" asked Sam.

"Susie works in a convenience store," said the redhead and I'm a real estate agent. What do you guys do?"

"We're salvage divers. We do underwater recovery and environmental work," replied Sam. We're up here doing a little preliminary work for a pipeline company."

"Sounds exciting," said the redhead. "I'll bet you guys have got a lot of really neat stories to tell."

"It's mostly a pretty boring job," said Eddie. "Early in the morning when you'd rather be doing something else, you gotta jump in the water and then start prying on hatch covers and stuff. It's usually cloudy and overcast and sometimes kind of windy. It's no fun at all, but it pays pretty decent because of the hazardous angle and the fact that you need all kinds of training and certification."

The women smiled and Sam ordered two more Budweisers and two more Captain and cokes. After two more drinks the blonde said. "Well, we've got to go get settled into our room. You guys want to help us with our bags?"

"Now there's an invitation that's way too good to pass up," said Eddie. "We'll meet you at the motel."

The two men stopped at a party store and picked up a fifth of Captain Morgan's Spiced Rum, a twelve pack of Budweiser and a couple of liters of Coca Cola. The girls were waiting for them out in front of the motel. There wasn't much in the way of luggage to help them with, just a couple of small overnight bags. "How long did you say you were staying?" asked Sam.

The girls just giggled.

As the evening wore on, the blonde began asking more questions about diving adventures saying, "You surely must have had some exciting dives in your lifetime." She came over and sat next to Sam on the couch.

Sam told the story about the time he had a crayfish run up his arm and it startled him so much that he spit his regulator out. He was diving alone and was at the bottom in sixty feet of water. He had a rough time retrieving the regulator and getting it cleared. The episode really scared him and the very next day he went out and bought a backup regulator that he wore on a loose rubber strap around his neck. To this day it remains part of his equipment and it still accompanies him on every dive.

"Expecting anything like that while you're here? How deep will you be diving?" asked the redhead.

"Actually we don't know exactly how deep we'll be diving but I think it will be less than sixty-five feet. Pretty shallow by diving standards," said Sam.

"I thought you said you would be diving on a pipeline," said the blonde. "You should already have that information."

Sam popped another beer tab. He was beginning to feel a significant buzz brought about by the half dozen Budweisers he'd consumed so far. "Well, I kinda lied about that. We're actually searching for an old shipwreck."

"Treasure hunters?" asked the blonde.

"Not sure," said Sam. "The guy that hired us says it's museum stuff but I sorta think it's something else."

"Like what?"

Sam hesitated, trying to clear his thoughts. "Well, I think it might be some kind of gold or silver coins and stuff. Don't know for sure. Just a hunch."

The blonde snuggled closer to Sam. "Now we're getting somewhere, baby."

CHAPTER 28

Gypsy had become much easier to work with since his two hirelings had attracted unwanted attention. Snyder made it clear that Sam and Eddie were Gypsy's responsibility and that he would be held accountable for their actions. Gypsy argued that they were grown men with minds of their own and he couldn't control their actions.

"But I can control their paychecks," responded Snyder. "And if I don't like what I see, I can terminate them."

Gypsy clearly didn't like being subjected to pressure and spent most of a day brooding in his room but by the next morning he seemed to have things worked out in his mind.

He greeted Jacob Marley at breakfast in the restaurant. "Ready for a little workout today?"

"Sure thing," replied Jake. "When and where do you want to start?"

"Well," said Gypsy. "Snyder says we can use his fishing boat but I don't think we need it. The last dock on the east end of the marina is pretty much vacant and I figure we can mark off a small area with diver's buoys and we'll have plenty of room to do everything we need to do. The water's plenty deep enough and it's a whole lot calmer right here in the harbor. Why don't we meet there in a couple of hours?"
"I'll have all my gear," answered Jake.

The sky was clear over Little Bay de Noc today and unlike the monster whitecaps on Lake Michigan the light ripple in the harbor glistened like diamonds under the summer sun. Jake patiently waited on the dock admiring the array of boats gently tugging at their mooring lines, a few with people aboard either scrubbing or fixing things. None of them appeared to be preparing to get under way. Footsteps on the dock jolted him back to reality.

Gypsy was walking in his direction and pulling what looked like an oversize wagon containing the new search gear. George Snyder followed behind carrying three life rings with dive flags.

"Where are your two helpers?" asked Jake. "I know they're not cleared to dive but they could be helping out."

"They're not here," said Gypsy. "Didn't make it back to their rooms last night. I don't know where they are."

George spoke up. "I checked with the Sheriff's office this morning and they've got nothing, so at least we know that they weren't in an accident or didn't get arrested or anything like that. They'll turn up."

Gypsy moved the conversation away from the two missing divers. "Let's get started," he said as he unpacked the equipment.

Jacob took the three diver flag markers and placed them at the edge of the dock. He dove into the harbor and then pulled the markers off of the dock one at a time and placed them in a semi circle in the area that Gypsy pointed out to him. After they were all anchored in position, he climbed back up on the dock and checked out his diving equipment. "I'm ready," he declared.

Gypsy slipped into his scuba gear and waved Jake into the water as he jumped off the dock. George handed Gypsy the surface penetrating radar unit.

The two men swam away from the dock and after a brief discussion the disappeared below the surface. They repeated the process with the side imaging sonar system and the dual frequency side scan sonar. The process lasted about three hours and yielded one open end wrench that must have been dropped in the harbor over sixty years ago and an automotive window crank that was even older. When everything was packed back in the wagon, Gypsy pointed at Jake and gave Snyder a thumb's up and said. "As soon as I get this stuff stored away, I'd like to borrow your car and go looking for our two wayward children."

Snyder said. "I'll drop the keys off at your room but I've got to tell you that my patience is wearing thin with those two." "I know, I know. Mine too," responded Gypsy.

When Gypsy approached his room he saw two men sitting outside his door in plastic chairs. They were laughing and drinking Budweiser.

"Where the hell have you two been?" said Gypsy. "I thought I told you to lay low and stay out of trouble."

"Hold on there," said Sam. "We didn't do anything wrong and we didn't get into any kind of trouble. We just got lucky. Met a couple of women. Any problem with that?"

"Bullshit," shot back Gypsy. "You guys are on a short leash and you know it. One more screw-up and you'll be on a plane headed back to Key Largo."

"Hey," protested Eddie. "It was nothing. We were only a couple of miles up the road and it was just the four of us. No problems, just fun."

"What do you know about these women?" asked Gypsy. "And what did you tell them?"

"We didn't tell them anything," said Sam.

"You must have talked about something," said Gypsy. "Did you mention that you were diver?"

"Well yeah," admitted Sam. "But that's about it. Why should we hide it anyway? It's a perfectly legitimate business y'know."

Gypsy was fuming. "You know perfectly well that our job here is sensitive and we can't be talking about it with anybody. I thought I had that drilled into your thick heads."

"Be cool," said Sam. "We didn't give away no secrets. Hell, we don't know any secrets."

Gypsy turned to see George approaching. "Looks like our friends here decided to check out the local talent last night and got themselves tangled up with a couple of unfettered women. No harm done. Hopefully."

George winced. "I sure hope you guys didn't let alcohol loosen your tongues. You know that this is a very discreet operation. I stand to lose my contract if things become public knowledge."

"Your secret is safe with us," replied Sam "We won't say a thing. We can't because we don't know anything."

CHAPTER 29

Vinny sat in the motel room with the blonde and the redhead listening to their report on last night's escapades. "Okay what'd you get?'

The blonde spoke first. "Well, you were right. These guys are here looking for the treasure. But they've been told something different, probably to keep them from getting too excited. They really don't really seem to know too much. Hired hands, if you know what I mean.

The redhead added. "And they're not diving around Poverty Island. Their boss has them looking in a spot that's clear on the other side of Lake Michigan."

"Really?" said Vinny. "I'd sure like to know what that's all about. Everybody stays close to Poverty Island. But I was kind of wondering about that too. Those guys were asking if there were any promising shipwrecks farther out in the lake. I gotta wonder just what kind of information they've got."

"Like I said," interjected the blonde. "These two are pretty clueless about the exact nature of the treasure. They think it's the big one but they can't be sure. Kept talking about some guy called Gypsy like he's their leader or something. They're saying that he wouldn't be involved if it wasn't something big and that he'd only be interested if it was pretty much a sure thing. But their employer told them that they're looking for museum artifacts… keeping them in the dark."

Vinny silently considered what he'd heard and then said. "Do you suppose you could find those two again? I'd like to find out who they're working for and see what I can find out about him."

"Sure we could," said the blonde. "We as much as told them that we'd be having lunch at the Buck Inn every day while we're in town. You can bet that they'll come looking for us again. We made them feel pretty special last night and they told us so."

"Besides, we know where they're staying," said the redhead. "The place is pretty much the headquarters for next week's water front festival. And it's got a restaurant and nightclub so that would give us a good excuse for being there and I'm guessing that they at least have their breakfast there. We can check it out in the morning."

"Yeah," said Vinny. "And with any luck their boss will be with them. I don't want to go with you because if all three of us showed up it would start them thinking and adding things up. Ya think you can get any pictures without them knowing."

"Absolutely," answered the blonde. "I'm really good at making it look like I'm talking on my phone while I'm snapping pictures. Do it all the time."

It was shortly after eight-thirty in the morning when the two women walked into the Little Bay restaurant. There were at least a dozen people, mostly older couples scattered throughout the spacious dining room. Most of them had a coffee cup in one hand and a newspaper in the other. None of them looked up when the pair walked in.

Sitting at a table that was off in a corner yet commanded a full view of the room, the blonde remarked, "I didn't think anyone read newspapers any more."

The redhead looked around. "I'd say that people born before nineteen fifty-five are still hanging on to the old stuff and they're the ones who have breakfast early in the morning. Come back in a couple of hours and you'll see tablets, smart phones, and iPads all over the place."

"You're probably right," answered the blonde.

"Coffee?" asked the waitress who held the pot in her right hand and two menus in her left.

"Buckets full," responded the blonde, smiling as she accepted the menu.

The girls opted for the breakfast buffet, filled their plates and had just sat down when Sam and Eddie came through the door accompanied by a big burly guy wearing dark sunglasses and a bushy beard.

"Gotta be Gypsy," whispered the redhead.

The blonde nodded. "No question couldn't be anyone else. I'm glad he wasn't one of the guys that we had to entertain."

Without looking around the men buried their faces in the menus and ordered their breakfast from the waitress. They chatted quietly while waiting for their order. The blonde managed to get four quick pictures of the one presumed to be Gypsy without being noticed.

Just about the time that their food arrived, two more men, an older guy with curly steel grey hair and a younger athletic looking fellow walked in. As they headed to a table near the women, Eddie, in a loud voice said, "Good morning mister Snyder. Morning, Jake."

The redhead began writing notes while the blonde busied herself trying to look absorbed in a telephone conversation as she kept turning her head in order to focus the camera lens on the new arrivals.

Suddenly, Sam noticed who was sitting across the dining room. The look on his face was one of alarm. He quickly shifted his gaze to avoid eye contact.

The blonde smiled and waved but Sam acted as if she wasn't there. It occurred to her that this Gypsy guy might be the problem or maybe it was the two men who just walked in. Sam must have realized that he had revealed way too much the other night and was worried that Gypsy or the other guys might find out. Vinny would be interested in hearing about this reaction. It confirmed her thoughts.

More people began filing in, among them was a group of three men, a woman and two small children. One of the men, the woman, and the kids were African-American, obviously a family. They greeted Sam, Eddie, and Gypsy with a nod and "Good morning," calling them by name, including Gypsy. And then they stopped to chat with that Snyder guy addressing him as George and said hello to his pal Jake before moving to a nearby table, the blonde's camera phone busily shooting away the whole time.

The redhead added George Snyder's first name to her notes then leaned across the table and whispered, "Vinny's gonna really be impressed with all this stuff. Maybe we should renegotiate our fees."

The blonde laughed and replied. "I think we should hang around and follow these guys. All the rooms have outside entrances so we'll be able to get all the room numbers if we're lucky. Hopefully they won't all leave at once and scatter in different directions."

Sam, Eddie, and Gypsy were the first ones to leave. The redhead waited until they were outside the door and then she stole a peek down the sidewalk that flanked one wing of the motel. Sam and Eddie had turned in just a few doors down but Gypsy kept walking almost to the corner before entering his room. The redhead hurried down the sidewalk and noted the room numbers before returning to the restaurant. When she rejoined her blonde friend, she was pleased to see that all the other subjects of interest were still dawdling over breakfast.

The blonde took the next shift as George Snyder paid the bill and he and Jacob Marley headed for the door. The fact that Snyder carried himself like a man with authority and that he so casually picked up the tab reinforced the notion that this whole affair was his personal project. The words 'Top Man' were penciled in next to his name. The two men had rooms right next to each other on the branch of the motel that extended out toward the bay. The room numbers entered in her notebook, the blonde rejoined her friend in the dining room.

The status of this last group was less clear. They didn't appear to be divers and they certainly didn't give off vibes as being on the board of directors. They could be investors or perhaps some kind of advisors but they would be included in the report simply because they seemed to know all of the other players. The two ladies made sure to get all of these room numbers as well.

The girls felt certain that they had nailed down all of the main characters and maybe lassoed a stray or two. They headed back to the Best Western.

Vinny was waiting when they got there. After going through all of their notes and listening to their reports, Vinny felt that they could be on to something big. Judging from the reaction that the blonde described when Sam recognized her, he determined that Gypsy and all of the others would be off limits as a source of information, at least for now. If he was to learn any more it would have to come from one of those two paid divers who didn't seem to know exactly what was going on. But maybe they knew a little more than they thought. Or, better yet, maybe they could be persuaded to dig a little deeper and pass their findings along. After all, they were simply contracted employees and might be tempted by a more promising offer. He'd concentrate on squeezing out every fact and every speculation that they harbored.

Vinny was glad that he'd found these two women and stayed in contact with them. He first encountered them about four years ago in a high end businessmen's bar near Milwaukee where he observed them hustling customers. They were so smooth that he was the only one who realized that they were working together. As they left the bar, he confronted them in the parking lot telling them exactly what he had observed. Although he didn't identify himself, the girls assumed that he was a cop and asked what he wanted to just forget everything he'd seen. These girls were pros and had contingency plans for every situation. Vinny assured them that he didn't want to cause them any grief but said he could help them make some really big scores instead of this nickel/dime gig that they had going now. He offered to be their agent.

"Sorta like a pimp?" said the blonde.

"Well," said Vinny. "I wouldn't put it that way. You two look way too high class to be hookers. I'd call you entertainers, you know, like Madonna."

The girls laughed and the redhead handed Vinny her phone number saying. "I'll tell you what. You find us a really sweet deal and we'll try it. If it works, you've got a couple of partners. Sound good to you?"

"Trust me," replied Vinny. "I'm gonna make you guys rich.

They worked together off and on with each adventure paying off generously. Vinny seemed to have a knack for finding rich and vulnerable targets who could easily afford a couple hundred grand to protect their reputation or privacy. The trio had even managed to fleece a head coach in the National Basketball Association for close to a half million. The relationship had indeed been a profitable venture and when Vinny called them a few days ago saying that he had a potential blockbuster going in northern Michigan they didn't hesitate to jump on board. So far everything was looking rosy. Time for the girls to go back to work.

CHAPTER 30

George and Jake took advantage of the sunny morning to climb aboard George's fishing boat and take a quick boat ride out into Lake Michigan. They left the harbor at sunrise and had not mentioned their plans to anyone else. George felt that they needed to get away from the other guys so that they could talk openly and share all of their concerns and fears as well as dreams.

The water on the big lake was far from calm this morning but not nearly as angry as it had been for the last couple of days. If it continued settling down at its current rate, it would be as smooth as a mirror in a couple of mornings. They could probably even dive tomorrow but waiting another day would give the sandy bottom a chance to quiet down and improve the underwater visibility.

George's fishing boat was actually a Donzi and built on an offshore ocean racing platform. The hull was no stranger to choppy seas. As they bounced around in the playful waves George asked. "Have you got any feelings about the guys we're working with?"

Jake answered. "Well, I'm pretty darned sure that Michael O'Conner and his cop buddy McCoy are rock solid. I'm not the least bit concerned about them. But when it comes to Gypsy and his two diving buddies, I have a few question marks. I'm not concerned about them causing any confrontational type problems but I haven't seen anything that makes me feel comfortable about their honesty."

"I know what you mean," agreed George. "Gypsy has never been crazy about following the rules. He about flipped out when he found out that I had a lawyer involved. And his two friends seem to smell something besides museum artifacts. They're asking way too many questions. If I had this to do over again, I'd be using just you and the guy that I originally hired, you know, Charlie, the guy who was murdered. Gypsy and those other two would never even have been here."

"Do you think it's possible that any of those guys had anything to do with Charlie's death?" asked Jake.

"Gypsy was the only one here when Charlie was killed," said George. "And he was supposed to be headed over to Charlie's cabin the night that Charlie was killed but said he got sidetracked and went to the casino instead."

Jake stared at George for a moment. "Have you told anyone else about that? I mean, it sure sounds suspicious."

"You know, I never gave it a thought. I guess I just believed what Gypsy told me. After all, he sounded innocent and sincere when he told me the story. He came off as pretty nonchalant about it. It never occurred to me that he might be lying. Maybe I should mention it to that Sheriff's deputy."

"Well," said Jake. "Maybe we should at least talk it over. I wouldn't peg Gypsy as a murderer either. He's too laid back and just doesn't seem like the aggressive type. But you can't always tell what a guy is really like by his outward demeanor."

His eyes still fixed on the horizon, George nodded.

Jake continued. "I know that you'd like to keep this project moving and that everything would grind to a halt if Gypsy happened to get hauled in for questioning. You pretty much need him at this point. There's no way you could depend on those other two guys to take up the slack even if they do get cleared for diving. It's really up to you but you could hold off until we at least get a fix on what's on the bottom over there." Jake waved his arm toward the east.

"You make a good point," said George. "But I still wish I'd have thought this thing through a little more thoroughly. Things would be a whole lot less complicated."

"Are you sure that the two hired divers don't know what you're looking for?" asked Jake.

"Pretty sure," said George. Gypsy insists that they have no idea and I've never said it's anything other than historical relics."

"Then why don't you just let them go?" suggested Jake. "Me and Gypsy can handle whatever we've got down there. And there's a lot less chance of trouble if you get rid of the extra baggage. If Gypsy balks, it will tell you something about his intentions."

"You've given me a lot to reflect on, young man," said George. I'm glad we came out here, just the two of us. It gave me a chance to do some clear thinking. When all this is over I'd like to talk about your future with my company. Right now, it's all me running it but... well you might be way too rich to think about ever working again."

George swung the bow back around to the west and raced the waves back to Little Bay de Noc.

CHAPTER 31

Gypsy joined Sam and Eddie for breakfast at the restaurant and then told them that he'd be busy getting things set in case things were quiet enough for diving tomorrow and so they would be on their own. Before they parted ways, Gypsy made sure that they understood that they were on thin ice with George Snyder. "Hell, I had to argue like crazy to keep him from firing you after that stunt you pulled the other night. Staying out like that without telling us what you're doing is pretty damned irresponsible."

"Oh come on," argued Sam. We don't work for that guy twenty-four hours a day. What we do on our own time is our business and we don't have to answer to anybody for it."

"Suit yourself," said Gypsy. "I'm just telling you how he looks at it. And he's the guy writing the paychecks. He even pays you your full salary on days when the water is too rough for diving and when you're not medically cleared to dive. Not many employers will do that. If he decides you're more trouble than you're worth, he'll likely dump your asses. Just don't say I didn't warn you."

"We won't be out looking for trouble but I don't see any need to just sit in our rooms watching television all day either. You called us up here because we're good divers and that should be all anybody expects from us." Sam stopped himself short of hinting that he knew anything about the Poverty Island treasure. "C'mon Eddie, let's get out of here. We've got a day or so left to enjoy ourselves before we go back to work. Maybe we can find those women again."

Eddie was all smiles as they left the restaurant.

Michael was heading out to the dock to make sure that everything on his cruiser was still okay when he ran into Gypsy on the pier.

"Hey there," said Gypsy. "Did Snyder mention anything to you about going anywhere in his boat today? It's not tied up in its slip."

"No, as a matter of fact he didn't say a word about it," answered Michael. "Have you tried calling him?"

"Not yet," said Gypsy. "I just now noticed that his boat is gone." Gypsy dug out his cell phone, turned his back and walked away while he tried to reach George.

George answered on the third ring and Gypsy could tell from the background noise that he was underway somewhere in his runabout. "Where you at?" asked Gypsy.

"Just coming back into the harbor," answered George. "Me and Jake just took a little ride to have a look at the lake conditions. Things are improving. I'm thinking that we might be able to do a little diving tomorrow but the bottom might still be riled up a bit. I'll talk to you when we get ashore. Looks like we'll be tying up in about ten minutes."

"I'll be waiting at your slip," answered Gypsy.

When George returned to his slip he found Gypsy waiting to accept the mooring line and secure the boat next to the dock. Jake hung the fenders over the port side and jumped onto the starboard dock and fastened those lines. The boat safely nestled in its home, the three men gathered at the end of the pier to discuss tomorrow's plans.

"I'm thinking just the three of us can take my little boat over there and, if things look promising we can come back with the rest of the gang on the big boat the following day," suggested George. "Considering that the bottom will likely still be stirred up and the visibility limited, I don't want to waste everyone's time. We can probably handle a preliminary dive with just a couple of people and a video camera."

Gypsy, looking out over the bay leaned on a tall piling and asked. "Are you thinking of cutting the other guys out? I mean, why don't you want them along?"

"Not necessarily," answered George. "Although I will admit I'm not happy about their lack of professionalism. My thoughts about tomorrow have nothing to do with them. I just figured we'd be lean and mean and get more things done if we had less people to trip over."

Gypsy nodded. "Guess you're right. I'll let the guys know but they won't be happy."

When Gypsy got back to his room he noticed that Sam was walking out to the rental car and waved him over. Sam trotted down the sidewalk and asked. "What's up?"

"I want you to bring all of that video gear down to my room," said Gypsy. "Looks like I'll be doing some diving tomorrow and I'll need it."

"Why can't I just bring it with me in the morning?" protested Sam.

"Because you ain't coming along," said Gypsy. It's gonna be just me and Jake and George."

"What does that mean?" asked Sam.

"Hopefully for you it doesn't mean anything other than you're not coming because you can't dive. George was pretty emphatic that it would just be the three of us."

Sam shrugged. "Whatever. I'll go get Eddie and we'll bring the stuff right over." He walked away shaking his head.

Within an hour Gypsy had the underwater video camera and two hundred feet of communication cable stacked neatly on the spare double bed in his room. He was glad that he'd be diving tomorrow, he needed the break in tension. He had the definite feeling that Sam and Eddie would soon be packing their bags for the trip back to Key Largo and they were the source of his anxiety. It might be all for the best. After all, they could watch the store back at Premier Salvage Divers and maybe pick up an odd job or two. Their maverick style wasn't a problem back in the laid back Florida culture but it sure wasn't working out in the structured mind of George Snyder.

Sam and Eddie jumped in the car and headed toward town. "Man, there sure ain't much to do around this place," commented Eddie. "Especially since the casino is off limits."

"Nothing is off limits, " barked Sam. "I'm sick and tired of somebody else trying to run my life. We're grown men and, as long as we're not breaking any laws, we can do any-thing we want. If Snyder doesn't like it, he can fire us."

"I think he's going to let us go anyway," said Eddie. "The writing is on the wall. He's got another diver who just happens to be his buddy so it really looks like we're the odd men out. But we shouldn't quit, we're making too much money for that. I say we keep taking the two-fifty a day plus the free room and meals until he says, 'adios.'"

"I agree," said Sam. "But I'm still not going to let him tell me where I can and can't go and what time to be home at night. I'm an employee, not a slave and I won't be treated like one."

"We can go to the casino if you like," said Eddie. But I'd like to stop by that Buck Inn place and see if the girls are there. They said they'd be having lunch there and it's almost noon.

Sam swung the car around and set his course for the Buck Inn.

The place was doing a pretty big lunch business when they came through the door. Table servers were scurrying everywhere with trays full of burgers, onion rings, and draft beer. Looking around, they spotted Vinny sitting at the bar nursing a coke. He smiled, raised the can in a toast and both of the men nodded. When their eyes adjusted to the light, they scanned the room but didn't see anybody they knew.

There was one empty table by the far wall and the two men grabbed it. The waitress was surprisingly fast delivering the menus. Sam told her to bring a couple of Budweisers while they decided what to order. After their big breakfast neither man was too hungry so they eventually settled on appetizers.

Eddie was just mopping up the last of the mini-tacos when the door swung open and the blonde sauntered in followed by the redhead. After a quick glance around the bar, the redhead spotted them and tapped her friend on the shoulder. Both girls smiled and made a beeline for the table. "Mind if we join you?" asked the blonde."

Sam was already on his feet holding a chair for the blonde. Eddie followed suit with the redhead. Unlike Sam and Eddie, the girls were hungry and ready for a meal. The two men drank beer and made small talk while the women devoured lunch.

"Looks like we're gonna have tomorrow off too," said Sam. "The Lake won't be too rough or anything like that but the boss figures he can get along without us for the day."

The blonde had a puzzled look on her face. "Are you being fired or anything like that?

"Let's just say that our future with Mister Snyder is somewhat cloudy at the moment," said Sam. "Gypsy, our dive-master says that we've still got jobs but the field looks mighty crowded to me. They have another diver on the team now and they just might be able to get by with just two guys."

"Is this new guy a more experienced diver than either one of you?" asked the redhead.

"It's a little more complicated than that," answered Eddie. "Ya see, me and Sam have been injured and we're not medically okayed to dive yet. We've got another physical scheduled for day after tomorrow and if we get cleared we'll see what happens."

"So," said the blonde. "If you don't have to work tomorrow, you're free to party tonight. Right?"

Sam smiled. "Oh, baby."

Like the last time they followed the girls to their motel, Sam and Eddie stopped for a bottle of rum, some mixer, a twelve pack of beer, and a bag of ice. And like the last time, they found the two women waiting in the parking lot.

Once they got in the room, the blonde didn't waste any time getting to the point "So what are your plans if you get canned? If you really think you're searching for gold can you just walk away from it?"

"Got that covered," answered Sam. "I have the coordinates for the search grid. I'm sure I could get close enough to find whatever's down there if I need to. The problem is that they'll be out there looking at the same time."

"I'm sure there are ways to handle that too," answered the blonde.

Eddie chimed in. "If we find it, we're gonna need some pretty heavy duty equipment to get it off the bottom. We can't be workin' outta no rowboat."

"That must really be some treasure you're looking

for," said the redhead. Sounds like you'll need some kind of salvage ship."

"That'd be the right way to handle it if it's what we think it is," said Sam.

"What do you think it is?" asked the blonde.

"Something big," said Sam

"Really big," added Eddie.

The blonde opened a Budweiser and handed it to Sam. "Let's drink to your dreams and hope they come true. We've got some partying to catch up on."

CHAPTER 32

Dawn broke under a cloudless sky. The wind had subsided over night and even the colorful pennants over the pier entrance remained motionless. At eight o'clock in the morning, the temperature was already in the mid seventies with the promise of upper eighties in the forecast. Gypsy joined George and Jake on the dock, the wagon with the video cameras dragging behind him. He was hoping to avoid any questions about Sam and Eddie because, once again they were no-shows at the motel last night.

"Looks pretty quiet out there," said Gypsy. "If it stays that way, we should have a productive day."

"Nothing on the radar to make me feel different," said a smiling Jake. "I can't wait to get started."

George hefted the cooler full of sandwiches and iced tea over the side of the boat. "How's our problem children coming along?" he asked. "Can't help noticing that they're not here to help us get going even though they're still on the payroll."

"Actually, I didn't ask them to be here this morning," said Gypsy. I wanted to give them some time to think about why they're not coming along with us today."

George gave out an exasperated sounding sigh. "I'm not trying to punish them or send any kind of negative message. I said yesterday that my only intention was expedience. Maybe I'd better stop by their rooms this morning and talk to them."

`"They aren't there. They were headed out to some restaurant in town to try their never ending breakfast bar. I guess they ran across the place yesterday and wanted to see if it was as good as they heard," lied Gypsy. "You'll have to catch them when we get back. They won't be able to come with us tomorrow either because they're scheduled for a follow up visit at the hospital. Sam says that doctor told them that they might be declared fit to resume diving. Both of them claim to feel fine."

"That's actually encouraging," said George. "If they behave themselves and they're physically capable, I'll keep them on the team. But if they keep screwing up and jeopardize the sensitive nature of this operation, I won't be able to take any chances with them."

"Fair enough," said Gypsy.

Jake was already loading the video equipment onto the boat, being careful to keep the camera protected as he stowed it in one of the live wells. "We should be ready to shove off any minute," he declared.

Gypsy was the last one aboard, staying behind to cast off the mooring lines. He threw his heavy looking satchel on board and followed it into the boat. "I'm ready."

George fired up the big twin Mercury engines and pointed the bow toward open water. They were off and running. On the way across the lake Gypsy questioned Jake quite extensively about how he could be so sure that he had pinpointed the location. Jake looked over at George and, only after seeing the big gray head nod did he turn back to Gypsy.

"Well," said Jake. "My great grandfather was considered the best navigator to ever sail the Great Lakes. I'm not exaggerating, it's been documented in Great Lakes history books. Anyway, back in nineteen twenty-nine it looks like he was aboard the tug that was in the process of recovering the cargo at Poverty Island when the Coast Guard decided to intervene. Apparently the tug had a big head start on the Coast Guard boat, probably close to two hours. They were almost all the way across Lake Michigan and were able to keep an eye on the pursuit. The skipper knew that he couldn't outrun the cutter so he had my great grandfather get a precise fix on their location and then they cut the tow ropes and air lines and let the crates sink again. They did all of that while the Coast Guard was still too far away to see exactly what was going on. Then they set their course in a northeasterly direction and ran parallel to Beaver Island. The government boys didn't catch up to them until they were almost to Garden Island. By that time they had dumped all of the other evidence like the severed air lines and such. The Coast Guard didn't have anything tangible to charge them with. But they insisted that they put ashore at Charlevoix and put the tug in an impound status with an armed guard for the rest of that summer. The crew was allowed to go home but they were all technically under arrest. They released the boat in October and then escorted it all the way back to Toledo. There were never any formal charges but the investigation remained active. According to my great grandfather, the skipper didn't make any entries in the log book until he was back home. The location was recorded in a cryptic code and was never entered in the log. As soon as they were back in Toledo, they locked all of that stuff up in the company safe. When the tug got back late in the fall, it was still labeled as evidence for the government and its use was prohibited as long as the investigation was in progress. The salvage company hauled it out and put it on some cribbing in the yard. It's still there."

Gypsy remained silent through the whole story and then he asked. "Why did you guys wait so long to get back into this thing?"

It's like this," said Jake. "The government kept their investigation open but, from what I can tell, they wouldn't answer any questions about their progress. They just kept the salvage company in the dark for about seven years and then finally sent a letter saying that the investigation was being closed with no further action and no explanation. By that time my great grandfather had retired and the tugboat skipper had moved on to a new job. Most of the personnel had changed and so had the company philosophy. The main focus of the business had changed as well. The boat had been on dry land so long and so many repairs would be needed that it wasn't worth restoring to duty. With no salvage tug to work with, they turned their attention to the land transportation world that was expanding at a breakneck rate in those days. The manufacturing industry had discovered trucks that were not limited by railroad routes. The whole industry was changing because the trucking companies could now service them. Admiral Salvage recognized that someone would have to keep the trucks on the roads and they flourished by servicing the trucking industry. Both my father and my grandfather were employees back then."

"Seems like a shame that no one followed up," said Gypsy.

"From what my dad told me, both my grandfather and he were discussing it and then the Second World War came along, my grandfather joined the army and went to war. He was wounded at Bastogne and spent the rest of his life in a wheel chair. That was the end of those plans. Besides, after my great grandfather died, there was nobody around that even remembered it. The only reminder was that old rusty tugboat propped up on timbers in the yard."

Gypsy gave it some time to sink in and then asked. "What spurred the new interest?"

Jake laughed. "It was all mister Snyder here," he said pointing at George. "He bought out the old Admiral Salvage Company a couple of years ago and gave me the job of figuring out how much metal is in that old tug so that he could sell it for scrap. I was in the process of tearing it apart when I came across this old notebook stuffed inside the command console. That's where the trail started and it's taken us right to here.

"Hell of an interesting story," said Gypsy. "It would explain why nobody has found any treasure over by Poverty Island. People have been hunting over there for around a hundred years. Your story about the salvage tug ties right in with one of the legends but it puts an entirely different spin on it. I sure hope you've got it right. As a matter of fact, I'm counting on it."

"Well, I'd be willing to bet that we'll have better luck listening to my great grandfather's directions than we would following the crowd. You can see how it's worked out so far for the guys pursuing the local folklore."

Gypsy and Jake used the journey across Lake Michigan to go over their diving gear time and time again the way professional divers do. George piloted the boat with an eye on his GPS and finally dropped the anchor in the exact place where the target coordinates crossed. "Forty-six feet under the keel," he declared.

Gypsy, glancing at his own GPS, said. "This is just about where we were on our first trip over here."

"Within fifty feet," answered George. "If the figures are right, we're right on top of it now."

"I'd like to begin with a few pictures," said Gypsy. We can attach the cable right to my laptop and load all of our videos directly to it. We can review the pictures when we break for lunch." Jake nodded and dug the video camera out of its storage case.

The two divers pulled on their wet suits and slipped over the side.

CHAPTER 33

Sam woke up on this sunny morning with merciless hangover. It was seven thirty and everyone else was still sleeping. He stumbled into the bathroom and climbed into a searing hot shower. Experience told him that, after a night of drinking it was the quickest path back to the land of the living. There was still nobody else awake when he emerged from the bathroom. He scribbled a quick note that included his cell phone number on the motel notepad and then quietly woke Eddie up. The two men snuck out of the room without disturbing the women and headed back toward Little Bay Marina.

"Think we still got jobs?" asked Eddie.

"They had big plans today," said Sam. "My guess is that they haven't even missed us."

It was time for breakfast when they pulled in to the motel parking lot. Sam left the car in front of his room and they walked over to the restaurant. The server found them in a quiet corner of the dining room and took their order for corned beef hash and poached eggs. After they were served and the waitress was gone, Sam began the conversation. "You know those girls really got me thinking last night. If we could figure a way to run those other guys off, we could have the treasure to ourselves."

"Yeah but we're not even a hundred percent sure that we're looking for real treasure," said Eddie. "It might be just what Snyder said it is; museum artifacts."

"I know," said Sam. "But I can't help thinking that there's a lot more to it. I mean, why would Gypsy be involved if it's just historical junk? Call it a gut feeling but I just know that it's gold."

"I suppose you could be right," said Eddie but I don't see where we can do anything about it. I mean we can't just push them guys out of the way. One of them is a cop, don't forget."

"I know," said Sam. "If we decide to go it on our own, we've got some heavy duty planning to do. And we're gonna need money. These things take more than just our diving tanks and wetsuits."

"Right, we've got some thinking to do if we're gonna buck the system," said Eddie. This ain't gone be easy or simple."

"I know," replied Sam. "And we don't have a lot of time. We've got to stay sober today and go see the doc in the morning. Clearance for diving will have to be the first step. Maybe we can get aboard that big boat in a couple of days and have a look for ourselves."

"Yeah," said Eddie. "All they got with them today is a video camera and if the treasure isn't sitting right up on top of the sand, they ain't gonna find anything."

Sam waited until the waitress refilled their coffee cups before he continued. "The way those girls talked, you'd believe that they had some sort of organization behind them. I mean they sounded as if they had the resources to take on this project. I think we should take a closer look."

Sam and Eddie spent most of the day in conversation without any resolution to their dilemma. There just didn't seem to be any answers, at least none that would work without a lot of outside help.

As mid day drifted into afternoon they decided to camp out on the dock and wait for Snyder's boat to return from the day's adventure. It was around six-thirty when they finally saw the bow rounding the point and heading for the pier.

The businesslike expression on Snyder's face made him hard to read and so, after securing the boat in its slip, they waited for him to speak. "Ahoy there," said Snyder, his face breaking into a smile. "I trust that you two made good use of your day off."

"Just trying to take it easy," answered Sam. "Want to keep our blood pressure on an even keel for our physical exam tomorrow."

"Did you see anything over there?" asked Eddie.

Gypsy answered. "Not sure. If there's anything there it's buried in the sand but there's an intriguing looking mound that I want to take a closer look at. We didn't have any metal detecting gear with us today. We'll try again tomorrow. I sure hope that you two can be ready by the next day."

"We're planning on it," said Sam. Neither one of us has had memory issues, headaches, dizzy spells, blurred vision or any of the concussion symptoms. I'd be awfully surprised if we don't get cleared right away."

George Snyder was standing on the dock with his hands on his hips. "There's plenty of work that needs to be done and you guys will probably be a big part of it. Hope for the best."

Sam and Eddie made sure that they had a nutritious supper and spent the evening sitting on the dock nursing iced tea and trying to figure a way to worm their way into the treasure ahead of George Snyder and Gypsy. They came up blank.

CHAPTER 34

Michael and McCoy were the first two customers when the restaurant opened at five o'clock for breakfast. The place filled up surprisingly fast as the first calm day presented itself. The boating and fishing enthusiasts had been deprived of their open water for the better part of five days and couldn't wait to experience the undulating motion of their water craft. They were kicking their day off with a good breakfast.

McCoy asked the waitress for coffee and then loaded up his plate at the breakfast buffet. When Michael joined him with his own impressively heaping plate, he began. "Well, today is our first official day as treasure hunters. I hope that Snyder was right about them finding something promising on the expedition yesterday. He said it was just a rise in the bottom where the sand had piled up on top of something but at least it's a place to start. He says that it's within twenty feet of the exact spot that old Harry Marley pinpointed."

"I can't claim to know how to read a lake floor but there has to be a reason for the irregularity," said Michael. "Today will be a learning curve for you and me and I'm sure we'll see, or at least hear about some interesting things. I can't wait to get started. I ordered a bunch of food from the catering service back in the kitchen." He pointed back over his left shoulder. "They said it would be all ready by six o'clock so we can grab it on our way out."

The two men paid their breakfast tabs and then picked up the provisions at the kitchen door and headed out to the dock. George and Jake were on their way in to the restaurant as Michael and McCoy were leaving. "What's in all the bags?" asked George.

"Well," Michael began. "There's a pasta salad, a variety lunchmeat, swiss cheese, Italian bread, bananas, apples, plums, and a few other things. Got some chips and dip and a bunch of different soft drinks along with a couple of twelve packs of bottled water. We shouldn't go hungry today."

George smiled and shook his head. "You're like my mother."

Michael gave the boat a thorough inspection as the sun was breaking over the horizon. Meanwhile, McCoy busied himself stowing the groceries in the refrigerator and pouring the ice over the bottles and cans in the big plastic cooler, By seven o'clock everything was ready for the day's task and Gypsy was headed down the dock with his scuba rig over one shoulder and a gear bag hung over the other. George and Jake were close behind with all of their equipment as well. Within ten minutes everything was aboard and stowed and Michael had the engines warming up.

Other engines were being fired up all over the marina as the fishermen prepared for their day of trolling for Walleye, Salmon, and Lake trout. The harbor was full of happy faces this morning.

Michael brought the big boat slowly out of its slip and pointed her toward the open lake. The sun reflected off of the smooth water and warmed teak decks. Once they were actually on Lake Michigan, Michael and Jake climbed the ladder to the fly-bridge where they occupied the twin command chairs. Jake recited the coordinates of their destination from memory as Michael plugged them into the boat's GPS.

"How are you and Gypsy getting along?" asked Michael.

"Gypsy seems to have an 'arm's length' clause in his personality," responded Jake. "He doesn't want anybody too close to him, even those two guys that he brought up from Florida. From what I've seen they don't entirely trust him and there seems to be a hint of friction between them. Eddie and Sam are tight with each other but Gypsy is a little bit aloof."

"Gypsy seems to be that way with just about everybody," said Michael. "Maybe that's just his personality."

"But guys like that usually have some sort of reason for being that way," said Jake. "Could be insecurity or lack of self confidence or..."

"Something to hide?" interrupted Michael.

"Yeah, that too," said Jake. "But I wouldn't rush to judgment on Gypsy. He's consistent so it's likely the way he's been for his entire life."

"I still want to keep a close eye on him and you should too. If he does anything that bothers you while you're diving, be sure to let us know," said Michael.

They were interrupted by McCoy climbing up to join them on the fly-bridge. "I'm not making this thing too top heavy, am I?" he asked "Wow, the view from up here sure is different."

"It's particularly helpful if you're backing into a slip," said Michael. "You can see everything. How is everybody doing down on the main deck?"

"Everything is holding up just fine. Any idea what our ETA is?" asked McCoy.

"I figure we're about thirty minutes out," replied Michael. I was just going to holler down to Mister Snyder. He wanted me to keep him advised."

"I'll let him know." Jake got to his feet and offered his seat to McCoy. "Here you go, all warmed up for you. It's time for me to get down below, get all of my checks done on my diving gear and climb into my wetsuit."

After Jake was out of earshot, Michael said. "Jake doesn't seem too worried about Gypsy but I'm not so sure. He hasn't shown any signs of getting out of line but we're just into our first day of searching. If we find something, we could be tied up for weeks just digging it out of the sand. If he's going to get testy, that's when I'd expect it."

"I wouldn't let my guard down in any case," said McCoy. "If he's dangerous, he'll pick his own time to show it and it may very well be when you least expect it."

"I'll keep trying to avoid paranoia," said Michael. "I want this to be a fun adventure for all of us and would hate to see something or somebody spoil it."

"So far things are just fine," said McCoy. "If I see a change coming, I'll let you know."

CHAPTER 35

Sam and Eddie reported to the clinic at nine o'clock in the morning. After checking in, they found two seats together in the crowded waiting room where they spent close to forty minutes marking time until their turn came up.

The physician's assistant that finally attended them checked the standard vital signs and then sent them to the lab for further testing. The next step was an EEG which the nurse explained was a lot like an EKG except they were measuring some sort of brain activity. Then there was one more test called a PET scan and then they returned to the waiting room. It was around twenty minutes later when the lady behind the counter called their names and asked them to come to the window. She handed them each a letter saying that the tests showed that no further restrictions were necessary. They were off the hook.

The two men decided to celebrate but agreed to shut things down early so they could be ready to join the treasure hunt in the morning. It was high noon when the entered the Buck Inn. The two girls were already there sitting at their regular table. They waved as the guys came through the door. Within minutes the four of them were toasting Sam and Eddie's return to active duty.

"I suppose we won't be seeing too much of you now that you'll be going back to work," said the blonde.

"Oh, we'll be wanting to stay in touch for sure," said Sam. "Especially if you've got connections that might be helpful to us."

"What's that supposed to mean?" asked the blonde.

"You sounded like you knew of a way to help us chase this thing without our current employer. It even sounded like you knew a way to move him out of our way."

"Anything is possible," said the blonde. "Yeah, we have some solid connections that make things happen but whether we contact them depends on just how serious you guys are."

"I suppose a lot depends on how things go for the next week or so," said Sam. We'll be putting in some long hours over the next few days and I'm sure that we'll have a much better picture of the whole operation and maybe a clearer idea of just what we're looking for. And from what I've seen, this lake kicks up pretty regularly and there are bound to be days when we can't operate on the water. If you girls plan on sticking around for another week or two, I'm sure we can show you just how serious we can be."

"Let's see where it goes," said the blonde. "We're ready and we can move things right along when the price is right."

"I'm afraid there can't be any partying tonight though," said Sam. "We're going to have to get back to the marina so we can greet our returning adventurers."

Sam and Eddie were waiting at Michaels slip when the boat arrived just before sunset. They took the lines and heaved them over the pilings like the pros they were. Gypsy was the first one off the boat and he was smiling. "You guys must have good news or you wouldn't have been here waiting for the boat."

"Yep," said Sam. "We're off probation. We can both go back to work tomorrow."

"Great," said Gypsy. Because it looks like we've found something. Not sure what it is yet but we got some really solid pings over a pretty good area and it's all metal, both ferrous and non-ferrous. We only had to move our position four times and then we were right on top of it. It was less than a hundred feet from the exact location we were given."

"Is it the stuff you've been looking for?" asked Eddie.

"Too soon to tell," said Gypsy. It's all buried pretty deep in the sand. We're gonna need to use the water jet to find it. We should get closer tomorrow."

George Snyder climbed onto the dock. "Did I hear you guys say that you're ready to go back to work?"

"Sure did," said Sam. "When do we start?"

"Right now," said Snyder. "You can begin by giving Michael a hand cleaning up his boat so that it's ready for tomorrow. I'm headed over to the restaurant to order some food for tomorrow's run. According to the weather service there's another small storm cell headed this way and it's expected to blow through here in three or four days. Not supposed to last more than a day or so and things look pretty clear after that. But I'd sure like to make some headway before the front gets here."

"We'll get right on it Mister Snyder," said Sam. "We're pretty experienced at cleaning up after ourselves when we get back to port. We'll have it done in no time."

The two men jumped aboard and each took a large plastic trash bag from Michael and headed in different directions picking up refuse. Within a half hour they had the boat in showroom condition and Michael was both pleased and impressed. "Thanks, guys," he said. If we keep after these chores, this is going to be a very pleasant experience."

"Nothing to it," said Eddie. "We got a system."

Gypsy returned to the boat just about the time they finished their chores. He was towing his wagon loaded with a couple of one hundred foot coils of air hose and a stainless steel water jet. Sam and Eddie helped him load all of the equipment onto the afterdeck before declaring their work finished.

Gypsy, Sam and Eddie made their way to the motel restaurant for an evening meal. George and Jake followed Michael and McCoy to their balcony.

CHAPTER 36

Chinese take-out was on the menu for this evening's outdoor dining. George, Jake, Michael, and McCoy joined Otis and Marla for the feast outside their rooms while the twins commandeered everybody's fortune cookies and giggled over the profound prophecies that they found hidden inside. "I could sure get used to this lifestyle," said Marla. "Ordering from the carryout menu and eating off of paper plates with plastic throw away flatware. It's every housewife's dream."

"Well," said Otis. "What sort of riches did you uncover while you were out there today?"

"We don't know yet," answered George. "But it looks pretty promising. Gypsy and Jake here mapped out a grid where they were getting some really solid signals bouncing off of something that was definitely metallic buried under the sand. Tomorrow we're going to try blowing enough of the silt and gravel out of the way and see if we can actually get an eyeball on it."

"What do you think it is?" McCoy directed the question at Jake.

"There is definitely a ferrous component to it because it attracted our magnets," answered Jake. "But there's more to it than just iron or steel because the draw on the magnets wasn't as strong as you'd expect for that much mass. I figure that it's probably an area about four feet high by four feet wide by close to twenty feet long. At least that's the way our surface penetrating radar saw it."

"Think it could be the gold?" asked Otis.

"Keeping our fingers crossed. The biggest part of it's non-ferrous," replied George. "I never dreamed that we'd get a hit like this so soon. I'm bracing myself for a disappointment but I can't deny that I'm pretty excited."

"I have a lot of faith in my great-grandfather's navigating skills," said Jake. But it wasn't him that wrote about gold in the logbook. All he did was chart the location of where they dropped their tow. He can take credit for telling us where it is but not for what it is."

"Is that your official disclaimer?" asked George.

"I'm afraid it is," answered Jake.

"Not to change the subject, but has it been tolerable working with Gypsy?" asked Otis.

"So far, so good," said Jake. "He's pretty much all business down on the bottom. He doesn't show any emotion at all. Can't read him."

"I know I'm sounding like I'm somehow obsessed with the guy," said Otis. "But when we had that meeting the other day, he took his glasses off for a few seconds and I saw something in his eyes that instantly alerted me. It's like I know him from somewhere but I sure don't ever recall running into him. If we've ever crossed paths, I'm sure it will come to me. But until that day, he's on my 'no fly' list. I'm just suggesting that you keep your eyes open and make your own assessment."

"I think that just about everybody has warned me about Gypsy," said Jake. "I won't go to sleep on him. Promise."

"I've watched him quite closely these past few days," said George. "And he's done nothing at all out of the ordinary. But like Jake, I'm not going to allow myself to be lulled into a false sense of security."

"While you guys have been out playing treasure hunting pirates, me and Otis and the kids have been enjoying your beautiful lakeshore," said Marla. "We all went to the gift shop and bought snorkels and dive masks and we've been exploring the lake, at least until it gets to be over three feet deep. Are there any big fish out there? All we've seen is minnows. But they're enough to scare the kids out of their wits"

"I'm not sure what you'll find in this little bay," answered Michael. "But there are some really big fish out in Lake Michigan. They say that some of the Sturgeon run somewhere around seven feet long."

"It's settled then," said Marla. "We'll be staying close to shore.

And the kids will have to be content with collecting clam shells."

CHAPTER 37

Today held the promise of being the clearest and warmest day of the summer. The sun rose like a flaming ball in the sky and the temperature was already climbing through the seventy-five degree mark when the boat left the pier at a quarter past seven. It carried a full compliment today, four divers along with Michael, McCoy, and George. The boat was large enough that it still didn't feel crowded even with seven full grown men aboard. Gypsy sat in the first mate's chair nursing a bottle of water while Michael, McCoy and Jake climbed to the fly-bridge. George occupied the skippers chair and Sam and Eddie retreated to the salon where they turned on the air conditioning. "It seems to be starting out fine," said Eddie. "Nobody's uptight and it's as if we haven't missed a beat."

"Don't get too comfortable," answered Sam. "We're still on Gypsy's shit list and we ain't too solid with old man Snyder either. Let's just see how it plays out over the next couple of days, especially if we find something real valuable. I want to see how they act if they smell gold."

Their conversation was interrupted by Gypsy who stuck his head in the door and told them that it was time to start setting up the gear that they would be needing for today's dive. The three of them retreated to the afterdeck where Gypsy fired up the high pressure air compressor and began connecting hoses to the hand held water jet. Eddie asked why Jake wasn't down here helping out and Gypsy sharply rebuked him saying that Jake had done all of the work up until now and it was their turn to pitch in a little bit. Both Eddie and Sam raised an eyebrow at Gypsy's comments.

They arrived at their destination under a brutally clear sky with the sun beating mercilessly on their backs. Gypsy, Sam, Eddie, and Jake couldn't get into the cool water any too soon. McCoy handed them the water jet and all four divers disappeared into the deep blue water.

Once on the bottom, Gypsy took the first shift with the water jet. The high pressure stream pushed sand, silt and stones out of the way and stirred up a huge cloud of sediment and residue. He could only keep the nozzle running a few minutes at a time because all visibility was gone almost immediately. The four divers took turns handling the unwieldy water canon until it was time to head to the surface for new air tanks.

After a short break, they went right back to work. By the end of the day, the team had opened an enormous hole in the bottom of the lake and still had not been able to see anything although their surface penetrating radar told them that they were very close. It was slightly disappointing that they hadn't been able to see anything and they knew that there would be a certain amount of backfilling overnight, but they were still optimistic as they reeled in the air hoses. It had been tedious and boring work. Tomorrow promised more of the same but it would be another day and they'd all be another day closer to being multi-millionaires.

Michael stopped at the gas dock, topping off the fuel tanks before returning to his berth. George supplied the credit card for the gas. The routine seemed to work efficiently. Jake pitched in on the cleanup when they returned to port and things were shipshape more quickly than they were last night. Gypsy returned to his room alone. George and Jake made plans to have supper with Michael, McCoy, Otis, and Marla while Sam and Eddie opted for the bar.

"What'd ya' think?" asked Eddie.

"Gypsy didn't seem too excited," said Sam. "But I couldn't help but notice that Snyder was keeping real close tabs on our progress and that Michael guy and his cop buddy were looking right over his shoulder every time we came up for air. Those guys acted like they were expecting something big to happen. Oh yeah, and I managed to get all the new GPS coordinates logged in to my unit."

"All I've seen so far is a lot of dirt and crap," said Eddie. "My wet suit is hanging in the shower and I've already rinsed the crud out of it three times. This has been a dirty job up to this point. We'd better hit something solid pretty soon."

Sam's cell phone rang. He answered it and the voice on the other end said, "This is Susie. How did your day go?"

"I guess you could say we were busy," said Sam. "But it wasn't too productive. We gotta go back for more of the same tomorrow. It's slow going because everything is buried under the sand. You might say we're in the excavation phase."

"Do you have a feel for what's down there," she asked.

"At this point, not for sure," replied Sam. "I'll have a much better idea once I can actually see something. Right now it's mostly radar pings."

"Well, you've got my number and I'd appreciate it if you'd keep me posted. I've made some phone calls and there is someone interested in helping you and he has resources."

Sam's ears perked up at the new information. "You can bet I'll be staying in touch."

"Anything good?" asked Eddie

"Could be," responded Sam. "That was our blonde friend and she as much as told me that she's got the connections that we need to handle this thing all by ourselves. Sure beats working for a couple hundred dollars a day when you're looking at close to a half a billion, don't it?"

"Since you put it that way, I'd say everything is cool," replied Eddie. "It's still awful hard to believe any of this is real and I guess I won't really be convinced until I can hold something in my hand that glitters like gold."

"I'm betting that you'll see that day within the next week or so," said Sam. "The weather reports show another system that will likely blow us off the lake for a couple of days but it's nothing serious. Hopefully we'll have everything uncovered before that happens."

CHAPTER 38

Today looked like a carbon copy of yesterday. Eddie commented that he never thought that the weather could be so hot this far north. The mercury had reached ninety yesterday and surely seemed to be headed right back there today. The surface was flat and friendly as the big cruiser knifed its way eastward through the blue water across Lake Michigan. Another thing that Eddie was not prepared for was the fact that you could lose sight of land on the Great Lakes. The sheer size of the world's largest fresh water reservoir certainly impressed him.

It seemed as if everybody returned to the same space on the boat that they occupied yesterday. Three men on the fly bridge, two at the command station and two more in the salon. It was comfortable for all and it worked.

"Think we'll see any crates today?" asked Eddie.

"I'm hoping," said Sam. "If we have the kind of day we had yesterday, I figure we'll make some good progress. The lake stayed calm all night so I'm not expecting to have to start over in a lot of places. The hole might look a lot like we left it yesterday afternoon."

"I think we'll be just fine," said Eddie. "These lakes might have currents but they're not like the ocean, they don't have tides. The bottom should be pretty much undisturbed."

It was a little quicker getting into the water this morning because they had all had a day of practice yesterday. The four divers were on the bottom within twenty minutes of setting the anchors.

Gypsy took the first shift with the water jet again today. He may have worried some people with his questionable character but he certainly didn't shy away from hard work. The site had backfilled only slightly overnight and so it wasn't like they were starting over. Progress was brisk today. By the time they broke for lunch and fresh air tanks, they had uncovered the rough shape of a long container. Conversation was brisk and lively during the break.

"What do you think?" asked Eddie.

Gypsy just shrugged and said, "We'll see."

Sam said. "We've definitely found something and from the shape I'm seeing down there, it's not just a big rock. Man made without a doubt. But I'm not getting too excited just yet. It could be nothing more than an old steel hull fishing boat."

"Could be," said Jake. "Quite a few of the old gill netters were like that. Started out as wooden hulls but were later covered with sheet metal. It helped them deal with the ice flows in the spring. A lot of them were abandoned back in the sixties though when the ban on gill nets went into effect for non-native fishermen on the Great Lakes so they're scattered all over the bottom in just about every one of the lakes."

Gypsy seemed to be listening intently. When Jake finished speaking, Gypsy said. "I'm pretty sure that this isn't an old fishing tug. It's not wide enough and definitely not long enough. If it's a boat, which I seriously doubt, it's a rowboat made out of solid iron. Hopefully we'll have some sort of answer before the day is over."

The quartet of divers started the second half of their day with renewed enthusiasm. They had developed an effective system of dealing with the clouds of silt created by the water jet and it helped things move along faster with less debris constantly obscuring their vision. By the end of their work day they had unburied one corner of what looked like a large crate. I was impossible to be sure because it was heavily encrusted with millions of tiny shells. The covering yielded very slowly to Eddie's attempts to chip it away with the heavy bladed Abalone knife that he carried strapped to his lower leg. They finally gave up in frustration and surfaced, swimming back to the boat.

"Zebra Mussels," said Jake as he sat sipping a large Gatorade. "They're all over the Great Lakes and they attach themselves to everything, even each other. Probably somewhere between two and four inches thick on whatever it is that we've uncovered down there. We're gonna need air chisels."

"I'm afraid he's right," chimed in Gypsy. "I'd suggest that we get the whole thing exposed first and then worry about getting the surface cleaned. Probably gonna need a couple more portable air compressors and some air tools. We can most likely rent all of those things but it might take a few days to round up everything we'll need. Blowing more sand will give us something to do until we have all the stuff necessary for the next phase."

"If you can come up with a list of everything you need, I'm sure Otis wouldn't mind making all of the rental arrangements," said McCoy. "He's not spending his whole day out here on the boat with us, so he has the time."

"I'll get with Gypsy after we dock and as soon as we have the boat back in shape. We'll come up with a plan. I let you know later, " said George.

The following day brought more of the dirty and boring job of blowing the sand away from the sunken treasure. The team spent eight full hours taking turns with the water jet and at the end of the day they were standing in a hole about five feet deep and working to feather the edges back at least another ten feet to avoid the possibility of cave-ins and back filling. The object that they had uncovered took on the rough shape of least four or five square containers that were somehow lashed together. The metal detectors were screaming off the charts, indicating that the content of the crates was just about solid metal. Gypsy and Jake knew exactly what that meant while Sam and Eddie were awash in speculation.

Once the on board housekeeping was done, the trip back to the marina involved three separate conversations in three different locations on the boat. George and Gypsy agreed that things looked promising but agreed to keep their enthusiasm restrained. Jake, along with Michael and McCoy up on the fly bridge speculated that they had found the object of their search and also agreed to keep their anticipation low keyed.

Down in the salon, Eddie and Sam argued over what it was that they were uncovering. Eddie insisted that it was the lost gold while Sam insisted that they not jump to conclusions. "It could easily be civil war artifacts. Things like guns and canon balls and cavalry sabers. Those kinds of things would set off wild signals on the metal detectors too."

"Yeah but are they that valuable?" asked Eddie'

"They would be if they're confederate relics," answered Sam. "Besides, none of the other guys are jumping up and down celebrating. That should tell you something."

When the boat reached the harbor and all seven men were standing on the pier, Sam asked. "Well what do you think? Have we found something important? Valuable?

George responded. "All we know at this point is that we've come across some cargo containers and they seem to contain metallic contents."

"I called Otis on our way back in," said Michael. "And he has two more air compressors and four nice air chisels. We'll be able to start carving the outer crust away tomorrow. In another few days we should have a good idea of what we've got down there."

"Better hope for some big time progress tomorrow," said McCoy. He held out his cell phone for all to see. "This new front will probably hit here tomorrow evening and from what I can see, it will likely shut us down for at least one day, maybe two."

Gypsy shook his head. "Damned Michigan weather."

CHAPTER 39

Taking time to load and lash down the new air compressors, the group started out about a half hour later today. Once on the bottom, the divers split into two teams, one on each side of the seashell covered mound. Even using air powered tools, progress was agonizingly slow. Layers of dislodged shells covered to bottom of the excavation and constantly needed to be cleared away with the water jet. The work was very tiring and the men needed frequent breaks. Jake had the best explanation for the fatigue. "You have to multiply your effort by a factor of three when you're working underwater. Just the extra energy that it takes to move your arms adds a lot to the strain. Working underwater can be very tiring."

Concentrating on one end of the structure, by day's end the team had exposed about two square feet of what appeared to be a wooden crate made of heavy rough sawn beams and banded completely with a two inch wide ribbon of grey iron. The corners of the containers were protected by iron caps held in place with long spikes. Sam wanted to try prying the caps off but Gypsy killed the idea immediately. When they got to the surface Gypsy admonished Sam for wanting to violate one of the most time honored rules in salvage recovery. Never disturb a container until you have it safely on dry land.

"What's the matter with you?" barked Gypsy. "You're like a little kid with a Christmas present. Just wait."

"But that could be two weeks away," protested Sam.

"Tough," said Gypsy. "Besides, it's none of your business what's inside them crates. All that stuff belongs to some museum. Even George Snyder don't own it. We're all just worker mules."

The weather radar showed that the front was steadily approaching and the crew agreed to start back to port a little earlier today. There was a slight chop on the surface of the lake as they headed back to their marina. Mother Nature was sending her scouts ahead to warn boaters about the leading edge of the violent front that would be passing through in a matter of hours. They entered Little Bay de Noc running into a steadily increasing headwind. By the time they had the boat docked and tied down, white caps were showing up on the open water.

In spite of their anxiousness to see what was in the newly discovered crates, everybody acknowledged that a day off was a welcome pause in their busy schedule. Michael and McCoy could enjoy a little more of Otis and Marla's company, exploring Escanaba and watching the kids eyes light up as the carnival arrived in town and began setting up in the marina parking lot. George could conduct a conference call with his attorneys. Sam and Eddie could get back together with the pretty blonde and redhead, and Gypsy could sit alone in his room searching his brain for a way to make the treasure his and his alone.

Sam called the blonde a little before dinner time and suggested that the four of them might get together tonight. The lady readily agreed and they made plans to meet for dinner and see where things led from there.

They met at a family type restaurant called Drifters where the conversation soon turned to the diving expedition. The girls listened intently, occasionally exchanging glances. They also made sure that Sam and Eddie new they were welcome to spend the night with them and agreed to meet at their motel after a few cocktails.

When the four of them settled into the motel room, it was obvious that the girls wanted to talk more about the treasure. They asked dozens of questions, most pertaining to the contents of the crates. Sam recognized it as a fact gathering mission and decided to head it off. "Just what exactly are you trying to find out and why?"

"Well," said the blonde. "You told us that you suspected that this was a treasure hunt from the very beginning and that you felt as if you were being frozen out. We said that we might be able to help and that's all we're trying to do here."

"What have you got in mind?" asked Sam.

"Well," said the blonde. "We have a friend who has access to a big boat, a fully equipped fishing trawler powerful enough to pull a half mile of fish filled net. And he has a lot of local connections. He could possibly have the boat that you're working on quarantined and restricted to port. You know exactly where this treasure is so we could slide in and haul it out of there while your employer is arguing his case in front of a magistrate."

Sam whistled. "How soon do you need our answer?" We just might want to bring Gypsy on board with this. It's his style."

"Right," agreed Eddie. "It would be a lot easier if we include Gypsy. After all, he's the guy who got us involved."

"That's up to you," said the blonde. "How much work do you have to do out there in the lake before you can move the stuff to shore?"

"Minimum of a week," said Sam. "Probably closer to two." Eddie nodded in agreement.

"Call us as soon as you can then, we need an answer. Our partner can be impatient at times."

Always curious and constantly on the prowl for more facts, Jake used his day off to do a little exploring and found himself at the historical museum and archives building. He inquired about any information that the archives might have on the Poverty Island wreck and the archivist replied, "That old story certainly has been revived recently. There were a couple of guys in here within the last week or so asking about that same legend. I believe they may have been divers, you know, treasure hunters. I told them what little I knew and then offered them the chance to discover something new for themselves but they decided that it was too much work."

Jake smiled and asked, "Really? Why would there be any extra work involved?"

"Follow me," said the lady and she led Jake to a room where row upon row of musty smelling books lined the shelves and several cardboard boxes sat on the floor. She showed him one section where the shelves were catalogued by date. "According to the story, this event occurred in eighteen sixty-three although some argue that it was at least a year later while others say that it was earlier. I have partitioned this one area of unread reports and diaries from that three year span. Some of the stuff is from corporate records and some of it from private citizens. Some of it is even boxes full of loose papers. If I'm not mistaken, there may even be a family Bible or two in the pile. We have no idea what's in there because nobody has ever read it."

"Would you know if there anything in there like old ship's logs or anything like that?" asked Jake.

"Very well could be," said the archivist. "You're welcome to have a look. Most of this stuff came from people cleaning out attics after their grandparents died."

Jake sighed, pulled the first volume from the shelf and took it over to a reading table. He opened the cover and began scanning the pages. By the end of the day, he had gone through about twenty percent of the books and binders without finding a single reference to the shipwreck. He tentatively approached the archivist's desk. "I don't suppose you ever let people check your reference material out like library books, do you?"

"It kind of depends on what it is," responded the young lady. "If it's something that earns a lot of local interest, we like to keep it here so that it's available to the general public. If it's something that nobody cares about, we can let it out for a couple of weeks. You interested?"

"Absolutely," said Jake. What do I need to do?"

Twenty minutes later Jake was heading back to the motel with four large boxes in his trunk and the back seat of his car piled high with musty smelling literature.

CHAPTER 40

Sam and Eddie left the girls right after a quick breakfast in the motel restaurant. There was no more conversation about sunken treasure, just a little small talk about strange encounters that the divers experienced in the waters off the Florida Keys. It was light banter punctuated by occasional laughter. Eddie picked up the tab and the two men headed back to Little Bay de Noc with hopes of a warm reception from Gypsy.

It took a lot of talking to get Gypsy to agree to go to lunch with them at the Buck Inn but Sam eventually persuaded him to leave the comfortable surroundings of the marina. "It's important and we need to be in a place where none of the other guys might overhear us. It's something very private."

Over their protests, Gypsy insisted on riding his motorcycle to the lunch meeting. Once inside the tavern, Sam led the trio to a table in a very secluded corner, passing the bar where Vinny sat watching them.

After ordering burgers and beer, Sam began. "We've known one another for a long time and me and Eddie know that it's not like you to come all the way up to Michigan for a job unless it was a blockbuster deal. We think that there's a lot more to this venture than we've been told. We done a little snooping around since we been here to see if there were any local rumors and you'll never guess what we found out."

"I know where you're headed," said Gypsy. "I'm still listening."

"Then we were right?" commented Eddie.

Nobody responded and Sam continued. "Everybody in this area knows about that treasure, hell, Escanaba is a big part of the legend. Anyway, the UPS driver who delivered all of that search gear to the motel has been spreading the word that there's a new treasure hunting crew in town and that they look pretty professional. We're no secret around here. People have been talking to Eddie and me, asking questions. We didn't have to play dumb because we were dumb, didn't know nothing about any treasure. Eventually we heard the whole story."

The waitress arrived at the table with a huge tray filled with burgers, fries, and beer. They waited for her to leave.

"Anyway, one of the stories we heard that there was a tugboat back around eighty years ago that actually latched on to all that gold and got it all the way to the surface. Story goes that they dropped it back to the bottom because they saw the Coast Guard closing in on them. That's what the natives are saying anyway. Everybody in these parts assumes that it was cut loose right about where they found it. We found something that sure looks like crates full of gold but it's clear across Lake Michigan, not within fifty miles of where everybody else is looking. Sounds like someone has uncovered new information"

"That's right," said Gypsy. "Keep going."

"Well," said Sam. "That Jake guy worked for a salvage company that did marine salvage way back in the last century. I heard him and Snyder, his boss talking about an old tugboat that was sitting on a cradle in their storage yard.

I'm wondering if that could be the tugboat that the old story talks about."

"If you're looking for more money, don't make any big plans," said Gypsy.

"We're looking for all of it," said Sam.

Gypsy stopped eating his hamburger and sat quietly for a minute. "You'd need lots of equipment and a really good plan," he said. "You got all that stuff?"

"We might have," said Sam. "We've been doing a little homework on this thing."

"Why didn't you come to me earlier?" asked Gypsy.

"C'mon," said Sam. We weren't even sure whose side you were on. Hell, you were keeping all kinds of information from us. What were we supposed to think?"

"You're talking to me now and you've already said way too much to turn back so you'd better tell me everything. It sounds interesting but you've got a lot of selling to do."

"We've made some connections," said Sam. "Looks like we've might have a line on a fishing trawler. It could very well have cranes and everything. We could lift the crates one at a time and swing them on to the deck. The rest would be easy."

"There's a lot more to it than just running out there and loading it on a boat," said Gypsy. "We've got Snyder and his gang to deal with and they aren't going to just stand back and watch."

"Looks like we can get that handled too," responded Sam. "Our connection claims that it can be arranged to have that big cruiser beached for a few days. You know, some sort of legal technicality. We just have to tell them when we're ready."

"This 'connection,'" said Gypsy. "I want an introduction."

"We can make that happen," said Sam.

Thundershowers were predicted for later in the afternoon and the blustery winds added credibility to the forecast. That didn't stop Otis and Marla's ten year old twins from insisting on one more ride and the merry-go-round. "But you've already ridden it four times," protested Marla.

"We know, but it's fun," answered the girls.

Otis showed up to join Marla on the bench with two paper cones of cotton candy, both pink. "Maybe this will coax them off of the ride," he said.

Michael and McCoy had been over at the shooting gallery challenging each other's marksmanship and impressing the Carney with their skill. Now they wandered back to the kiddie ride area to hook up with Otis and Marla.

"Been a pretty warm day so far," said McCoy. "And it's predicted to stay that way. If this storm blows through quickly, we should think about having one of our legendary patio parties up on the balcony this evening. We can invite George Snyder and Jake."

"Sounds like fun," said Marla. I've found some new cocktail recipes I'd like to try. You guys can be my guinea pigs."

Michael dug out his cell phone and punched in George's number. After a brief conversation, he slipped the phone in his shirt pocket and said. "Seven o'clock on our balcony. It'll be a dinner party, carry-out only and George says he's buying."

"I'll feed the kids first, around five thirty," said Marla. "Carry-out only."

At seven o'clock sharp, there was a knock on Michael's door. George and Jake showed up carrying plastic bags full of fried chicken, biscuits, and mashed potatoes with gravy. "Compliments of the Colonel," announced George. "Everybody enjoy your day off?"

Otis said. "Me and Marla are about worn out from trying to keep up with the kids all day. Carnival rides are just too tempting when you're ten years old."

"Mike and I spent a little time on the boat this morning," said McCoy. "You know, just checking stuff out, doing a little cleaning, and making sure that everything is in good shape. It's all fine. Then we just hung around the motel and eventually explored the carnival."

George polished off a drumstick and then said. "I spoke to my attorney today and he sounded pretty optimistic. He's found some cases that solidly support our position. He feels like we've got some really good precedents. Just waiting to pull the trigger."

Otis looked over at Jake who hadn't said a word since he walked in. "How about you Jake? Had a productive day?"

"Pretty boring, actually," said Jake. Been reading all day and have discovered absolutely nothing."

"You might try reading something a little more interesting," laughed Michael. "What were you looking for?"

"It's probably nothing," said Jake. "But when we uncovered that first crate down there in the lake, I saw something that looked familiar and I wanted to check a few things out."

"Jake, you never cease to amaze me," said George. "Let's hear it, the whole story."

Jake began. "Way back when Admiral salvage was first thinking about returning to the marine recovery business, they approached me and asked if I'd be comfortable running that side of the business. I had been going to college and taking business management courses at the time so I jumped at the opportunity. There were still a lot of reference manuals in the store room from the old days when it was a big part of their business. They must have known that they would be searching for the Poverty Island treasure because a lot of the books dealt not only with the legend itself, but with shipping precious metals and how to prepare them for shipping. I didn't know why it was there at the time but there was a whole section bookmarked in one of the volumes on shipping containers. It dealt with the crates that were unique to France. And the gold we are looking for originated in France."

Jake cleared his throat. "When we first uncovered that crate out there and I saw the iron corner cap on the container, it rang a bell. I knew I'd seen it before. Luckily, I had scanned all of those reference books to a flash drive and so I had a quick look on my laptop when we got back on shore. Sure enough, it was typical of French built crates in the mid eighteen hundreds. But what really bothered me was that the cap looked like it had been disturbed, as if someone had removed and replaced it at one time."

"Wow," said George. "So what were you reading today that might help solve your mystery?"

"As far as I can tell," said Jake. "The gold was loaded on a ship in France for shipping to the confederacy. The only scheduled stop along the way was right here in Escanaba where the cargo was transferred to another ship to complete the voyage and it was that second ship that was sunk near Poverty Island."

So just what were you looking for?" asked Michael

"I have no idea," answered Jake. "That's why I visited the historical society and archives here in town. I found about three hundred years worth of uncatalogued documents in the archives that have never been reviewed. Some of the stuff is private diaries and I've already come across two ship's logs but they had nothing to do with the treasure ship. I'm not even a third of the way through everything so there's no telling what I might find."

"Found anything encouraging so far?" asked Michael.

"If it's true, I may have found something very significant," said Jake. "In one of the private diaries there's an entry about a lone survivor from a ship that was sunk off of Poverty Island about the time that our treasure ship went down. The story says that the unidentified man was so terrified, he wouldn't talk about what happened and didn't want anyone knowing who he was or where he came from. The owner of the diary said that the family that rescued him told him that he could stay on a relatives' remote farm and no one would ever find him. The guy made up a new name and that's where the account ended. But I've been able to identify the owner of the diary and hopefully can track down some of his descendants."

"I can help with that," said Michael.

"I have found absolutely no reports that talk about any survivors," said George. Here's hoping you can find more detail. How long do you think it will take to get through all of it?"

"It depends on how much time I have to work on it," answered Jake. "We'll probably be back out on the water starting tomorrow, so I'll just have evenings available for reading. You never know how lucky I'll get when I'm going through all that stuff. Hell, there's a good chance I won't find anything at all. It's a fishing expedition."

"Well don't give up," said George. "But, geeze, I hope you don't find anything saying that it was all a joke. I'd hate to think we're chasing ghosts."

"Oh, I still believe that there's gold in those crates," said Jake. "I'm just the curious type so I always check out everything I do."

"That could be a good thing or a bad thing," said Otis.

CHAPTER 41

"They're ready," said the blonde.

"How ready?" asked Vinny.

"You know about their friend called Gypsy, right?" asked the blonde.

Vinny nodded.

"They're meeting with him today," said the blonde, "and from what we've heard about this guy, he's too greedy to pass up the deal."

"Why would they want to include him?" asked Vinny. "It's just one more person to share with and besides, we've already got enough people to pull it off."

"I think they're a little scared of him," said the redhead. "They claim that he's an old friend but I think he may have something hanging over their heads that they don't want revealed. These guys aren't boy scouts."

"I'm just not crazy about adding people who I don't know. Hell, I don't even know Sam and Eddie except for a couple of bar room conversations," said Vinny. "Call me paranoid but I like being careful."

"The weather's supposed to be good tomorrow so I expect they'll all be back out on their search site," said the blonde. "I suggest that we let them get most of the digging done before we make our move."

"Oh, absolutely," said Vinny. "I can only have their boat impounded for a day or two, three at the most. We've got to be ready to move and move fast when the time is right."

"We'll be ready," said the redhead. She slipped the fifteen round magazine into her Glock model nineteen. "I'm ready now."

"I have the boat lined up and it's ours for at least the next forty-five days," said Vinny. "You girls and me are going have to learn all the ins and outs of running a commercial fishing boat. I've had some experience; worked at the family fishery when I was in high school but I'm going to need a little bit of brushing up. I'd say that we'll be doing some cruising just about every day. Maybe a couple of trips into Green Bay and possibly a trip out into Lake Michigan down towards Manitowoc or some place like that. We've got to be able to manage the boat with just the three of us. At one time I was able to run a boat like this all alone so I know we can handle it."

"We're supposed to meet the guys tomorrow night over at the Buck Inn," said the blonde. "Are you going to be there?"

"Yeah, probably," said Vinny. "But when I introduce myself as their partner, I suggest we pick a different bar. We're all becoming too well known in that place."

The blonde fixed herself another spiced rum and coke and then said. "The guy who owns that big cruiser over at Little Bay marina is kind of new at running a boat that size so they always return to port before dark. All of that might change if he starts feeling comfortable with his seamanship. According to Sam, he's some sort of private detective and his partner is a Detroit cop. Neither one of them seems to be a rookie sailor but they aren't pros either."

"In that case," said Vinny. "We'd better just assume they'll both be packing. Cops always carry their gun and so do private detectives. We'd be smart to keep that in mind"

"I'm sure that we'll have some kind of answer from them tomorrow," said the blonde. "But there's a chance they'll bring this Gypsy character with them. He's a really scary looking guy. Dresses like an outlaw biker with all the tattoos and muscles and always wears dark sunglasses, even in the restaurant. We've never met him but Sam says he's solid."

"Be careful around him," said Vinny. "Try to get a good read on him. I don't need any surprises."

When the girls arrived at the Buck Inn, they were relieved to see that it was just Sam and Eddie waiting to greet them. "Hey, how was your day?" asked the blonde.

"More of the same," said Eddie. "Chipping away at Zebra Mussels all day. My arms are ready to fall off and I've got blurred vision from all the vibration."

The girls laughed. "Have you talked to your friend yet?" asked the blonde.

"Yep," said Sam. "Had a nice conversation with him yesterday. It looks like he's all in with us. He wants to meet with your connection before he makes any commitments though."

"I don't blame him," said the blonde. We can set something up whenever you're ready."

"How about tomorrow?" asked Sam. "Gypsy wants to get all the details he can and he insists on meeting the main guy."

"We can do that, is eight o'clock okay?" she answered. "Our connection wants it to be at a different place though. He wants to meet at Ernie's Pub. It's an Irish place in the downtown area, right on Ludington Street."

"What's the matter with meeting right here?" asked Sam.

"We've been here too many times," said the blonde. "We're worried about the locals making too many connections. It's just a precaution. If the location bothers you, feel free to pick the place yourself."

"It'll be just fine at this Irish place that you picked out," said Sam. "Maybe they'll even have corned beef there."

"Something else that I have to tell you," said the blonde. "Our contact is going to look familiar to you because you've already met him. His name is Vinny."

Silence hung in the air for quite a long time before Sam finally spoke. "I don't like it. The whole thing smells like a set up to me. I hope you've got a good explanation to go along with your little surprise."

The blonde stretched her long suntanned legs and began. "Vinny grew up in this town and has lived here most of his life. His dad was a commercial fisherman up in Bessemer and moved his whole business down here around forty years ago with the specific goal of finding that treasure. Vinny began hunting for that gold when he was eight years old tagging along with his father. Eventually he made it his life's goal to find it and won't let anything stop him. He's not really the greedy type so he's more than willing to share the fruits of his research for just a reasonable share of the money. A lot of people have tried to take advantage of Vinny's researching efforts and generosity and over time, he's become suspicious of anyone claiming to want to help him find it."

Understandable," said Sam. "He's probably spent over forty years investigating every rumor and chasing millions of hot leads that have got him nowhere up to now. But if he's smart he probably understands that he might already have the answer in his hand but can't see it."

The blonde continued. "When you guys showed up and were searching in a completely different area, it made Vinny sit up and take notice. He actually followed that big Chris Craft Roamer one day until he saw you setting out your dive flags. That's when he really got interested and asked us to talk to you."

"Are you trying to tell us that all of our partying with you two wasn't just fun and games up to that point?" asked Eddie

"Not really," said the blonde. "Vinny was keeping an eye on you from the first time you walked in here. He makes sure that he checks out everybody who's looking for that treasure. But you two especially interested him because you were obviously not local and didn't know anything about the gold. That meant that you were hired divers and most likely professionals. He called us in to get close to you and see just how much you really knew. When you started talking about the other side of Lake Michigan, it really raised a flag in his mind. Nobody hunts for the treasure over there. Nobody. That's why he had to know more. And now he's pretty sure that you may be on to something and he's not about to be left out in the cold. That's the honest to goodness truth."

"I'm still not crazy about it," said Sam. "It's just too sneaky if you know what I'm saying."

"Hey, I didn't have to tell you any of this," said the blonde. "I'm trying to be up front so that you know you can trust me. When Vinny followed you out there, he noted down the coordinates. He knows exactly where you've been diving and could pull this whole thing off without you guys if he wanted to. I'm telling you all of these details so that you'll understand that we're all full partners in this deal.

Right now, with that other bunch, you're nothing more than employees."

Sam sat looking at his hands. "I suppose you could be right but what guarantees do we have?"

"I'm sure that Vinny will lay all of that out for you if you're still willing to bring your friend along and meet with him."

Sam responded. "I can't promise anything without talking to Gypsy first. The things that you just told me might just run him off."

The redhead spoke up. "Do the best you can and call us when you know something."

"Will do," said Sam.

CHAPTER 42

The water was still and the sun blazing over the dive site. The anchors were both in place although there was little chance of drifting in the calm air. Gypsy was the first man in the water followed by Jake. Sam an Eddie tagged along a few minutes later. The visibility was very good and almost no backfilling had occurred during their day off. Within an hour the crew was once again moving forward. They were getting close to halfway through the heavy crust of Zebra Mussels and were picking up the pace. Every one of them was looking forward to having this bone jarring phase of the operation behind them. They broke for lunch with all of them in a good mood.

"Four or five more days like this and we might be ready to start fitting floatation collars," said Jake. "My big concern is whether or not this boat has the power to tow that much weight."

"I think we can move it all right," said Michael. "My main worry is keeping it from ramming us when we stop."

"A long enough tow line will solve that problem, gives you room to get out of the way," said Gypsy. "We do it all the time in Florida."

The noon time conversation remained light and the divers went back to work with refreshed enthusiasm. Except for air tank changes, they remained on the bottom until almost four o'clock when it was time to call it a day. By then they had one crate close to a hundred percent exposed and it looked a lot like they could cut through the lashing and separate the containers if necessary. For now though, they thought it best to leave them bound together.

On the trip back to the marina Sam and Eddie busied themselves cleaning up the daily mess that a diving operation always left behind. The high pressure air compressor was thumping away, refilling the spent air tanks. Gypsy had agreed to talk to them after they were all ashore and could find a little privacy. Sam tried to prepare Gypsy saying that the deal still looked promising but a little more complicated than they had originally thought. Gypsy shut down the conversation saying that they'd talk later.

Jake took on the job of cleaning and organizing the salon area of the boat while George climbed up to the fly bridge to chat with Michael and McCoy.

"I think we're far enough along for my attorneys to file my claim with the State of Michigan," said George." The Coast Guard or Department of Natural Resources could become involved at any time and I'd like to be protected by a court order if they do. I'll call my lawyer as soon as we're within range of a cell tower." George glanced at his watch and then at his cell phone. "I'm hoping I'll have a signal soon. My attorney is prepared to move as soon as I give him the okay. The court is only open for about another forty-five minutes."

"Is your attorney still optimistic that you'll prevail?" asked McCoy.

"He claims that it's a lock," said George. "Based on our argument and the precedents that we'll be presenting, the ruling seemingly has to go in our favor. There will certainly be appeals but they take time and by then I hope to have the gold safely locked up."

"That's an interesting point," said Michael. "Just where can you find a place secure enough to store about a half billion dollars worth of gold?"

"I'm sure that the banks will be knocking at my door," said George. "The key is to get it stashed away before the government decides they want to confiscate it. The banks will all help you fight that kind of action but if it's simply sitting on your back porch, your yard will be full of military vehicles in a heartbeat."

Michael handed his phone to George. "Here, use this. It's a satellite phone and you can call from anywhere. I wouldn't want to see tanks and armored personnel carriers moving down your block."

George smiled and accepted the phone. He referred to the list on his own phone and hastily dialed the number. After a short conversation he handed the phone back to Michael and said. "It's as good as done. My lawyer is in the courthouse right now and has all the paperwork in his brief-case. He says he'll be able to catch the clerk before she heads home and get it logged in today. Thanks a lot."

Michael was getting more confident in his seamanship daily and this afternoon he guided the big cruiser into its slip without a single bump or a scrape. "Perfect landing," commented McCoy.

As soon as the boat was declared fit and secure, Gypsy, Sam, and Eddie all headed for Gypsy's room where Sam and Eddie filled him in on everything they knew up to this point, including the fact that Vinny had been watching them very closely from the first day he met them. Gypsy listened intently occasionally interrupting to ask for clarification of a point or situation. He allowed both men to finish before he spoke. "I'm not a hundred percent comfortable with everything you've told me but it doesn't sound too far fetched either. As a matter of fact it kind of makes me curious. I'd like to fill in a few holes and I can see a lot of them. When is this meeting supposed to be?"

"Today at eight o'clock," said Sam. "Supposed to be in an Irish Tavern down on the main drag. I understand that there are some quiet corners in the place where we can have some privacy."

"Call 'em," said Gypsy. "Tell 'em we'll be there."

Vinny and the girls were already seated at a table in a dimly lit corner away from the kitchen and the restrooms so that there would be minimal foot traffic past their table. Vinny was all smiles as Sam made all the introductions. Everybody seemed pleased at getting things started. It was only Gypsy who remained expressionless.

"Sensitive eyes?" asked Vinny pointing at Gypsy's ever present wrap around sunglasses.

Gypsy nodded and sat down. "So what have you got for us?" he asked.

"As I understand it, you guys are all working for a salary, correct?"

"That's right," answered Gypsy.

"What I'm offering is full and equal shares for everybody," said Vinny. "According to my calculations, that should come out somewhere near a hundred million dollars each."

Sam and Eddie both sighed in harmony while the blank look on Gypsy's face never changed. "I assume you've got a plan."

"Absolutely. I've been over it a thousand times," responded Vinny. "It's about as foolproof as it can get."

"Lay it on me," said Gypsy.

Vinny pulled his chair closer to the table and spoke very quietly. "First, I need you guys to tell me when the treasure looks like it's ready to be moved. I'll need at least a day or two notice. I've got a local political connection who owes me a couple of favors and I'll have her contact the Coast Guard with some trumped up emergency story about that Roamer cruiser that you guys have been using. That will get the boat red tagged and it will be restricted to the harbor until they can conduct an inspection. Following me so far?"

"How much time will that buy us?" asked Gypsy.

"At least two days, probably three," said Vinny.

That ain't much," said Gypsy.

"When you see the equipment I've got, you'll say it's plenty," said Vinny. My dad was a commercial fisherman and not long before he retired, he bought a big fishing boat. It's a forty-eight foot stern trawler with a big steel ramp and a really powerful winch. Familiar with those?"

Gypsy nodded and an almost imperceptible smile crossed his lips. "Can we have a look at this here trawler?" he asked.

"Too late today but we can run over there tomorrow," said Vinny. "It's about an hour and a half from here, tied up at dock in a ghost town called Fayette on Big Bay de Noc. Meet me in the parking lot of the Buck Inn and we can all ride out there together. What time can you be there?"

"If we keep the same schedule that we've been on up until now," said Gypsy, "figure on six o'clock."

"Done. That will give us plenty of daylight," said Vinny. "Now let's eat. I'm buying."

CHAPTER 43

As had recently become the custom, Michael and McCoy along with George met Otis and Marla on their balcony for dinner and cocktails. Marla had just tucked in the twins in their adjoining room and left the door open. Jake promised to join them later after he'd had a chance to go over more of the large pile of historical information. The twins had split their day between the beach and the carnival and had gorged themselves on corn dogs and elephant ears. Marla had balked at the deplorable menu choices at first but eventually caved in to the persistent pressure that only a pair of ten year olds can bring to bear. This evening the adults would dine equally unhealthy bratwurst and macaroni salad from the motel restaurant carry-out menu.

"So how's the treasure hunt going?" asked Marla.

"Actually, none of us has seen it, except on the computer screen" replied George. "Other than those cloudy images, all we know is what our divers tell us. It all seems encouraging though. I'm getting used to having four guys down there on the bottom and I'm sure that it's putting us way ahead of where we would have been. To answer your question, it's going great."

"Yeah," added Michael. "Me, McCoy, and Mister Snyder, we just sit up on the boat all day and spend our time gabbing or looking over the side. But today I was just glad that there's air conditioning in the salon and I actually took a short nap. We spend most of our time getting the exchange tanks ready for the divers. We go through sixteen to twenty tanks a day. Besides the one on the diver's back, we have twelve spares and have to keep them fully charged and ready to go."

George spoke up. "Frankly I'm tired of having every breath I take being consumed by the treasure hunt. Let's talk about something else. Otis, you've been a cop for a long time. How about a few detective stories? Are you involved in crime prevention?"

Otis smiled. "The term crime prevention is pretty much a joke. Oh, maybe better quality locks, state of the art alarm systems and the presence of endless surveillance cameras may have cut down on a few burglaries but the criminals just find other ways to steal your money. Crime prevention programs don't prevent crime they only change the method. Laws don't prevent crime either. Laws simply define the crime so that the cops have some sort of guidelines for arresting the crooks. You keep hearing about how violent crime is on the downswing. That's because technology has allowed the criminal to steal your identity, suck your bank account dry and never have a clue as to what you even look like. Then they disappear into cyberspace and we haven't learned how to catch them yet, at least not all of them. It's a different world these days. Back when I started, we had beat cops and we walked the streets. We knew just about everybody on our beat and knew who we needed to check in on from time to time and we knew who needed a close eye. When a crime was committed on our beat, we generally could narrow the search down to a handful of guys, even in the rough neighborhoods. We recognized tendencies and we knew habits. And we were aware of which guys hung out together and who their friends were as well as who they considered their enemies. We were also pretty good judges of just how far any of our special interest guys might go. It's all different now. There are still the physical social circles in any given neighborhood but technology has allowed them to hunt down new victims throughout the entire nation and beyond."

"So I suppose you consider the old beat system a superior process," said George.

"Let me put it this way," said Otis. "It had a whole lot less unknowns. It was dangerous. Dangerous every single day, but you knew it and you walked your beat on high alert the whole time. Every day was an eight hour adrenaline rush. But, back then the beat cops solved more crimes than detectives do today."

"How long were you a beat cop?" asked Michael.

Otis paused. "I think it must have been about four years and then I transferred into the motor division, you know, motorcycles."

"Sounds like a summertime job," said Michael.

"Not at all," answered Otis. Any time the temperature was twenty degrees or higher and roads were mostly snow and ice free, we were required to ride. We did mostly traffic and escort duty. They wouldn't let us get into pursuits unless there were more than three of our cars involved in the chase."

"But you're a homicide detective now," said George. "How did you transition into that?"

"I had applied for detective early on," said Otis. But like all low seniority cops, I had to earn my stripes. I worked in a lot of different divisions, some on the street and others in administration. I didn't find any of them dull and I learned new things everywhere I served. I even worked in…" his voice went silent.

"You okay?" asked George.

"Yeah, sure," replied Otis. "I just had one of those lightning bolt moments where a bad memory flashed across my consciousness and then it was gone as quickly as it came."

"Can't remember what it was?" asked George.

"It wasn't in my brain long enough," replied Otis. "I was talking about the different divisions I worked in and I don't even remember where I left off."

"Maybe it will come to you," said George.

"Maybe, but I doubt it," answered Otis.

A soft knock on Michael's door announced the arrival of Jake.

"C'mon in," welcomed Michael. "The Bratwurst is still warm and there's sautéed green pepper and onions to pile on them. Dig in."

"Find anything new today," asked Michael.

"Well, sort of," answered Jake. I was able to track down the family of that shipwreck survivor. At least I know who he was and I know that he eventually married the farmer's daughter and that they had kids. Their grandchildren still live in the area but I wasn't able to find any contact information. Anyway, I got hold of the county archivist and she knows the family. She said she'd forward my email address to the grandson and he could contact me if he wants. Kind of iffy but it's all I've got at the moment."

"At least you've got the archivist on your side," commented McCoy.

"Actually, I think she kinda likes me," said Jake. At least that's how her body language reads."

Michael shot him a puzzled look.

"Something we studied in business school," said Jake.

Marla laughed heartily at the exchange. "I can see that you guys have a lot to learn about women."

"Seems like some of us are mind reading today," said McCoy.

"I'd be satisfied if I could just read my own, sure wish I could get my mind around whatever that fleeting thought was," said Otis.

"Did I miss something?" asked Jake.

"We all did," answered Otis.

CHAPTER 44

Sam and Eddie had an early breakfast with Gypsy. The two of them bombarded Gypsy with questions about his take on Vinny's offer.

"There's still more to see," said Gypsy. "I want to be sure that the boat he described is exactly what he says it is. If it's a true stern trawler, it might be perfect for what we need to do. But if it's one of those lightweight outrigger trawlers, it won't work. You guys know what I'm talking about, we've all worked off of stern trawlers when we were on big jobs down in the Keys."

"Sure," said Eddie. "I guess we'll know tonight."

Sam finished off his orange juice. "But today all I can think about is six solid hours shaking my brains out on the end of that air chisel. Anybody besides me having blurred vision from all that vibration?"

"I think we all are to some degree," answered Gypsy. "But if I were you, I wouldn't mention headaches or anything like that in front of Snyder. He's liable to insist that you go back to see the doctor."

As if on cue, George Snyder and Jake walked into the restaurant. They waved, walked over and sat at the table next to the three divers.

"Ready to have at it for another day?" asked George.

Gypsy didn't look up from his plate but Sam answered. "I suppose so. I'll sure be glad when we have all those mussel shells chipped away. I didn't expect anything like that when we first got here. That's what's taking all the time."

"How much more?" asked George. "About four or five more days?"

"Three at the most," said Gypsy. "Now that we've broken through the outer crust, they're starting to come off a lot faster."

Michael and McCoy came through the door and went directly to the counter where the cash register sat. A waitress appeared from the kitchen carrying two plastic bags that smelled suspiciously like fried bacon. Michael paid the bill, looked over at his partners and hollered, "We'll see you on board." They hustled out of the restaurant and headed toward the pier.

It was another productive day and, in spite of the close proximity there were no disagreements or arguments among the group. A large part of that might be attributed to the upbeat encouragement of Michael and Jake and the fatherly manner of George Snyder. The harmony led to steady progress on the task at hand. By the end of the day they had uncovered the remnants of the floatation collars that had been installed by the crew of the Maumee Princess. Jake brought a few shreds of the old canvas covered rubber to the surface so that he could study them.

"This is style kind of float collar Admiral Salvage used. There were still a few of them in the warehouse up until the auction sale that they had when they were liquidating. We'll have to clean all of this garbage off of those crates if we want to be able to attach some new ones."

Gypsy nodded in agreement while George turned the tattered old fabric over and over in his gnarled hands. "Good work," commented George.

McCoy had both anchors on board within minutes, the stern anchor first. He was still rinsing them under the hose when he heard the engines start up. In almost no time, Michael had the vessel on course back to Little Bay de Noc and they were underway.

It was a pleasant trip across the calm lake and Michael picked up his cruising speed slightly and shaved a full ten minutes off of the trip home. The boat was put to sleep for the night under its protective canvas by five thirty and everybody went their separate ways.

As soon as Gypsy got to his room, he took a quick shower, put on fresh jeans and called the number that Vinny had given him last night.

"Looks like we'll be a little bit early," he told Vinny. We're headed out the door right now."

Vinny drove a big GMC Denali with three rows of seats. He and Gypsy rode up front with Sam and the blonde behind them and Eddie and the redhead in the back seat. "Me and the girls have had the boat out on the lake the last couple of mornings," said Vinny. "They're getting the hang of managing the boat just fine. They're already like a couple of old sailors. We're at the point where they run everything and I just sit back and keep an eye on things. This morning I didn't have to open my mouth, even when they docked it."

Gypsy grunted his approval. "You a diver?" he asked.

"Since I was twelve," answered Vinny. "I've made dives all around Poverty Island and have done quite a number of deep water dives. I've logged thousands of hours of bottom time."

They pulled into the historic village of Fayette, Michigan. Vinny explained that it was mostly State Park property with just a few privately owned parcels.

Snail Shell Harbor, with its limestone cliffs is nothing short of breathtaking. Even Gypsy seemed impressed with its beauty. "Nice," he said.

The town of Fayette was originally a quiet little fishing village that later became an iron smelting center servicing nearby iron ore mines. Eventually the hardwoods of the Garden Peninsula, needed for the production of charcoal were depleted. And then a couple of major fires hampered efforts to keep the smelting plant in continuous operation As technology moved along, Fayette and their traditional ways were quickly left behind. When the iron business left, so did the economy. Residents bailed out leaving behind their homes and their history. Fayette officially became a ghost town.

Today, Fayette is mostly a tourist destination featuring its historic limestone buildings and its picturesque harbor. It doesn't attract a lot of attention because it doesn't have a glamorous history or benefit from vigorous promotion. It's known as a pleasant and quiet place to visit, picnic, and take photographs.

The big trawler was all but hidden from view tucked into a small inlet on the east side of the harbor. "This is still family owned property back here," Vinny explained. "Me and my sisters share the deed. The boat is usually leased out to a commercial fishing outfit but they ended their season early due to illness and the lessee for the fall campaign doesn't take over for a month and a half. Until then, it's all mine. I haul it out for the winter and that's when I do all the maintenance."

"Let's have a closer look," said Gypsy as he opened the door of Vinny's SUV.

The six of them headed for the dock as Vinny fished a heavy ring of keys from his pocket.

Vinny opened the hatches to expose two large Detroit Diesel engines. "All the horsepower you'll ever need and low hours on those motors too. The fuel tanks have been topped off so we have a fifteen hundred mile range. The tour took them to the back of the boat and the heavy steel ramp that angled down toward the water where it met industrial size rollers to assist dragging a heavy load aboard. Off to one side, a gantry crane stood at the ready, capable of lifting twelve tons on demand.

Sam whistled when he saw the massive capacity of the vessel. The large afterdeck work area looked as big as a basketball court.

"No frills," said Vinny. "It's strictly a work boat and a very capable one."

Gypsy maneuvered Vinny away from the rest of the group where he could talk privately. "What's with the girls?" he asked. "This doesn't look like your standard salvage crew."

"I'm not into salvage," said Vinny. "I'm into opportunity and having these girls along sure broadens my range of my opportunities."

"I'm assuming that you make a lot of your own opportunities," said Gypsy.

"You catch on fast," said Vinny. "There's a lot of money out there and an obscene amount of it is in the hands of foolish men. And men like that are very fond of women like these two." He pointed at the two women standing with Sam and Eddie.

So you're a hustler and these are your assistants," said Gypsy.

"I guess that pretty well describes it," said Vinny.

"I think we'll be ready for you in about three days," said Gypsy.

"So it's a done deal?" asked Vinny.

"Let's move it forward," said Gypsy.

CHAPTER 45

After doing extensive research, Marla decided to take advantage of the babysitting service that the motel provided to free her up to go out dancing with her dashing husband tonight. Otis welcomed the thought of a romantic evening with his beautiful wife. They have been married for over twenty years, some better than others and they grew as a family. Their bond had become strong enough to overcome the unbelievable stress that being a cop brings to a marriage. But tonight they'd be celebrating just being together with close friends, both old and new. They had a reservation for a table for six at the Ship's Anchor. The weather was gorgeous tonight, in the upper seventies so the glass doors would be raised and they'd be dancing beside the sparkling blue waters of historic Little Bay de Noc.

Five people showed up at seven thirty, George explaining that Jake had made an important connection with some local people and would be along as soon as he could comfortably break away.

George started the conversation. "So Otis, did you ever catch that thought that blew through your mind last night? The alarmed look on your face when it happened has made me very curious."

"You know," responded Otis. "I actually dreamed about that last night. I still can't remember what it was or any details at all. But I remember that it scared me."

"I think there's a name for that," said McCoy. "Shrinks like to label everything. They've done studies on that sort of thing and it seems to me that I read somewhere that it's something that you'd really rather not remember."

"That's part of the problem," said Otis. "I've got this weird feeling that it's something important and important right now; today. Why can't I bring it into focus?"

"Maybe you're trying too hard," suggested Michael.

"Well, I hope you try even harder to put it out of your mind, at least for tonight," said Marla.

Otis laughed and they all ordered cocktails. "The bartender is not nearly as pretty as the one we've become accustomed to," said George. He raised his glass in a toast to Marla.

Jake joined the table at about eight o'clock, panting with enthusiasm. "I just left the grandson of the only survivor of the Poverty Island wreck. He's resurrected the original family name of Lemieux and asked me to try to reconstruct his grandfather's adventures.

"Cool," said Michael. "I wonder if there's anything interesting that he might be able to contribute to the legend we're uncovering."

"I didn't tell him about everything we're doing," said Jake. "I only told him we were researching the shipwreck and surrounding circumstances. But he offered me some stuff that might really prove to be helpful."

"Like what?" asked George.

"Seems that his grandfather kept journals on every part of his life, something he learned as a child. The grandson let me borrow them" said Jake. "We got into the one about the pirate raid on that sixty foot schooner. Seems that one of the pirates took a shot at him and when the musket ball whizzed past his head, he pretended to be hit and fell over the side. He swam around the stern of the ship and when he was satisfied that nobody noticed him, he set out swimming for the island. He didn't quite make it but one of the island residents had been watching through a telescope and rowed out to grab him. He was totally exhausted when the guy pulled him into the boat."

"Did he mention the gold?" asked George.

"There's no reference to any kind of treasure or what the cargo was in what I've read so far but I've barely scratched the surface."

"As if you don't already have enough old paperwork to sift through," said Michael. "Did you used to look forward to doing homework when you were a kid in school?"

Jake laughed. "I actually think that the old sailor purposely avoided mentioning anything to do with that ship other than to explain how he survived the massacre. He doesn't even give the name of the ship he was on or what the attack was all about. According to his grandson, he lived up until nineteen twenty-one and kept a diary right up until the day he died. The grandson says he opened up a little when he got older. That's when Marc Lemieux, his real name came out. Before that, he lived under the name of Jean Blanchet, something he just made up. He must have had a powerful reason for hiding his real identity for almost sixty years though. I'm hoping to find some clues in his journals."

"You sure have a strange taste in entertainment," commented McCoy. "We really don't need to know all that stuff. We know where the treasure is."

"You never know," said Jake. "I'm liable to find anything in there."

"How close are you to getting it off the bottom?" asked Otis.

"Fortunately, the bottom twenty percent or so of the crates were buried in the sand before the Zebra Mussels invaded the Great Lakes," said Jake. Once we get all the shells cleaned off, we'll be able to blow away the rest of the sand using the water jet and then start fitting the floatation collars. I figure that we'll be ready for that in probably three days. And then it should take the better part of another day to inflate them. We'll most likely be underway most of that night and reach our destination about dawn the following day."

"So you're saying that you think you'll be swimming in gold by the end of the week," said Otis.

"I'll save you a nugget," said McCoy.

"Have it made into a nice ring and put a couple of rubies in it," teased Marla.

Otis turned to George and asked, "Where do your divers hang out when they're not working? They never seem to come near the rest of us. Are they just anti-social or do they not like us?"

"Near as I can figure, they feel like outsiders because they're Florida guys," said George. "Heaven knows I've invited them to just about everything. They don't even always go to breakfast with us. They all seem cordial enough when we're out on the boat. Never any arguing or anything like that. I guess you'd have to say that they're just... different."

"Any idea where they are tonight?" asked Michael. "I think I saw all three of them pulling out of the parking lot not long after we got back in to port. They seemed to be in a hurry to get somewhere but none of them said anything when we were working today. It's almost like they were on a mission and running late. I suppose they could have been going to a restaurant somewhere, Heaven knows you can get awful hungry after working on the bottom of a lake all day. But then maybe they just wanted to get somewhere while there was still some daylight."

"Call me a conspiracy theorist," said McCoy. "But I don't trust them. It's obvious that Gypsy is their leader. Neither one of the other guys hardly utters a peep when Gypsy's around. He does all the thinking and they follow orders. That's the way mobs work and it worries me. The fact that they always wander off to parts unknown as soon as we're ashore is a bit bothersome too. I've spent a lot of years studying criminal behavior and these guys fit the mold. I'll be keeping a close eye on them."

"Not exactly my field," said George. "I'll leave that stuff up to you. I'd like to think that everything will continue going along like clockwork."

"Speaking of a graceful operation, how are you planning to lift the crates out of the water?" asked Otis.

"That's been handled," said George. I have a twenty five ton crane waiting for us. It's already in place just behind the seawall over at that place I'm buying in Charlevoix. Way back when I worked for the trucking company I went to school to become a crane operator. Like most trucking companies they were pretty diverse and were closely linked to the construction industry. They had all sorts of equipment in their yard. I ran their various cranes all one summer while their regular operators were on vacation. They said I was a natural, could dip a teabag with a sixty five ton lattice boom rig. I still belong to the operators union and so I had no problem renting a unit."

"Sounds like you're not leaving any loose ends out there," said Otis.

"Nope and my lawyers are on the docket to present our case just about the time we'll be raising the treasure out of the water. My guy is ecstatic about the judge that we drew. He says that this judge is a guy who's known for bucking the political machine. He seems to get a kick out of putting the government in its place, a real crusader. We're really optimistic, on a roll, so to speak"

"Kinda hard to believe that everything is going so smoothly," said Michael. "I'm waiting for it to all blow up in our faces. You know, the Murphy's Law thing."

"Inevitable," said Otis. "Nothing ever goes off without a hitch. Destiny doesn't allow those things."

"I'm keeping my fingers crossed just the same," said George. "This whole project started out pretty rocky, especially when my diver got murdered. But things are clicking now and I want it to stay that way."

CHAPTER 46

It was shortly after eight o'clock when Vinny pulled back into the parking lot of the Buck Inn. Gypsy, Sam, and Eddie got out of the Denali and headed in to the bar for a quick bite to eat and a beer before making their way back to the motel. Hungry after a full day's work, they all ordered from the dinner menu and waited quietly, looking around the room to make sure that no one was paying any attention to them while the waitress delivered their drinks Gypsy insisted that they keep still until after their meals were served and the waitress had moved on to other customers.

"Well, what did you think?" asked Sam.

Gypsy looked around to be sure that no one in the bar could hear their conversation. "I'll tell you right now that I don't trust your friend Vinny. I know his type and he's in this strictly for himself. The girls are nothing but pawns. He's using them just like he plans on using us."

"So how are we going to shut him out?" said Sam.

"We won't, not right away," said Gypsy. "He'll come in handy for a while but then he'll need to be removed because he'll be coming after us."

"What do you mean by that?" asked Sam.

"Think about it," said Gypsy. "The only thing he really needs us for is to keep him up to date on what we've been doing so that he can make arrangements to get our crew out of his way when the time is right. Then he'll need help with the diving and recovery. We're salvage divers, tailor made for the job. Once the gold is safely aboard the trawler, we become excess baggage."

"I see what you mean," said Sam. "But we'll need him for a little while because he has to handle the trawler."

"That boat of his is made for fishing but it's almost an identical twin to a salvage boat that I worked on when I first got in the business down in Key Largo same engines, same winch, same everything. It looks big and scary but the pilot house sits up nice and high with a panoramic view. The controls are easy to use and the boat itself is quite responsive. I don't expect any trouble at all. I used to run that boat all by myself back then. I'll handle that end of the deal as soon as Vinny's out of the way."

"Are you saying that we're going to have to kill them?" whispered Eddie.

Gypsy took a long swallow of beer. "How bad do you want the Gold?"

When they got back to the girl's room, Vinny opened the conversation "I need to know just how deep you girls are willing to go with this project,"

"As far as I'm concerned I'm in it all the way, no matter what it takes," replied the blonde.

"What if it comes down to killing someone?" asked Vinny.

The redhead spoke up. "It wouldn't be the first time."

Vinny stared straight ahead, not sure how to react.

"You don't know us as well as you thought you did," added the blonde. "Just what have you got in mind?"

It took Vinny a few seconds to compose himself. "This is a treasure that I've invested a lifetime in. It's something I've been obsessed with as long as I can remember. I always knew that I couldn't salvage it all by myself but I'm not willing to hand over half of it just because these guys are helping out. After all, they're only hired hands for somebody else. They don't have a dime tied up in this project between them and they had absolutely nothing to do with locating it."

"What about us?" asked the blonde. "Are we just worker bees to be sacrificed once the honey is in the hive?"

"Of course not," barked Vinny. "We've been partners for a long time and have been through a lot together. I'll never cross you guys. I hope you feel the same. You've done way too much for me. We're family."

"Let's hear your plan," said the redhead.

"It's going to take all three of them plus myself to get the crates loaded onto our vessel. Probably going to take at least half a day just getting everything rigged and floated to the surface. From there all we have to do is winch it up the ramp and get it tied down on the rear deck. We'll get underway as soon as we have everything on board. I had thought about heading to a remote harbor up on Georgian Bay in Ontario but now I'm thinking that crossing an international border might be too risky. Right now I'm leaning toward taking everything down to Detroit. There are some abandoned warehouses and docks down there and I think I know a guy who can arrange a discreet location for us. He doesn't need to know what we're up to. He's used to dealing with smugglers coming across from Canada and he knows better than to ask any questions. I'll contact him tonight.

"Where does the murder part come in?" asked the blonde.

"That's the touchy part," said Vinny. I figure that it will be right after we get everything on the deck and as soon as we're out of sight of land," said Vinny. "I don't want any eye witnesses and I don't want to wait for them to decide that they can have everything to themselves. If I've got them pegged right, they have something up their sleeve. Gypsy is the most dangerous one so I'll take care of him. Do you girls think you can handle your boyfriends?"

The redhead smiled. "Mine's gonna be easy."

CHAPTER 47

Michael, McCoy, and Jake were struggling to get the bulky float collars loaded into the back of the cruiser.

"I'm sure glad that this boat isn't six feet shorter," said McCoy.

"I figure that each one of those crates is going to weigh in the neighborhood of three to five tons," said Jake. "It's gonna take a lot to lift them off the bottom and we'll have to be helping by trying to rock them back and forth with pry bars. If we can get at least three lift collars around each crate, it will make it a little easier."

"Planning to float them one at a time?" asked Michael.

"Definitely," said Jake. "We'll keep them loosely tethered to one another so that we can tow them but there's just no practical way we'd be able to get them all to the surface in one piece."

When do you expect to install these things?" McCoy pointed at the floatation collars.

Jake stroked his chin. "With any luck, we'll have enough of the Zebra Mussels chipped away by the end of the day to begin separating the chests. We might even be able to get the cables cut today. There's enough of a gap between them to squeeze the float collars through and then we can start inflating them one at a time. I'm guessing we can be that far in about two or three more days."

George appeared on the dock and said that he had just run into the other three divers at the restaurant and that they would be along any minute. "Looks like we're going to get an early start this morning," he said.

"We sure have been blessed with some calm weather," said Michael. "It's given me a chance to get used to handling this boat. I'm pretty comfortable with it right now."

The voices of Sam and Eddie interrupted the quiet morning as they made their way toward the boat. With all hands aboard, the lines were cast off and the big Roamer headed toward the rising sun.

Today's efforts were extremely productive. The crew finally chipped away the last of the Zebra Mussels and were able to cut through the rusty cable that had held the crates together for almost ninety years. Jake finished off his day by grabbing the waterjet and blowing away the sand at the base of the first crate, exposing the bottom edges for the first time, while the other three divers brought all of the floatation collars down and tied them off to old cable which was still mostly buried in the sand. When they got back aboard the Roamer they held a short meeting with George to bring him up to date.

There was just a hint of excitement in Gypsy's voice as he offered the first assessment. "The first crate is ready to break away from the others. I suggest we get a couple of float collars around it and inflate them to see what effect they have. It's my guess that it will take at least three of them to lift it. We can tether it to the others to keep them all together."

"How much time will that take?" asked George.

"It depends," said Gypsy. "If we have the same kind of day we had today, I'd estimate that we could have the first crate isolated and floating free by lunch break. With any luck, we might have another one all rigged and ready to start inflation by the end of the day. The next day we could possibly have all five separated and off of the bottom. They'll have to be all tied in a series and anchored so that they don't move overnight. And hopefully by the day after tomorrow we can complete the inflation and put them under tow. It's a lot of weight. I sure hope that this boat can handle it."

Michael responded. "According to the people I've talked to, she should be able to handle it. We're not going to be able to travel fast though and I'll need a lot of helm response time. Turns are going to be tricky. It looks like it will be mostly a straight line to Charlevoix. I'm just worried about getting into the harbor." "It might be easier than you think," said George. "It's actually just a little bit south of Charlevoix and the entrance looks like you're going into a river mouth. There's a sign at the entrance that says, 'Private harbor. No trespassing.' You enter directly due east and it widens out within a quarter mile with a thirteen hundred foot straight dock on the south shore. You'll see the crane sitting there. I'm sure you can handle it."

Michael had the boat back in its slip by just after five thirty. By six o'clock the cleanup was finished and the overnight canvas was all in place and zipped. It had been a good ten hour work day.

The gang went their separate ways to take warm showers and get ready for their evening meal. As had become almost standard as of late, Gypsy, Sam and Eddie jumped in the rental car and headed out of the parking lot. McCoy and Michael stood on their balcony and watched them head in the direction of downtown. "Maybe they just wanted to get away from the crowd," said Michael. He pointed at the ferris wheel and other attractions that sat at one end of the parking lot. "Lots of people and lots of noise."

"Yeah, right," said McCoy. "I might just follow them if they take off like this again tomorrow night. I'd sure like to know where they're going and, even more than that, I'd like to know what they're up to."

CHAPTER 48

Everybody was anxious to get underway this morning and they actually cleared the harbor and were headed out to Lake Michigan before dawn. The cloudless sky presented a fiercely bright sunrise making it difficult to see what lay ahead.

Cruising on full plane, they arrived on site in slightly under three hours. The divers were over the side as soon as the anchors were set. The calm seas of the past week had made visibility better than usual this morning. Gypsy and Sam had a floatation collar fitted to crate number one within the first half hour while Jake and Eddie concentrated on getting the second crate fully exposed. By the time their lunch break rolled around, the first crate had two floatation collars firmly in place and they were ready to start installation on the second one as soon as number one was out of the way.

They planned their afternoon strategy over ham sandwiches and iced tea on the afterdeck of the cruiser. "We'll take the air lines down with us," said Gypsy. "Let's start with the high volume compressor and see how long it takes to get the first one moving."

Jake already had four pry bars lashed together and was lowering them over the side on the end of a long rope. "There are plenty of good size rocks laying around down there to use as fulcrums. With all of us working on it, we should be able to rock it back and forth."

When the crew returned to the submerged crates Gypsy immediately attached the air hose to the upper floatation collar and began inflating it. When it reached a point where it was firmly constricted around the crate, Gypsy disconnected the hose and plugged it into the lower collar. Then all four of the divers picked up their pinch bars and wedged one end under the crate and pulled down on the other end like a lever. They had to deflate their buoyancy compensators in order to have any effect. They struggled for over fifteen minutes before there was any movement at all but then the crate began rocking back and forth. Eventually it moved about a foot away from the other crates.

With Sam's help, Gypsy installed a third floatation collar and began inflating it. It was just enough to raise the crate a foot off of the bottom. Gypsy, obviously pleased had the crew build a pile of rocks underneath the crate and then deflated the collar enough to allow the crate to settle onto its new base without sinking into the sand.

By the end of the day, the second crate had been worked loose from the sand, moved a short distance and was ready to float. The remaining three crates had been cleared of sand and debris and awaited further action.

The divers were exhausted when they returned to the boat but every one of them was smiling. "Looking real good," commented Jake. "We might be able to start moving things by the day after tomorrow."

George broke out a twelve pack of Budweiser for the long trip home and the crew happily toasted the day's success.

Instead of heading back to his room after securing the Roamer in its slip, McCoy went straight to his car where he waited for Gypsy, Eddie, and Sam to embark on their daily journey away from the motel. He followed at a discreet distance and watched as the car carrying the three men pulled into the parking lot of a large rustic looking log building that bore a sign saying "The Buck Inn."

"Hmmm," muttered McCoy. "Maybe just getting away from the motel food."

A man stood waiting at the door as Gypsy approached the bar. He stopped to talk to the stranger and they chatted for several minutes. After talking for a short time, the conversation became much more animated and took on the appearance of an argument. It quieted down as quickly as it had erupted and all four men entered the bar, Gypsy holding the door for them.

McCoy sat outside for about another ten minutes and then decided to break off his surveillance. If Gypsy spotted him it would set off too many alarm bells. He headed back to the motel.

Once inside the Buck Inn, the quartet chose a table in a corner with both Gypsy and Vinny sitting with their backs to the wall. There were no protests from the other two men.

"Where's the girls?" asked Eddie.

Vinny shot him an icy stare. "This is a business meeting and they weren't necessary."

"We need your guy to act tomorrow," said Gypsy. "In two days we'll be ready to start moving things and then it will be too late."

"Like I told you outside," said Vinny. "The boat won't be allowed to leave the dock after tomorrow. You've got to trust me."

"I just need you to understand that we can't afford any slip ups."

Vinny sighed. "It's all arranged. The Coast Guard Commander will get his orders right after you sail tomorrow morning and should have a man waiting when the boat returns tomorrow night. The coast Guard has no idea about what's really going on, they'll simply be following orders."

"You'd better be right," said Gypsy.

"What will they be holding the boat for?" asked Sam.

"All vessels that carry passengers for hire, must be inspected and certified seaworthy by the Coast Guard and they take it very seriously, said Vinny. "You guys have got four air compressors strapped down to the deck and each one of them needs to be certified as well. You're also filling scuba tanks and they all need to be hydro-tested and approved. There's a lot of stuff to check out and it might take three or four days to get it all blessed, even longer if they find any discrepancies."

"Figure on everything sailing right through," said Gypsy. "This Michael O'Conner, he's right on top of everything."

"Okay," said Vinny. But I'm still betting it will be at least three days."

"With any luck, we'll only need one," said Gypsy.

CHAPTER 49

The trip back to the motel was full of lively conversation. "He's going to turn on us," said Gypsy. "I can see it pretty clearly now."

"How can you be so sure?" asked Eddie. "I didn't notice anything that would suggest that."

"You'd better open your eyes," said Gypsy. "He told us that the Coast Guard had no idea that this was a set-up. The Coast Guard isn't that stupid. He's not telling us everything."

"So what do we do? Call it quits?" asked Eddie.

"Of course not," said Gypsy. "Let's see what happens tomorrow, Do you guys both have guns?"

"Naturally," replied Sam. "Should we be packing?"

"Not while we're on the boat with Snyder, Jake and that cop," said Gypsy. "We need to keep our noses clean when they're around. But when we hook up with Vinny and his girlfriends, we'd better be ready for anything at any time."

"I can't see myself shooting the girls," said Eddie. "They've been so friendly and so full of fun up to this point."

"It might not come to that," said Gypsy. "But the smart money says to be prepared. And if you need to shoot, don't hesitate"

Back at the motel Vinny and the girls sat scattered around the room each with a cocktail in their hand, rum and coke for the girls and bourbon and water for Vinny.

"So, how did it go?" asked the blonde.

"Seems, like it's following the script," said Vinny. "I've got our guy lined up to meet the boat when they return to port tomorrow. He's got the official Warrant Officer uniform and everything. It should go off without a hitch. The ticket is pretty official looking too. It should be. It's a real citation that a buddy of mine boosted when he was at the Coast Guard station up in Grand Marais. We're good to go."

"What will become of our friend after he serves the summons?" asked the Redhead.

"Just leave that to me and don't ask questions," replied Vinny.

The redhead smiled. "I suppose this means that we go into action the day after tomorrow then. I'm ready and I can't wait for the turmoil to begin. My juices really get flowing when I can spill some blood."

"Sounds like you'd enjoy doing all the killing," said Vinny.

"I can if you want," said the redhead. "I'm more than willing."

Vinny shivered for a few seconds and then continued. "Here's how it has to work. I figure it will take a little over half of a day to haul all the crates up over the ramp. As soon as we get them aboard, I plan to start moving. We'll sneak northward between High Island and Whiskey Island and then head east through the Straits of Mackinac and then follow the coastline down to Detroit."

"When do we get rid of our extra passengers?" asked the blonde.

"I'm not sure yet," said Vinny. "We certainly can't wait for them to make the first move but we have to be aware of our surroundings. We have to be careful because I don't want to attract any attention with the sound of gunfire."

"Are you sure that anyone would even take notice?" asked the redhead. "I mean people shoot off of boats all the time. A lot of skeet shooters practice over the water. Besides we might be just far enough offshore that nobody would hear us anyway."

"I agree that the sooner, the better," said Vinny. "We'll just have to play it by ear."

"Why don't you just let us make the call?" asked the blonde. "We should be able to get a pretty good feel as to how jumpy they are."

"I don't need any surprises," answered Vinny. "Remember I'm the one who has to handle Gypsy and I've got the feeling that this isn't his first go around."

"How about if I just yell, 'Hey Vinny' before we start shooting?" asked the blonde. "Not very original bit it's about the only thing I can yell without arousing suspicion."

"I like it," said the redhead. "Hey Vinny, boom, boom, boom. Three dead ex partners and we're on our way."

"You girls scare the daylights out of me," said Vinny.

After a quick shower McCoy joined the rest of the group on the balcony where Marla was experimenting with new cocktails. Bartenders guide in her hand and a determined expression on her pretty face she asked, "You guys ever tried a 'Yellow Bird'?"

"I have the feeling that we will before the night is over," commented Michael.

The laughter was led by George Snyder who was in top spirits tonight. He insisted on Caribbean music and tropical drinks tonight, perhaps in anticipation of retiring to Trinidad. "Tomorrow could very well be our last full day on the current dive site. We were so fortunate to find everything so easily. Let's drink a toast to Harry Marley whose expertise in celestial navigation made all of this possible."

"Here, here," said Michael. "And to his great grandson, Jacob Marley who used all of his dark and cryptic talents to decipher the code that led us to the exact location."

By the way," said McCoy, "Where is our resident boy genius?"

"He'll be along shortly," said George. "He's in his room reading the diaries of an old man who survived a pirate attack. As soon as his head starts swimming from that crazy Frenchman's ramblings, I'm sure he'll want to join us for a couple of drinks."

Since the twins were still awake and full of energy, Otis decided to order from the Rice Bowl Inn, the restaurant that provided the most entertaining fortune cookies. He ordered shrimp Chop Suey for Jake.

At about eight o'clock, Jake joined the party and observing all the laughter, he remarked. "You guys certainly know how to enjoy life,"

"Don't be fooled," said Otis. "Me and McCoy, we're on vacation and you're supposed to let yourself go when you're enjoying a holiday. When we return to the reality of a cop's world, all the smiles disappear."

"Anything new show up in your research today?" asked Michael.

"Nothing helpful, at least not so far" answered Jake. "The guys English wasn't too good but he was determined to become as American as he could so he even kept his journals in English. Mostly he just raves about what a wonderful place America is. But somehow I get the feeling that he wants to say something important so I guess I'll keep on reading."

"Is it a pretty thick book?" asked McCoy

"Actually it's three pretty thick books," said Jake. "If there's anything important in there, I just hope that it's not on the last page."

CHAPTER 50

George and Jake were the first ones out on the dock this morning. They had wiped the overnight dew from the canvas, removed it and had it stowed before Michael and McCoy arrived.

"You guys in a hurry this morning?" asked Michael

"Just trying to share the load," said George. "You guys don't have to do all the work."

The other three divers showed up with matching enthusiasm. It seemed obvious that everyone wanted another early start. The big Roamer with its passengers was soon gliding across the calm waters of Lake Michigan.

Everybody worked just a little harder today and by the time lunch break rolled around they had two crates floating off of the bottom, the third was freed from the sand around its base and was ready to float, and Sam and Eddie had installed the first floatation collar on the fourth crate. The team surfaced for a quick sandwich and fresh air tanks. In spite of their intense working efforts this morning, no one was showing any signs of fatigue.

"Think we'll get it all done today?" asked George.

Gypsy shook his head. "We'll be close but it looks like we might need another hour or two tomorrow morning to have everything up to the surface and ready to move."

After a brief snack the men returned to their underwater task. Progress remained brisk partly because they had become accustomed to working together and teamwork had emerged from their efforts.

Michael sat with McCoy in the bright sunlight on the fly bridge. He had a laptop computer sitting open on top of the command console and he was staring at his satellite phone. "I'm pretty sure I can link to the internet through this phone. It's called tethering."

"Why would you need an internet connection way out here?" asked McCoy.

"Just thinking ahead," said Michael. "When we start towing all that stuff down there, we won't be making any better than eight knots at the most and I'll be dragging about a three hundred foot long tail. I wouldn't want to encounter another boat that might cross my path close behind me. There's an internet site that tracks all commercial vessel passages on the Great Lakes in real time and it will tell us what's coming and when. I'll want to keep a close eye on that once we get going."

"Sounds reasonable," said McCoy. "And you can get an internet signal way out here?"

Michael held up his cell phone. "With this I can connect to what they call a hot spot. It's a satellite phone. The signal bounces off of satellites rather than cell phone towers. Otis has one just like it. I kinda talked him into it so he'd never be out of touch. You should get one too."

"Maybe some day. I don't even have this 'smart phone' thing nailed down yet," said McCoy. "You know it's hard to believe that we're this close. Seems like we've been working on this for months but it has been only a little over a week."

"And you still don't trust Gypsy," teased Michael.

"Let me tell you something," said McCoy. "I've got a policeman's instinct and a very good one. It's very seldom that I get one wrong and Gypsy is one that I feel pretty strongly about. I've seen his kind hundreds of times over my

career and they all smell the same. That's one of the reasons
I'm packing every single day and if you're smart, you'll do
the same."

Michael smiled and lifted the bottom edge of his shirt
to reveal the grip of a Kahr K40 peeking out of an inside the
waistband holster.

"You're learning," said McCoy.

When the divers surfaced at the end of their work day
their near exhaustion was clearly evident. Sam and Eddie
stripped off their wetsuits and headed straight for the salon
to take a nap on the ride home.

Jake briefed the boat crew on their progress. "It looks
like we have all five crates broken free of the bottom. The
first three are all ready to go. Float collars in place and tied
together at twenty five foot gaps with a one hundred foot
lead to connect to the boat. The remaining two just need
to have one more floatation collar on each and then start
inflating them. I'd say that we can be ready to move with
about another hour and a half worth of work. The inflation will go much faster too because we can use all four
compressors."

Jake, Michael, and McCoy climbed the ladder up to the
fly bridge as was their usual custom. Jake would probably
doze off at some point on the way back to the marina.

Gypsy peeled off his wetsuit, grabbed a tee-shirt out
of his gear bag and settled into the first mate's chair across
from George who occupied the captain's chair. "It's going
pretty good on our end," said Gypsy. "What's going on with
you? By this time tomorrow we should have it all on dry
land. Are your lawyers ready with the paperwork saying that
it's your money?"

"Everything will be taken care of within the next two or three days," assured George. "We go to court tomorrow and we've got the right judge. It's pretty much a done deal. I'm comfortable with where we are and remember, I have more at stake here than anyone."

Gypsy nodded. "I wish I shared your confidence. Any idea how long this weather is supposed to hold?"

George looked at the sky. "The last time I checked out the radar there was nothing to the west of us all the way to the Rockies. My guess is that we won't be seeing any atmospheric disturbances for a couple of weeks and all we need is a day or so."

The sun was getting low on the horizon as the cruiser sailed back into the harbor. Michael maneuvered the boat back into its slip and it was only then that he noticed the man in a uniform walking toward the boat.

CHAPTER 51

"Hello there," said Michael. "Can I help you?"

The man in the Coast Guard uniform smiled. "You can if you're the owner of this boat. There are some small problems that may need attention."

George began shutting things down and getting the boat ready for the night. He spoke directly to Michael. "You go take care of whatever business he wants and me and Jake can close up the boat for you."

Sam and Eddie had their gear bags in hand and were already headed for their rooms. McCoy jumped onto the dock and walked over to stand next to Michael. Gypsy stood on the afterdeck with his hands on his hips and his eyes hidden behind the black wraparound sunglasses.

"Are you running charters off this boat?" asked the officer.

"Not exactly," said Michael. He pointed at George. "The boat is for sale and Mister Snyder there is a perspective buyer. Three of the men who were on board are his employees and Mister McCoy here is a personal friend of mine."

"According to all the information that I have, this boat has not had a marine survey in quite some time and has not been certified as seaworthy. I'm going to have to quarantine this vessel until it's been inspected and approved."

Michael's jaw dropped. "But we have important business in the morning. We need this boat."

"That's not a decision that I can make sir. I'll call it in right now and you might have a team out here to check you out as early as tomorrow morning. But I can't promise you anything. I've been ordered to deliver the citation and to take the boat out of service. I know no other details" said the Warrant Officer as he attached the impound tag to the bow mooring line. He handed Michael the citation. "You can call the number on here but it's after five o'clock and it's Friday so the only personnel on duty are emergency response teams. There won't be anybody in the office that can help you until Monday morning at nine o'clock."

"Why did you wait until now to drop this on me?" asked Michael. "Couldn't you have done it sooner so that I could have called somebody?" Michael made no attempt to hide the irritation in his voice.

The Warrant officer remained expressionless and his manner was calm. "I was here at nine thirty this morning but the slip was empty. If you attempt to take this boat out of the harbor, you will be in violation of a Federal law. Do you understand me, sir?"

"I understand," said Michael. He looked at McCoy and McCoy just shrugged.

George started to go after the Coast Guard officer but Gypsy reached out and grabbed him by the arm. "That treasure's been down there for over a hundred years. It ain't going nowhere. Another couple of days won't matter much. I wouldn't make a scene if I were you.

George took a few seconds to compose himself and let Gypsy's words sink in. "I suppose you're right but we're so close."

"I've had this same thing happen before," said Gypsy. "Things worked out okay back then."

George and Gypsy climbed out of the boat leaving Jake to finish up closing the canvas and joined Michael on the dock. "Let me see that citation," said George. He examined the paper document, handed it back to Michael and said. "I'll go good for any fines they impose." Then he turned and stalked off toward his room.

Gypsy stopped in at Sam's room and found both Sam and Eddie sitting there drinking cold Budweisers. "Don't overdo it tonight," he said. "We've got a big day ahead of us tomorrow. Maybe the biggest of all." Gypsy threw his gear bag on one of the queen size beds and opened it up. He took everything out and then lifted out a flat panel that had one side covered with foam rubber. "This is a false bottom. Give me your guns and we'll hide them in here." Sam gave him a puzzled look.

Gypsy stared at him. "We're going to be diving tomorrow and all of our gear bags will be up on the boat with those two dames. I'd be damned awful surprised if they didn't go through them while we're underwater." Sam and Eddie handed over their pistols and Gypsy stowed them, along with his own in the depths of his gear bag. He then replaced the false bottom and put his other belongings on inside before he zipped up the bag and said, "You'll only have one magazine full of ammo tomorrow. Make every bullet count. Oh yeah, and be ready to leave by five o'clock. Tomorrow is our D-Day."

Gypsy hurried back to his room where he sat down called Vinny's number. "Hello Vinny. Looks like everything is on schedule. The Coast guard showed up and did their job. We can meet you at your boat around six thirty. Is that okay?" He listened for a moment as Vinny agreed then said. "Okay, we'll be there."

Gypsy went out to his motorcycle in the motel parking lot and retrieved a small bundle from the bottom of one of the saddlebags. He took it back to his room and rolled it open on the desk until it exposed a small Kel-Tec PF-9 nine millimeter semi automatic pistol. As handguns go it wasn't one of Gypsy's favorites. It only held seven rounds, eight if you had one on the chamber and Kel-Tec is a relatively young company whose reputation as an arms manufacturer has not yet been established. Gypsy questioned things like the reliability, not the kind of concern you want to take into a firefight. The fact that he'd be getting it wet for a long time was unsettling as well. But there was no choice. He needed to keep in on his body at all times. Even while diving. On the other side of the ledger, its size made it highly conceal-able. But this gun would be a backup, a last resort and a question mark is decidedly better than an empty hand in a gunfight. He checked to make sure that it was ready to fire and gently slid it into the custom made pocket inside his wetsuit jacket and deposited a spare magazine into the slot next to it. He moved the Velcro hold down strap into place and hung the jacket over the back of a chair.

George Snyder, still fuming from the action of the Coast guard joined his new friends on the balcony for drinks and conversation.

"Why would they do something like that?" moaned George. "They could have just issued a warning and given us a week or so to comply. They didn't have to restrict us to port."

"Their rules are pretty strict," said Otis. "The bigger question should be, who turned you in?"

"What do you mean?" asked George.

"Think about it," said Otis. "There are hundreds of boats in the harbors around this town. Why was Michael singled out? In my experience in law enforcement most cases that involve compliance issues are initiated by a third party complaint. I'm not saying that there's a conspiracy but these types of instances are almost never random."

"But who?" asked George.

"That's the million dollar question," said Otis. "And one that can easily lead you to jump to conclusions. It's the kind of question you'll want to sleep on."

"It certainly can't be any of our crew. They know how close we are to realizing our dream and most definitely would not want to gum things up. It's got to be someone else. Someone who wants us to fail."

"Or someone who wants us out of the way over the weekend," said Michael.

"I hadn't thought of that," said George. "But nobody else knows what we're doing."

"I have an idea," said Michael. "Why don't we jump in your fishing boat and take a ride over to the dive site tomorrow, just you, me, McCoy, and Jake. If everything looks okay we can continue on over to that harbor in Charlevoix so I can have a look at it before I have to negotiate it while towing several tons of cargo. Besides I'd like a ride in your boat."

"What are you expecting to find out there?" asked George.

"I don't think we're expecting anything," said McCoy. "But we'd be foolish if we didn't keep our eyes open. There's a lot of money at stake here and taking chances is just plain dumb. You can't afford to assume anything. We haven't got anything better to do for the next couple of days and by then we could very well have our boat back. Besides, it's a good opportunity to check out the warehouse and see just how secure it looks. We can have a picnic lunch while we're at it."

George turned to Michael. "I couldn't help but notice that you specifically excluded Gypsy and his two friends when you suggested checking things out."

"I don't have a particular reason," said Michael. "It's just that those three are the only question marks in my mind."

"I think we're all in agreement on that point, at least to some degree," said George. "But Gypsy's been a model employee ever since the serious diving began. I was beginning to trust him a little more."

"I'm not saying you can't trust him and no one is condemning him or accusing him of anything," said McCoy. "It's just that you seem to regard Jake as the son you never had and me and Mike, well we go back quite a ways. We just don't know enough about Gypsy and maybe even less about his two friends. That's all there is to it."

"Whatever happens, I sure hope you have your answer soon," said Otis. I have to be back to work in four more days and McCoy only has a couple days more than me. I want to see what happens. You guys and your adventures have got me on the edge of my seat."

Jake showed up just in time to devour the last three slices of pizza. "You guys sure don't have a very diverse menu," he remarked.

"We like to keep it simple," said Otis. "And besides, I'm on vacation and you don't have to follow diets when you're on vacation. Everybody knows that."

"Are you saying that you like pizza?" asked Jake.

"Love it," answered Otis.

Michael outlined tomorrow's plan for Jake. "Sound okay to you?"

"Except for one thing," said Jake. "That Coast Guard officer hinted that an inspection team could show up tomorrow and there should be someone around to assist them if they decide to pop in."

"I hadn't thought about that," said Michael.

"Not a problem," said Jake. "I could take all of those diaries that I've been studying and go sit on the boat. It would be a quiet place to read without any distractions and I could pick up some sandwiches and pop at the Ship's Store. It's actually just what I need."

"Are you sure you don't want to come along?" asked George.

"You certainly don't need me for anything and we won't be cracking open any treasure chests. I think I'd have just as much fun reading the history of a unique old man. I'll stay with the boat."

Michael threw him the keys. "It's all yours, for a day anyway."

CHAPTER 52

Vinny had the Denali all packed and ready to go by the time the girls met him for an early breakfast. They were the only ones in the restaurant at this early hour. Most other people opted for an extra hour or so sleep on Saturday mornings. Vinny led them to a table in the corner.

"Big day coming up," said the redhead. "I can already smell the blood in the air."

"Boy you sure start early," said Vinny

"Don't mind her," said the blonde. "She always gets like this when she knows she's going to murder someone."

"I kinda got that drift," said Vinny. "Gives me the shivers to be completely honest."

"No need to worry," said the redhead. "I sort of like you and I almost never kill people I like."

"But what happens if you change your mind?" teased to blonde.

They all laughed but Vinny's snicker was decidedly shaky.

"Do you have all the details figured out?" asked the blonde.

"There's nothing that should be too difficult," said Vinny. "I'll be diving with them so you guys will have to handle everything topside. The hardest thing you'll have to do is run the winch and it's nothing more than a forward and reverse lever. Any time you need to run it I'll be at the surface hanging on to the ramp and I'll give you the signal to pay out the cable and then I'll let you know when to retrieve it. Once the load hits the ramp just put the lever in neutral and I'll climb on board and handle it for the last few feet. Your end should be pretty easy."

"What happens once we get it all on the boat?" asked the redhead.

"There will still be a lot of work that will have to be done," said Vinny "We've got to make sure that everything is lashed down good and solid and that will take all of us to get that done. The crates will be sitting on steel rails and we don't need them moving around, especially if the lake kicks up. Just that alone is going to take around a half hour. As soon as everything is secure, we can start the boat moving. Sometime during that operation, one of you is going to have to slip me my gun, and make damned sure it's ready to go. I'll let you know when I'm ready for it so keep it handy and out of sight."

"No problem said the blonde. I'll stick it in my fanny pack and pull my sweatshirt over it."

What about those guys?" asked the redhead. "What if they have guns too?"

"You can pretty much count on that," said Vinny. "They'd be foolish to come on board without them. But they won't be carrying. They'll be underwater all day and they'll want to keep their guns dry so they will be somewhere in whatever luggage they bring with them. It's up to you two to dig them out and put them somewhere out of reach. Otherwise we'll all have to depend on our quick draw skills"

"I'll throw them down in the chain locker" said the redhead. It's dark, dirty, and smelly down there."

"Okay," said Vinny. "Let's work on some signals. You'll have about twenty or thirty minutes when the four of us divers first go underwater. Hopefully that will be enough time to check out their gear bags and remove their guns. When we come to the surface I'll ask if everything is okay on the boat. You can let me know that you've got their guns taken care of by asking me if I'm ready to start working."

"Got it," said the redhead.

"Once we get everything on the deck, I'll need to get my gun back from you. I don't want it getting loose on me so I'll have a holster strapped on under my wetsuit. I'll let you know that I'm ready by saying we've got to make sure that we haven't forgotten anything. Then I'll act like I'm checking the load and as soon as I'm out of sight around the back of the crates, you can meet me there and hand it to me. Let me have a good look at our surroundings to make sure nobody can see what's going on before I give you the green light by saying that the job went easier than I expected. At that point I'll be ready when you yell, 'Hey Vinny.' That's when the shooting can start."

"This is shaping up to be a great day," said the redhead.

The trio climbed into Vinny's Denali and headed west toward the town of Fayette. The one hour trip gave them plenty of time to go over their plans dozens of times. Vinny reached over the seat and handed the blonde his Smith & Wesson M&P 40 saying. "Just put it away and don't touch a thing. I want it back exactly the way I handed it to you. All I'll have to do is pull the trigger."

"No problem," said the blonde. She deposited the pistol in her fanny pack. "Anything else?"

"Not at the moment." Said Vinny.

It was barely sunrise when they pulled in next to the big trawler. Gypsy and his guys hadn't arrived yet.

Vinny loaded three large coolers aboard the trawler. He had enough food to last four days for the three of them. He used a handcart to maneuver the crate carrying three AR-15 rifles and stowed them in a locked box under the vee-berths in the bow. "These are to protect the cargo once we get into port," he explained.

CHAPTER 53

Gypsy gathered his two partners and pulled out of the parking lot at ten minutes after six on a bright and sunny Saturday morning.

"Looks like another scorcher," said Sam.

"It's been a hot summer," answered Gypsy

"I wonder if the girls will be wearing bikinis," said Sam

Gypsy grunted.

"We're not really going to shoot those girls, are we?" asked Eddie

"As of now, we really don't know how big of a role they're playing in this thing," said Gypsy. "They could be nothing more than tools and totally harmless. But don't forget that they're the ones that came to you in the first place and laid out this whole scheme. They might be in it a lot deeper than you think."

"Yeah but that Terri is such a cute and cuddly little redhead," said Eddie. "I'm sure she's not dangerous. She's just too sweet."

Gypsy sighed. "That's the kind of thinking that can get you killed. Yeah, she's cute and all that but that doesn't make her any less treacherous. I'm telling you to be on your guard and don't hesitate to shoot if you need to."

"I know my job," said Eddie. "But I think you've got her pegged all wrong. At least I hope so."

"Do you really think the girls might be a threat?" asked Sam.

"Well, you guys know them a lot better than I do," said Gypsy. "But I've seen a lot of troublesome women in my lifetime and some of them can seem downright sweet until it's time for the fangs to come out. That's what makes them so dangerous, they lull you into a false sense of security."

"What about Vinny?" asked Sam. "You see him as a big problem?"

"I try not to underestimate anybody," answered Gypsy. "Some of the wimpiest looking guys can turn out to be the biggest threats. I'll treat him like he's Hercules and that way I won't be surprised."

"And then there's always the chance that they've been playing it straight with us all along and things will go just fine," said Eddie.

"Don't count on it," said Gypsy. "I've got a plan and we'd better stick to it. First of all we need to arm ourselves as soon as possible after we finish diving. The chance of being discovered is a lot less if just one of us retrieves all three guns. When we get aboard, I'll stow my gear bag in the head. I'll claim that I have to use the bathroom when we get done diving. With the girls on board, I've got a built in excuse to go into the head and close the door. I'll get the guns and pass them on. Eddie, I want you to wear that big abalone knife in your leg sheath. It looks like a normal tool when you're diving and it gives them something to pay attention to when you climb out of the water. Keep your eyes open for any unusual movement from any of those three."

"What do you mean by unusual movement?" asked Eddie.

"Things like them maneuvering to get behind you or anything that might give them a physical advantage. Things like them picking up a wrecking bar or anything like that."

"When would you expect them to make their move?" asked Sam.

"I'd say that it could come any time after they don't absolutely need us any more. My guess is that they'd want us out of the way at the earliest opportunity."

"And you think the girls might help him?" asked Eddie.

"Use your head," said Gypsy. "If they don't help, we've got Vinny outnumbered three to one. He'd be dumb to play those odds."

"What do you expect them to do?" asked Sam.

"My guess would be that their first task will be to find our guns and get rid of them," said Gypsy.

"But they're pretty well hidden," said Eddie.

"There are no guarantees," said Gypsy. "If they don't find anything they might just toss all three gear bags over the side just to play it safe. Either way we could possibly be without our guns and if we find ourselves in that position, it's up to us to do the maneuvering in order to gain advantageous positions. If it comes to that, we have to each pick a target and stay real close. Watch me and when it looks good I'll make the first move"

"I still think that the redhead is just too cute to be dangerous," said Eddie.

"Do you know where that port is that we'll be heading to in Detroit?" asked Sam.

"We ain't going that way," said Gypsy. "We'll be headed straight south to the Illinois Waterway and then down the Mississippi. I've got enough connections in Florida to hide the boat for the next ten years. I'm hoping it has a full fuel tank because those babies have a range of right about a fifteen hundred miles. I've got enough cash for one refueling stop and that should be all we need."

The car carrying the three divers wound its way down the picturesque Garden Peninsula and into the parking area next to the massive trawler riding at anchor and lashed to the pilings. There was a GMC Denali parked next to the dock and two women and a man were on the boat making preparations for getting under way.

"We're here," announced Gypsy. "Everybody take a deep breath and let's go to work."

Vinny leaned over the gunwale to wave them aboard. Gypsy went around to the back of the car and opened the trunk. Each of the men retrieved his gear bag and scuba equipment and set them on the expansive rear deck of the trawler. "Now this is the kind of boat I'm used to working from," said Sam. "Not as fancy as the one we've been using but a lot more elbow room."

Gypsy climbed aboard and immediately produced a tape measure and stretched it form the pilot house to the stern ramp. "About six feet to spare if we pull all the crates forward in two rows and the last one centered. We'll need to tie them together," he said.

"That's how I saw it too," said Vinny," "They're going to be pretty heavy and I'd like to keep them directly over the keel if possible."

While Eddie lashed down all of their equipment, Sam wandered over to one side and began counting the spare air tanks that nest in the long rack.

"Twenty," said Vinny. "And we have a compressor if we need it but I'm hoping that the whole underwater part of this operation won't take more than five or six hours."

"Sounds about right," said Gypsy as he picked up his gear bag and headed below. "Could be even less."

Vinny climbed up on the Captain's chair and fired up the engines. He hollered for the girls to cast off the lines and within five minutes they were away from the dock and headed toward the dawn.

CHAPTER 54

George and Jake were already seated in the restaurant and scanning their menus when Michael and McCoy walked in. McCoy spotted them first and led the way to their table.

"I'm surprised to see you here this early," said George. "This is almost like a day off. No hurry to get out there, we've got all the time in the world."

"I'm looking forward to riding in that fishing boat of yours," said Michael. "We should get out there more than twice as fast in that thing. What'll she do, anyway? Ever have her opened up?"

George laughed. "That's my toy. The first thing I did with it after I got it was to take it to a performance shop and have a few modifications made. It's got a lot more zip than it had coming out of the factory but the guy who worked on it told me that he couldn't go any farther without compromising the safety factors. Those hulls will take a lot but even a Donzi has its limits. But, to answer your question, I'm not sure just how fast it will go but I've seen seventy on the speedo."

"I'll put on my life jacket before you even leave the dock," said McCoy.

"It's not really that scary as long as I accelerate slowly, and it runs as quiet as a kitten. A whole lot quieter than that big Roamer we've been using," said George. "But if I put the spurs to it… hold on Nelly."

Michael laughed and turned to Jake. "See all the fun you're gonna miss today? Don't you wish you were coming along?"

"I'll be just fine," said Jake. "I don't mind at all. I'm enjoying that old man's life story and could even finish it by the time you guys get back. Besides, if the Coast Guard shows up, you'll be thanking me for helping speed things along."

"As long as you're happy, I'm happy," said George.

McCoy hefted a cooler full of bottled water and iced tea over the back of the boat while George went over his pre trip check list. With the lines cast off, McCoy and Michael settled into the nicely upholstered transom seats and George took his place at the center console. The sleek hull silently crept out of the harbor.

Once they were fully on plane and cruising at a respectable speed, Michael remarked, "You weren't kidding were you? This thing really is quiet when you're moving."

"Lots of space age sound insulation built into those engine cowlings," said George. "It was the speed and acceleration that surprised me the first couple of times I drove it. But then it's a Donzi, it comes with an offshore racing pedigree."

"Mine isn't nearly as peppy as this thing," said Michael. "I guess I've traded off performance for a little comfort and luxury."

There was very little boat traffic on the lake this morning, a sure sign that the five AM fishing reports had been less than enthusiastic. Aside from three small runabouts traveling at trolling sped, the only other boat they encountered was a stern trawler commercial fishing boat. It appeared to be on a similar heading with them.

"I sure hope he doesn't drop his nets on your treasure," commented McCoy.

"He shouldn't even come close," said Michael. "The water is way too shallow where we were working. He'll probably begin his fishing about five miles this side of our site and then drag straight north."

Leaving the trawler far behind them until it completely dropped out of sight, they continued until George's GPS told him that they were directly over the treasure. "It gives me chills to know just how close to a king's ransom I'm sitting right now," said George.

"It won't be long and you can start counting it," said Michael.

George didn't say anything but he circled the area twice and then put the boat into a graceful arc setting his course for Charlevoix. When he got near the coast, he slightly altered the direction until a small atoll known as Fisherman Island came into view. Soon there appeared what looked like a narrow river emptying into Lake Michigan. A sign on the bank identified it as the entrance to a private harbor.

"You won't have to do all that zigzagging that I just did," said George. "Now I have the precise coordinates of the entrance and so you'll be able to come on a straight line. The water in this channel is over eighteen feet deep and it stays at that depth throughout the harbor."

George guided his craft into the harbor entrance and straight into a large deep water lagoon, one side of which was a seawall guarded by a substantial looking dock.

Directly behind the steel seawall sat a yellow crane with its hydraulic boom neatly retracted, outriggers up tight against the body and four heavy duty wooden pads lying on the sod, spread out at the corners of the crane. The truck and trailer that had delivered the crane sat nearby. A gravel road followed the seawall and led past a large structural steel building with two tall vehicle doors and an electric meter mounted on the far side. The road continued past a slightly smaller version of the first building and then disappeared into the hardwoods presumably to connect with a county road somewhere in the distance.

George maneuvered his boat up to the dock and McCoy dropped the fenders over the side and threw the mooring lines over the pilings. All three men climbed onto the dock led by George who headed directly toward the biggest building. He fished a cluttered key ring out of his pocket and unlocked the door. "I'm negotiating a deal on this place," he said. "I've been wanting to buy it for some time but it took the owner a long time to agree to a sale. My legal staff is bargaining with his guys right now. I understand that we're pretty close. I'll be getting everything that's here."

George unlocked and opened the pedestrian door, walked inside and turned on the overhead lights. A propane powered fork lift sat against on wall on the spotless concrete floor and there were two high cube vans parked in the back of building. Both bore the black and red logo of The Road Wrench, mobile service, Inc.

"Wow, you sure are prepared," said Michael.

"I hope so," said George pointing at the two trucks. "Both of those box trucks have had the suspension beefed up to more than double their original capacity. I did that a long time ago when I had a special project going. I was bidding on some government contracts and I had to meet their specifications. It should be enough to carry at least two of those crates on each truck. And that fork lift over there is rated for seven tons. I think we've got everything covered."

"This place would be a smuggler's dream," commented McCoy. "What was it used for in the past?"

"My understanding is that it originally belonged to a guy from Beaver Island and he used to bring a passenger ferry in here but it didn't work out too well because it was too far away from any town. He spent a lot of money putting in this seawall and building this pier. I guess he went belly up and another outfit took the place off his hands and built these two buildings thinking of making it into a warehousing area, there's thirty acres of land with this parcel. From the looks of things, they never did anything with it except bring that forklift in. If you look at the floors, they're still like brand new, never had anything stacked on them."

"What are your plans for the place?" asked Michael.

"It would let me expand my business to northern Michigan," said George. "We do major repairs as well as the roadside stuff and this place already has two commercial quality buildings with eight inch thick reinforced concrete floors on it and there's plenty of room inside for a bridge crane. And when I bought out Admiral Salvage down in Toledo, it got me thinking about dabbling in marine salvage as well. This site would kill two birds with one rock. Besides, there's nobody like our company operating in this area. Fertile turf, if you know what I mean."

George locked up the building and led the other two back to his boat. As they climbed aboard and retrieved their mooring lines, George said. "We've got plenty of time and I'd like to top off the fuel tanks so why don't we run up to Charlevoix and we can have lunch while we're there. My treat."

"I'll drink to that," said McCoy.

George motored out of the harbor and followed the coast up to the city of Charlevoix. After stopping at a marina gas dock for fuel he traveled a little farther north and tied up in front of a very impressive waterfront restaurant called The Weathervane.

The ambiance in the place was dignified but relaxed. "We're off duty today so you two guys feel free to order cocktails if you wish. I never drink until after sundown." He picked up a menu and searched the seafood section, settling on the whitefish platter.

McCoy and Michael opted to split a pitcher of cold Killian's Red and then went back to studying the menu. McCoy eventually chose a small rib eye steak and Michael asked for the Chicken Florentine.

George pulled out his cell phone. "While we're in port, I thought I'd give Jake a call and see if anyone has showed up at the boat yet." He dialed Jake's number. After a short conversation he frowned, shook his head and ended the call.

"I'm thinking of having my attorney contact the Coast Guard on Monday morning and see if he can't get something moving. I'd like to get that stuff moved by Tuesday. No telling when we might run into a week long string of bad weather."

"As an enforcement officer, I can tell you that the Coast Guard probably would resent being pressured by some lawyer," said McCoy. "It's kind of like when somebody goes over your head without giving you a chance to get things done on your own. Insulting, if you know what I mean."

"I suppose you're right," said George. "I'll give them a day or so before I do anything that might upset somebody."

"I feel kind of guilty," said Michael. "I should have known that an older boat, especially one that has spent almost a decade sitting on dry land would need to be checked out. I know that the boat is in better than new shape and so do you guys. But there are a lot of other boats around that age that simply aren't safe and I suppose that the Coast Guard has to look at all of them."

"It's nobody's fault," said George. "It's just something that happened and it's water under the bridge. We need to learn from it and move on."

There was still a lot of daylight left when they returned to the boat. It looked like they'd easily make it back to the marina before sunset. When they pulled away from the dock, George suggested that they make another visit to their dive site about mid day tomorrow, just to keep an eye on things.

Michael and McCoy agreed and Michael remarked that they had plenty of time to run by there again on the way home.

"Good idea," said George.

CHAPTER 55

Marla was genuinely enjoying her vacation with Otis and the twins. Their days were being spent together as a family swimming in the clear waters of the northern lakes and building sand castles on the beach. Having a carnival with all of its bright lights and glitter in the parking lot near their room was both a blessing and a curse when you have two energetic ten year olds tugging at your sleeve. There were daily sightseeing trips through Michigan's beautiful wilderness as well as visits to historic sites and sampling upper peninsula cuisine. And when daylight gave way to starlight she could savor her role as hostess to the almost nightly get togethers with friends on the balcony outside their room. It was fun to laugh and mingle with other adults while being serenaded by the sounds of an active marina. And then there was the romantic dancing in the moonlight at The Ship's Anchor to the music that only a big band can provide. It was the kind of vacation that one wished would never end.

Otis, a creature of habit always liked to start his days with a five mile run on a quiet country road. While sightseeing with his family one day, he had found the perfect place for running. It was a few miles from town in farm territory. It seemed as if the agriculture in the area consisted of corn and grains like wheat and oats. There were a few dairy and beef operations scattered among the crop farms.

This Saturday was blessed with bright sunshine that had burned its way through the morning haze and bounced its rays across the stubble of a recently harvested oat field turning the straw to glimmering gold. Otis liked running in the sunlight. The image of the horizon far beyond the fields was broken only by the twelve story silos of the grain elevator; rural America's answer to big city skyscrapers and very often the main reason for the small village that surrounds it.

The sun was rising over Otis's left shoulder as he ran. Otis didn't carry an ipod or any sort of recorded music. He simply didn't like headphones and found ear buds to be irritating. Instead he entertained himself with his thoughts punctuated by the sounds of nature. The brilliant sunlight cast a keen edged shadow on the asphalt road. He concentrated on that silhouette as he ran. It stretched across two lanes of pavement blurred slightly as it crossed the gravel shoulder and then sharpened again as it climbed the ten foot tall cornstalks on his right.

The thought struck him like a lightning bolt and stopped him in his tracks. Otis stood there staring at a shadow that took him back in time by a full thirty years. The memories were vivid in spite of the gap in time.

Way back when Otis had just made detective grade, his first assignment was with the narcotics squad. In the old days it was common for the department to throw the young guys directly into the fire.

The city had started a push on narcotics arrests to appease a nervous city council and so the department did a lot of personnel shuffling in order to beef up the narcotics squad. They were borrowing manpower from every division. One of the young officers was a water search and rescue diver named Pingree Smith, "Ping" for short. He was the youngest member of the Harbormaster's division and not at all happy about drawing a street assignment. He reported for duty as ordered, but with an attitude. Otis drew young Pingree as his partner and during their first week together they had stumbled across a drug deal in progress. They surprised the offenders and each cop grabbed one dealer and had them spread out for frisking. Otis had his man up against the brick wall of an abandoned supermarket while Ping spun his prisoner in the opposite direction and had him spread out against a chain link fence across the driveway. Ping obviously didn't know enough to bring his man over to stand next to the other. Having the cops facing opposite directions was something that even rookie cops were suppose to recognize as a dangerous practice. Otis made quick work of his pat down and swiftly began putting the handcuffs on the offender.

The sun was at Otis's back that day and so the shadow of Ping and his prisoner was printed clearly on the brick wall next to where Otis stood. Otis kept one eye on his man and the other on Ping's shadow. And that's when it happened.

The shadow showed that the man that Ping was frisking seemed to be totally cooperating, his arms and legs spread as far as he could reach. And then the cop shadow drew its weapon, a department issued thirty eight special. Then the cop shadow appeared to spin the prisoner shadow around to face him and the sound of a gunshot shredded the morning sunlight.

When Otis turned around, the suspect was prone, quivering face down on the ground with a swelling pool of blood forming around his upper torso. Ping looked at Otis and said. "He tried to grab my gun out of its holster. I had to shoot him. Believe me, I had no choice."

Otis didn't respond but radioed for an ambulance and backup.

As with every shooting incident, the Police Department conducted a full investigation. During his interview, Otis described everything that he had seen and his version was corroborated by the drug dealer that he had been taking into custody at the time. The result was a second degree murder charge for Officer Pingree Smith.

It was a lengthy trial with the defense producing numerous character witnesses as well as the criminal record of the deceased. It seems that the drug dealer had been arrested numerous times and had a history of resisting arrest that included one assault on a police officer.

The result of the trial was a hung jury because the defense attorneys were able to convince the jury that looking at a shadow was not the same as being an eye witness. As they marched out of the court room Pingree's eyes locked onto Otis's and his smirk insulted Otis's sense of justice.

The prosecutors looked at the trail and decided that they'd probably never be able to get a conviction based on "shadow" evidence and so they elected to drop the case.

The police department was not quite as sympathetic and unceremoniously fired officer smith, stripping him of his pension and any other benefits.

The city was served with an unlawful death lawsuit and eventually settled out of court for close to a half million dollars.

Now, years after the fact, Otis stood alone in the middle of a country road staring at his own shadow on a row of cornstalks but seeing only those eyes that had mocked him in that courtroom decades ago. Those eyes belonged to Gypsy.

CHAPTER 56

"Sam. Eddie. Get down," yelled Gypsy as he crouched behind the gunwale.

"What's wrong?" asked Vinny.

Gypsy pointed at the fast moving vessel coming up from their rear. "I recognize that boat. It's Snyder."

"Looks like they might be headed to the same place we are," said Vinny.

"They're still too far away to see who is on board," said Gypsy. "But it wouldn't make much sense for them to be going out to the dive site. They only have one diver at the most and there's really nothing that one guy can do alone out there. Besides they wouldn't be able to tow anything with that boat. It's not built for that sort of thing."

"Well then where would they be headed?" asked Vinny.

Gypsy remained out of sight as the smaller boat past them at a distance of about a half mile. "The only thing I can think of is they might be checking to see if anybody is out on their dive site. If that's where they're going, I sure hope they're not planning to hang around there all day. We only need three or four hours and we can have the gold on board and be on our way."

Vinny opened a cabinet near the command console and retrieved a pair if binoculars and called out to one of the girls. "Looks like we're going to put someone on sentry duty. You two can take turns. Once we get out to the dive site we'll have to come up with some sort of signal so that you can let us know if any boat looks like it's approaching us. We can't take chances at this point."

The trawler rumbled across the big lake closing in on the specified coordinates. The suspicious runabout, with its faster cruising speed had long since pulled out of view. Now that they were near their target area, it was nowhere in sight.

"I wonder where they went?" said Vinny. "Are you sure it was them?"

"I couldn't make out any faces," said Gypsy. "They were too far away. But I haven't seen any other boats that looked like that one. It almost had to be them."

"The girls will keep scanning the horizon and if they see anything, they'll let us know," said Vinny. "Besides we'll be popping to the surface every fifteen minutes or so. I have to tell you that it makes me nervous just knowing that they could be out here somewhere."

"I hope they don't surprise us out here," said Gypsy. "But at the moment, they don't have any more legal right to that treasure than we do. It belongs to whoever hauls it out of the lake and claims it. Basically they can't stop us. But I'm still hoping that there won't be any sort of confrontation."

They reached the destination and Vinny released the twin anchors and their heavy chains followed them to the bottom. Sam and Eddie wiggled into their wetsuits while Vinny and Gypsy sorted out the heavy nylon slings that would be wrapped around the crates in order to haul them up the transom ramp.

The trawler only had two air compressors on board but they would be moving the crates one at a time and they should be able to get by nicely inflating two floatation collars at a time. Once everything was prepared, the divers walked out to where the transom ramp disappeared into the water and jumped off.

As soon as the men were below the surface, both girls began rifling their gear bags. Finding nothing in either Sam's or Eddie's satchel they turned to Gypsy's which had been left inside the head. The weight of the bag, even after emptying it made it immediately suspicious. The blonde reached inside and knocked on the bottom. It had a hollow sound and so she ran her fingers around the edges until she found a canvas loop. A slight tug and the false bottom broke free revealing two Glocks and a Beretta resting on a foam rubber pad. "My, my, look what I found," said the blonde. She quickly gathered up the guns, handed them to the redhead and reassembled Gypsy's bag, being careful to replace his clothes so that it appeared that nothing had been disturbed.

With the guns safely hidden, the girls returned to their guard duty sweeping the surface of the lake with the powerful binoculars.

It was about ten minutes before all four heads popped up out of the water. Vinny and Gypsy climbed up the ramp while the other two men remained in the water. The outline of one of the crates wrapped in float collars showed clearly just beneath the surface.

"How is everything going up here?" asked Vinny, as he looked around at the open water.

"Just great, so far," said the redhead. "The question is, when are you going to do some work?"

Vinny flashed a knowing smile and stepped forward to the winch and picked up the large hook on the end of the cable. He told the blonde to engage the reverse control and walked toward the ramp at the back of the boat carrying the hook as the cable payed out off of the spool. When he got to the transom he handed the hook to Sam and then directed the blonde to slow the winch down and finally told her to press the stop button. All four divers circled the crate, checking and double checking to be sure that it was rigged properly. Finally, Vinny instructed the blonde to turn the function switch to the inch mode so that the drum on the winch would roll very slowly, pulling the crate up the ramp an inch at a time. The old trawler creaked and groaned and the heavy load caused the stern to dip low toward the water.

Everybody cheered when the first edge of the crate broke the surface but it surrendered to the power of the winch and was soon completely clear of the water and slowly creeping toward the pilot house on two of the one inch diameter steel bars that served as rails. When the load was all the way forward Vinny disconnected the winch and the men went to work removing the nylon slings, deflating and removing the floatation collars, and getting the load ready to lash down.

As soon as everything was secure, Sam said. "Can we have a peek inside?" Both Gypsy and Vinny yelled, "No."

Gypsy spoke up. "Maybe after we have everything on board and locked down, but not now."

"The first crate went according to the script," said Vinny. "If the next four go that well, we'll be out of here in less than two hours."

Retrieval of the next two crates followed suit, floating to the surface with the aid of float collars and then riding slowly up the ramp and onto the other pair of steel rails that were welded to the trawlers rear deck. The process had now become routine and was done more quickly with less conversation.

After the third crate was strapped down, the crew took a break for a bite to eat and some bottled water. Working underwater for extended periods can be very tiring and even human batteries need to be re-charged.

Sam and Eddie both removed their wetsuit jackets during the break while Gypsy simply unzipped his about one third if the way down. As they sat having their lunch on the stacks of folded up floatation collars, Gypsy studied the two women and seemed to notice a slight change in their demeanor. It was a subtle change but troubling. They weren't nearly as cheerful as they had been earlier in the day. He excused himself to use the head. Once inside he locked the door behind him and immediately went for his gear bag. He could tell as soon as he lifted it that the guns were no longer there. His mind went into contingency plan mode and he exited the bathroom to find the redhead just outside the door. He gave her a convincing smile as if he hadn't discovered the missing guns and held the door open for her. "You're next," he said.

The redhead was visibly nervous as she went into the head. Gypsy listened at the door for a few seconds but there were no sounds coming from inside.

Gypsy got back out onto the afterdeck and asked Sam to help him get a couple of fresh tanks ready for the next dive. When he was sure that nobody was paying any attention to them, he told Sam about the missing guns and advised him that he and Eddie needed to position themselves to quickly overpower the two girls if anything at all suspicious happened. He'd keep a close eye on Vinny for any signs of trouble. "We've got to all go into action at the same time so make sure that you're fully aware of everything that's going on at all times and that the girls are less than an arm's length away. They won't try anything until the last two crates are loaded and tied down but after that, things could pop at a moment's notice. Now pass what I've just told you along to Eddie and make sure that nobody sees you two talking to one another."

When Sam approached Eddie on the afterdeck, Gypsy engaged Vinny in a conversation about securing the cargo. He talked about the risk of one or more of the crates slipping off of the rails if they weren't tied down firmly. "Those babies are heavy," said Gypsy.

"They're supposed to be," laughed Vinny. "They're full of gold."

The last part of the day wasn't quite as easy. The final crate had slipped out of one of the floatation collars and it took almost thirty minutes to get everything back in place and inflated. The load crawled slowly up the ramp and leveled out, straddling the center two rails as it crept forward to where it would be stowed. Vinny disconnected the winch hook for the last time and reeled in all of the cable. "This thing is rated for fifteen tons," he said. "I don't think anything less could have done the job."

The girls were hustling to get the tie down straps in place as Sam and Eddie began stripping off their wetsuits. Neither Gypsy nor Vinny made a move to remove theirs.

When the last latch was snapped closed on the tie down straps, Vinny said, "Let's make sure that we haven't forgotten anything before we throw the tarp over it."

The blonde disappeared around the back of the load as Vinny circled around from the other direction. The hand off was so smooth it could have been done in front of every-body and it's likely that nobody would have seen Vinny take the Smith & Wesson from the blonde and slide it into the Kydex holster under his wetsuit. He slowly wandered out from behind the load saying that everything looked good. It was only Gypsy who noticed that now Vinny's wetsuit jacket was unzipped.

Vinny climbed up into the pilot house and turned on the bilge blowers and sniffers. Then he walked back to the afterdeck and said, "When this boat has been sitting still for a while after being run, it sometimes takes a few minutes to get all the fumes out of the bilge. I'll be able to fire up the engines in about five minutes and we'll be able to get underway." He walked over to the starboard rail and looked out over the water. Then he did the same thing on the port side. Gypsy watched his movements with intense interest. After a sweeping examination of the surrounding waters, Vinny proclaimed. "That whole operation went a lot easier than I expected."

Gypsy's hand slipped inside of his wetsuit jacket.

CHAPTER 57

"I can't believe the weather we've been having," said McCoy "Kinda makes me wish you had a set of water skis."

"You'd break your neck," said Michael.

George had the boat cruising at a much more relaxed pace on their way back across the lake. "Anybody want to guess when the Coast Guard will show up at Michael's boat?"

"From the comment that Warrant Officer made, it doesn't sound as if they're too busy. Might be as early as Monday. By then you'll at least be able to call them and get an idea.

"I sure hope it's within the next couple of days," said McCoy. "I'll be out of vacation days by this time next week. I'd hate to miss out on the grand opening."

"And you'll be rewarded generously for all your help," said George. "You two have made me feel much more comfortable about what was becoming a very stressful enterprise."

"You don't have to pay me," said McCoy. "I came up here to help Michael get his boat going and that's basically all I've done."

"Nonsense," responded George. "You've been a great help to me. Both of you have."

McCoy stepped over to the cooler and pulled out a couple of cold beers, handed one to Michael and opened the other for himself. "You don't get one, George. You're the designated driver."

George laughed. "It's too early for me anyway," he said. "I'm from the generation that invented the five o'clock rule."

The conversation was interrupted by the ringing of Michael's satellite phone. He recognized the caller as Otis Springfield and answered with a cheery, "What's up?"

"McCoy with you?" were the sober words from Otis.

"Sure, wanna talk to him?" said Michael

"Yeah," said Otis. "Can you put him on?"

McCoy took the phone and put it to his ear. "It's McCoy, Otis. What do you need?"

Otis began. "You remember the other night when I told you that a thought flashed through my mind but I couldn't catch it? Well, that thought just hit me in the face."

"Let's have it," said McCoy.

"It must have been twenty five years ago or maybe even longer but a cop named Pingree Smith got booted off the force for unprofessional conduct. He killed a drug dealer during a routine arrest. Shot him in the chest, unprovoked. He got off the murder charge because the only two eye witnesses didn't have a direct line of sight. They were looking at shadows. The defense lawyer made a fool of the prosecutor at the trial. One of the eye witnesses was the drug dealer's buddy and the other one was me."

"I remember the case," said McCoy. "I didn't realize it was you though. That had to be five or six years before you and me started working together. I would've still been a beat cop back then."

"That's right," said Otis. "Anyway, that cop really rubbed my nose in the fact that he beat the rap but our internal investigation found him to be unfit for police duty and they canned him. He had been loaned to the narcotics division as part of a big push we were having, trying to round up street dealers. Lots of the officers on that program weren't streetwise cops and he was one of those. Up until then he had been working for the harbormaster division as a diver. His supervisor was Charlie Kelly."

McCoy let out a low whistle. "The guy they found floating in the harbor back at the marina."

"Exactly right," said Otis. "Can you see where this is going?"

McCoy said that he did.

"The last thing I remember about that rogue cop was him staring into my eyes when the jury verdict forced the judge to let him off the hook. And then last week when we were having a meeting with George and all of the divers, Gypsy took off those black sunglasses for a few seconds and we made brief eye contact. It was those eyes that lit up in my mind and then disappeared that night up on our balcony. I'll never forget those eyes."

"So you're pretty sure we've got a murderer in our crew," said McCoy.

"Absolutely positive," said Otis. "I'm assuming he's not with you guys at the moment."

"You assume correctly," said McCoy. "What's the next step?"

"I'm going to contact that sheriff's deputy," said Otis. "What's his name? Haynes? And let him know who Gypsy really is and about his connection to Charlie Kelly. There won't be enough evidence for an arrest but Gypsy can be labeled a person of interest and that's enough to open an investigation. And while he's at it, Haynes can see if there's any connection between Gypsy and that guy they found strangled in the front seat of his car."

"Is Gypsy there, in the motel right now?" asked McCoy.

"I didn't see him or either of his two friends in the restaurant this morning but they don't always have breakfast here when they aren't working with you guys," said Otis. "I know what their car looks like and I'm outside in the parking lot right now I'll walk around and see it it's here. Gypsy's motorcycle is always easy to spot so I'll look for that too."

"Looks like we may have been right about him," said McCoy.

"It's a cop's nose," said Otis. "I'll call you back if I find out anything more."

McCoy closed out the call and then went forward and sat between Michael and George and told them everything that Otis had relayed to him.

"This really complicates things," said Michael. "With Gypsy out of the picture, that means that we can't trust either one of his buddies either. That leaves us with one active diver and the treasure still on the bottom of the lake."

"Let's just hope that the Sheriff's Department does their job and keeps Gypsy and his pals out of the way," said McCoy. "We'll have enough problems with that Coast Guard citation and finding some new divers."

"Hiring a couple of divers may not be too difficult," said Michael. "My friend John, the guy who owns the marina, has a million connections around town and he should be able to help out with that."

Michael's phone rang again and it was Otis once more. "Yeah," answered Michael. "Do you need Otis or will I do?"

"You're fine," said Otis. "I just talked to Jake and he said that he saw the rental car with three guys in it pull out of the parking lot early this morning. He figured that they were just going somewhere for breakfast but they haven't come back all day. Gypsy's motorcycle is still parked where it was last night. That's all I have."

Michael ended the call and relayed the information. "Where do you suppose they went?" asked George.

"I have a thought," said McCoy. "Remember this morning when we were headed over here and we passed that fishing trawler? I wonder if that could have been them. I mean, we talked about how that Coast Guard visit could have been prompted by a complaint. What if they had a boat all lined up and just needed conditions to be right? They could've made a phone call and then made their move. You gotta admit with all of those crates floating just off the bottom and loosely tied together, it's a perfect set up."

George visibly paled. "Do you really think they're doing that? Sneaking behind our backs and stealing the treasure?"

"I wouldn't be surprised," said McCoy. "Just to be on the safe side, why don't you circle around to the north and come at the site from a different direction. If they are out there and watching out for us, they'll be looking for us to approach from a southerly direction. This boat is quiet enough that they won't hear us either."

George swung the boat to a northern heading and increased the cruising speed. Within a half hour they had rounded the north end of Beaver Island and had turned back south. Michael took a pair of binoculars from the command console and leveled them straight ahead.

"There's something there," said Michael. "I can't make

it out yet but we should be closer in twenty minutes or so. I'll keep an eye on it."

George increased the speed a little more.

"Just because Michael spotted something up there, doesn't mean it's them," said McCoy. "When we get closer, slow it down enough to see what's going on and who it is."

"What if it's them?" asked George.

"We'll confront them," said McCoy. "Unless you guys can think of something else. We're in a bad spot. We haven't recovered anything yet so it's still anybody's treasure. If we do nothing, they can just load up and be on their way."

"We might still be okay in a court of law," said George. "After all, I've financed the whole thing, led us directly to the gold and have overseen the entire project. And let's not forget that Jake is a direct descendant of on of the last people to be in possession of the treasure. But no matter what, we can't just let anybody else run off with it."

"One thing to keep in mind," said Michael. "It's an awful lot of money and there's a decent chance that Gypsy may have killed two men so far in his quest. That potentially puts all of us in danger."

As they approached the dot on the horizon it slowly materialized into a fishing trawler. It was the same boat that they passed on the way to Charlevoix. It had been on their dive site all day. Michael strained to see who was on board. "Looks like more than three people," he said. There's a big guy who looks like Gypsy but we're not quite close enough for me to make him out."

They were close to getting in range of the binoculars when some foreign sounds floated across the water. Pop, pop, pop, pop. A pause and then more popping sounds.

"Gunfire," said McCoy. "I've heard enough of that in my lifetime to know. Keep you heads down and see if we can get a little closer. Michael, call Otis and tell him to notify whatever jurisdiction Beaver Island is in that we have an active shooting going on out here."

CHAPTER 58

Gypsy watched as the redhead moved around behind Eddie while the blonde did the same with Sam. He already had the small nine millimeter automatic in his hand when the blonde yelled, "Hey Vinny."

The redhead immediately produced a Glock and fired a quick shot into the base of Eddie's skull. He never knew what hit him and was dead before his body landed on the deck.

Sam was quick enough to throw a backward elbow, catching the blonde flush on the jaw. Her first two shots arced skyward but the third one hit the redhead in the forehead as she rushed in to assist her friend. In the confusion, Sam was able to wrestle the pistol out of the blonde's hand and empty the rest of the magazine into her body as she tried to shield herself with her hands.

The action on the forward section of the cargo deck was only a slight distraction for Vinny as he glanced in that direction. But that was plenty of time for Gypsy to fire three shots into Vinny's throat before his pistol ever cleared its holster.

It was over in less than a minute and there were two dead men and two dead women lying on the steel deck.

Gypsy, still crouched in a Weaver shooting stance looked up at Sam. "You hit? You all right?"

"I'm okay," said Sam. "Looks like my old army training finally paid off." He was visibly shaking. "I sure didn't want to shoot her but there just wasn't much choice."

Gypsy grunted. "If you have any doubts, just take a look at Eddie. That woman certainly had no qualms about killing him."

Sam sat down on the rack full of spare scuba tanks. "Man, this is a mess. What do we do now?"

"The first thing we need to do is to get these bodies out of here," said Gypsy. "I think I saw some concrete blocks down below. Why don't you go get about eight of them and I'll look around for some rope. There's got to be some rope somewhere on this boat."

Sam obediently went down into the cabin and brought up two concrete blocks at a time depositing one pair next to each of the bodies.

Gypsy appeared from the sleeping quarters with a spool of nylon rope and an AR-15 semi-automatic rifle. "I'll give Vinny credit for one thing," said Gypsy. "He sure knew how to prepare."

Sam, still wearing his wetsuit pants drew his U S Army issue survival knife from the front pouch of his buoyancy compensator and began cutting the nylon rope into six foot lengths. Working silently, Sam and Gypsy tied one concrete block to each ankle of the dead bodies. When they were finished, they dragged the corpses over to the ramp and, one by one, slid them into the chilly waters of northern Lake Michigan.

"Do you think they'll stay on the bottom?" asked Sam

"They'll be fish food for at least a couple of months and by then it won't matter," said Gypsy. "Outside of Eddie, there's nothing that can tie the other three to us. Don't worry about them."

Sam and Gypsy each grabbed a swab bucket and scrubbed the areas of the deck that were bloodstained.

When they were done, Sam gathered up both buckets and took them back down below. Gypsy picked up the military looking rifle and walked back to the back of the boat to survey the area.

* * *

"Just take it easy," said McCoy. "See if you can maneuver around behind the boat. That looks like one of those fishing boats that's open at the transom so that they can haul fish nets up over the stern. Most of them actually have a ramp back there so that the nets can slide right up onto the deck. They haven't seen us yet and we'll be close enough for me to jump on board in a few minutes."

"You're not thinking of climbing into their boat, are you?" asked Michael. "You gotta be nuts."

"You called Otis and gave him our coordinates, didn't you?" asked McCoy.

Michael nodded.

"Then I would expect that we'll be seeing reinforcements pretty soon now. "I'll have help. Just get me close enough."

"I'm coming with you," said Michael. "Can't let you go without somebody watching your back."

McCoy directed George as they approached the trawler. They approached quartering the starboard bow and slowly circled to the rear. There was no sign of human activity as they passed nearby.

When they rounded the stern of the boat, a man could be seen bending over as if checking the tie downs on the most rearward of a line crates. The man seemed to catch the motion in his peripheral vision and suddenly stood straight up looking at them with a rifle in his hands. It was Gypsy and he was raising the rifle into firing position. Both Michael and McCoy instinctively ducked behind the command console but George responded by pointing the bow directly at Gypsy and slamming both throttles full forward. The boat instantly leapt ahead as if shot from a catapult. The sudden acceleration threw all three passengers onto the stern bench. With no one at the helm the boat hurtled forward eating up the fifteen yard gap in mere seconds. Just like in one of those stunt shows, the big Donzi hit the ramp and launched onto the cargo deck of the trawler. The entire hull was airborne about four feet above the surface of the trawler deck. The bow of the boat was the first part to make contact with Gypsy, hitting him just below the chin and violently snapping his head back while the keel of the boat climbed his chest. Its four tons landing fully on top of him. The boat slammed into the crates coming to a crashing halt. The sudden stop caused McCoy and Michael to somersault forward coming to rest in the bow of the boat. Michael was the first to recover, climbing over the side in time to see another man scurrying toward the cabin of the trawler. He gave chase and tackled the man just as he reached the entry hatch. McCoy was right behind him and helped restrain the man until he meekly surrendered.

A throbbing sound from the sky signaled the arrival of the Charlevoix County Sheriff's Department. Three men in SWAT team uniforms hurriedly clambered aboard the trawler and, with rifles at the ready and ordering everybody to lie face down on the deck. They all complied even though George still seemed a little disoriented after his ramming experience.

McCoy identified himself as a police officer and invited the deputies to remove his wallet from his back pocket and examine his badge and photo I.D.

One of the deputies spoke up. "Our information was that there was one regular police detective and one reserve officer."

"That would be me," responded Michael.

"How about helping us sort this all out," said the man who seemed to be in charge.

"It's going to be a long story," said McCoy. He pointed to Gypsy who still lay partially under the Donzi. "But the dead guy under the boat there is a suspect in two murders up in Delta County. And the ringleader of this whole affair"

Then McCoy pointed to Sam who was still prone on the deck. "This guy may or may not be an accomplice. I'd suggest holding him."

"What about the older guy?" asked the deputy.

"He's one of ours," said McCoy. "One of the good guys."

"The call was about a shooting," said the deputy. "Who was shooting at whom?"

Michael spoke up. "When I first put the glasses on this boat, we were still quite a distance away but it looked like there were five or six people on board but there were only these two when we got here. I'm guessing that the shooting victims have all been buried at sea."

"Can I talk?" asked Sam.

"What have you got to say?" asked the deputy in charge. "This is my boat," said Sam. "And everything on board belongs to me... all of it."

CHAPTER 59

Jake sat in the captain's chair with journals scattered all around him aboard Michael's cruiser. He chose one at random and opened the well worn cover.

The story began:

"For all who will read this, I am casting off the fictitious name of Jean Blanchet. My real name is Marc Lemieux and I have been hiding behind a false identity for more than fifty years. It is time for the truth.

I have an ugly story to tell, one of deceit and treachery and whose attributes chased me into hiding for all of these generations.

I was a young man at the time and employed by a marine transportation company. My job was simply that of a night shift dock laborer.

The company for which I worked was called upon to transport a top secret cargo from the port of Escanaba Michigan south through the Illinois Waterway and down the Mississippi River. I can't recall the final destination except that it was somewhere in the Confederate States of America. I assumed that was the reason for the secrecy. We were to offload the cargo from a French vessel and stow it aboard one of our ships for this part of the journey.

At the time, I didn't know why but the cargo transfer was scheduled for midnight. I reported to my job at the normal time and found a crew already at work and they were all strangers to me. There were five large crates lined up on the dock and the men were loading them with cases of musket balls along with a few smaller barrels full of canon balls. I thought that loading these items into large crates to be unusual because of the weight, although the crates looked substantial enough.

Our company had a modern steam powered crane for lifting heavy items aboard ships but we usually reduced loads like this into multiple, smaller containers for easier handling.

Even though I was a regular dock worker I didn't recognize a single person. None of my workmates were on the job that night. I thought I was going crazy.

And then my boss showed up and wanted to know what I was doing there. I told him that I was supposed to be there and then he said that all of the regular workers had been canceled for tonight and I said that nobody had notified me.

He asked what I had seen since I arrived and I told him about the musket balls and my thoughts about the extreme weight. At that point he told me to go to work and help load the cargo. He also told me that I'd be required to serve aboard the ship until it reached Chicago and that I would return to Escanaba on a stagecoach. I thought it was a strange requirement but I always did as I was told.

As far as I know, the cargo from the French vessel was offloaded to a series of mule carts. The mule train departed before we finished loading the schooner. I recognized the driver of the first cart as a man I had seen hanging around our dock for about a week.

It was dawn when we finally set sail and I was assigned the task of making sure that all crew members had biscuits and a ladle full of drinking water. It was a meaningless job and I seriously wondered why I was forced to join the crew.

We sailed into Green Bay and then east to Lake Michigan. As we entered the large lake just south of Poverty Island, I saw another ship riding at anchor. We approached the other craft and a boarding ladder was stretched between the two vessels. Many of the crew from the boat that I was on crossed over to the other ship. There were about six or seven of us left and we were all brought up on deck and lined up against the starboard side. Eight men with muskets faced us and one of them asked me what I had seen. I told him about the musket balls being loaded into the crates and that seemed to enrage him. He raised his gun and fired directly at my face. The ball missed me but passed through the bill of my cap sending it flying overboard. I followed it over the side and hugged the side of the ship, treading water. There was a lot more shooting and bodies were falling into the water all around me. I inched my way around the stern and swam away, keeping the other ship between myself and the schooner. I was about a quarter mile away when I risked looking back. Nobody had witnessed my escape but the schooner had a decided list, obviously having its hull opened up below the water line.

I kept swimming but soon fatigue set in. I was a strong young man in those days but even then, I had my limits. I became aware of the sound of oarlocks creaking and could hear the oars dipping into the water. I was almost unconscious when a strong pair of hand hoisted me aboard the dory. I was in and out of my mind for a few days when I awoke to find myself in the home of a fisherman in a place called Point Detour. I confided in him and expressed my fear of what might happen to me if I was found alive. He was sympathetic and sent me to work on a trusted friend's farm in Gladstone, Michigan. It is here where I still reside.

It was two months after my experience that I began to hear the rumors about a treasure of gold said to be worth millions of dollars at the bottom of Lake Michigan just off of Poverty Island. Piecing together what I know to be true, I can say that those crates that were sunk with that ship did not contain gold. That cargo was mostly lead and a few cast iron cannon balls. Only now do I understand why we loaded iron and lead into those crates. In order to complete the illusion they had to be extraordinarily heavy. As far as I know, the gold from that French ship was taken somewhere not too far inland. A treasure of that size would surely have attracted notice and since it has never been found, it is my assumption that it has been buried somewhere nearby. "

Jake let the book fall to his lap and said, "Somebody's going to be awfully disappointed."

CHAPTER 60

Otis, Marla and the twins joined George Snyder and Jacob Marley for breakfast on their last morning at Little Bay Marina. They were enjoying the big dining room of The Shop's Anchor seated at a large round table that commanded a view of the entire harbor. The morning sun sparkled off of the calm water as several of the charter boats made their way toward the big lake. The group had just finished their first cup of coffee when McCoy showed up. "Mind if I join you?" he said. They made room at the big table.

"I'm counting my blessings," said George. "Yeah, we missed out on the treasure but I learned a huge life lesson and I'll be better for it. I'm the only one who had any cash invested so the most that anyone else lost is their time."

"Except for the dead people," added McCoy.

"That's unfortunate," said George. "But the only ones I feel bad about are that retired cop and the marina handyman. They were the true victims."

"Agreed," said Otis. "We all learned a thing or two this past week."

"Well," said Jake. "Michael wanted to find out if his cruiser was dependable and seaworthy and it looks like that proved to be true."

"By the way, has anybody seen Michael this morning?" asked Otis. "He's not the type that likes to sleep late."

"He's out there," said Jake pointing out the window toward the harbor.

A small dinghy rocked gently in the water behind the stern of Michael's cruiser. Michael was kneeling on the center seat just putting the finishing touches on the big gold letters that scrawled across the massive mahogany transom of the stately Chris Craft. The words said, "Fool's Gold."

Made in the USA
Columbia, SC
20 April 2022

59137659R00154